BTZ   1/1~

BITTER ROOT

Visit us at www.boldstrokesbooks.com

By the Author

Forsaken

Bitter Root

BITTER ROOT

by
Laydin Michaels

2016

BITTER ROOT

ISBN 13: 978-1-62639-656-2

This Trade Paperback Original Is Published By
Bold Strokes Books, Inc.
P.O. Box 249
Valley Falls, NY 12185

First Edition: August 2016

CREDITS
Editors: Victoria Villasenor and Cindy Cresap
Production Design: Susan Ramundo
Cover Design By Melody Pond

Acknowledgments

Thank you to MJ, my rock, for always being in my corner, no matter the odds. Thank you to the fantastic, professional staff at Bold Strokes, you make dreams come true every day. Special thanks to Vic for all your help with the editing. Thank you to every dreamer out there, who finds a connection with the worlds we create. I hope to never disappoint you.

Dedication

For Gloria and Jerome 1945–2005, through your example, we learned to love. Live a lot, laugh a lot, love a lot.

PROLOGUE

Merley skipped through the shop looking for her papa. She had completed the signing in of deliveries at the dock, just like he asked her. He was supposed to take her to Conq's store to get a limeade, and she was excited to go because her best friend Rachel was going to be working the counter today.

Just wait till I tell her! She's not going to believe it. I still don't believe it. How did Papa rent the whole theater for my party? Who cares? We'll have all the popcorn and candy we can eat, plus we get to watch all my favorite movies. Julie Messier is going to turn green when she hears. Too bad she's a big ole mean thing. No invitation for her. It's going to be so much fun. Twelve is going to be the best birthday ever.

Life was so good since Mamma had married J.B. and he had become her papa. Before then, Mamma was as apt to knock her to the floor as to look at her. When her daddy died in the shrimping accident, it was like a bee got stuck in her undershorts. She was always mean. Merley pretty much stayed out of her way. She didn't want to make her mamma mad, so she mostly hid from her. J.B. had changed all that. When he started dating Mamma, she mellowed. She smiled again and even laughed from time to time. He gave Merley just about anything she asked for. He was the best papa in the world and he was all hers. *Take that, Julie Messier.*

She ran through the heavy wooden door to the back room, buzzing with anticipation, but stopped short. At first she wasn't sure what she was seeing. There was Papa, holding tight to the arm of their neighbor, Ransom Prejean. Papa had something in his fist, and as she watched, he slammed it across Ransom's face, opening a channel of skin and spraying blood all the way across the room. She bit back her scream, but not before both men looked her way.

She was frozen in place, but Papa moved toward her quickly. He grabbed her around the waist with one arm and used the other to wrap her small hand around the grip of a pistol.

"Take him out, baby girl. This scum tried to rip us off." He held the gun pointed at Ransom, keeping it from shaking in her hand. And then he squeezed her finger against the trigger before she could make a sound of protest. The gun jerked in her hand as the noise blasted through her. She watched the hole erupt in the center of Ransom's chest, more blood spraying out behind him.

She couldn't stop looking at his face. He looked just like that boy at school who fell into the coulee, his expression showing surprise and fear. But while the boy had quickly caught his balance and recovered, Ransom just melted into the bloody mess around him. Merley felt a sharp ache in her own chest, tight, like a knife going through her.

Am I gonna die too? Am I having a heart attack?

Papa spun her around so she was facing away from the carnage. "Look at me, Merley. You done a good thing here. That man was worthless and had to go. I'm proud of you, baby. Nobody cheats a Nerbass and lives to tell about it. Right?"

She felt herself coming loose then, drifting away from that place and its gore. She started shaking everywhere, her stomach all roiling and twisting. *What's happening? Papa? I'm going to throw up. So much blood. If I throw up, it'll get all mixed with that blood.* She felt hot tears burn down her cheeks. *What's happening?* Spittle hit her face, shocking her back to the present. Her papa was practically yelling in her face.

"You hear me, Merley? I'm proud of you, baby. You didn't do nothing wrong."

She struggled to reconnect, words choking out of her desert dry throat. "But...why? He's dead, Papa. Why?"

"You killed him, that's why. It needed doing, and you did it. Now, don't you fret none. I'm going to dump him so far out in the marsh that nobody is ever going to find him. It's a better thing him being gone. Besides, the gators need to eat too."

"But, Papa, what about Max and Ellie? He's their daddy. We gotta call the police, Papa. It was an accident. I didn't mean to hurt him."

He began to drag Ransom to the hatch in the floor that opened above his skiff tied up below the shop.

"Stop that foolish talk, girl. He was a terrible daddy to those kids. He's gone now and he's not coming back. We have to get rid of him so they don't take you to jail. Listen now. Get that bucket and mop over there and clean this place up. We don't want anybody to walk in and see what you did. There's some bleach on the shelf. Drag the hose up here from the hatch and wash it all away, baby girl."

I killed him. Merley's ears wouldn't stop ringing. As she hosed down the back room, she started shaking so hard the water splashed everywhere. *I killed him.* She watched the pink tinted waterfall slide from the edge of the hatch to mix with the salt water below. She filled a bucket with fresh water before climbing down the ladder to close the water valve. *I'm a killer.* Back upstairs, she poured more bleach than she needed into the bucket and began to mop the room. *I'm a murderer and my papa is proud of me.* She dropped the mop and sat heavily on the floor, legs dangling above the hatch. She felt cold, but her skin was clammy. Her head ached, and her stomach felt sick. The edge of her mouth started to twitch, and she knew tears were coming. She leaned forward as her stomach rebelled against what had happened and her breakfast hit the concrete floor. *Now I'll have to clean that up too.* She slid to the side and curled into a ball, giving in to the shock and grief of the situation.

Papa found her in that same spot an hour and a half later. He made his way up the ladder and swung her legs to the side to close the hatch door.

"Good job, Merley. I couldn't be prouder of you, girl. This is all for you, you know? One day this will all be yours. It's about time you became a part of this. You're almost twelve. That's old enough. Get me one of those ice chests from the last delivery. I want to show you our power."

She pulled herself down to the big dock and brought one of the small ice chests to Papa. He opened it and pulled out a handful of little zippered baggies. They had what looked like rock candy inside.

"This is it, baby. The key to the future. People buy this crap like they would die without it. All we gotta do is pay guys like Ransom to deliver it along with their shrimp. We box it up in the shrimp and send it on to the guys who sell it. It's like money from nothing, baby. It's all gonna be yours one day."

She didn't want it. She didn't want one bit of it. The ache in her gut and the hollow echo of that shot were all she felt. That night, she lay thinking about what her papa, the man she thought had made life better, was offering. She thought of Ransom's eyes, the smell of blood, and the way the metal was hot in her hand. Her mamma had ignored her during dinner, and Papa had kept shooting her a knowing smile that made her stomach turn.

The next few weeks were no comfort. Merley had her party, but it was bittersweet. She didn't feel like she deserved to be happy. She watched Ellie and Max Prejean at school. They were so sad all the time, and it was her fault.

I wish I could just tell them what happened to their daddy. I wish I didn't have to feel like this. And now I have to work at the bait shop every day. Even Sunday. It's like J.B. doesn't want me out of his sight. Why's he always watching me? What does he think I'm going to do? He's made sure I'm stuck here. What else does he want from me?

Merley hated the new life she was forced to live. J.B. made things even more horrible. Six months after the shooting, he opened a seafood processing company next door. Now they could ship more of their little surprises to even more places. He made other people disappear too. She didn't have to pull the trigger, but she had to watch, too many times. She washed away so much blood she became almost numb to it.

At least I didn't know them and I don't have to look at their kids every day. It was small comfort, though, as guilt continued to eat away at her.

The week before her fourteenth birthday, Merley was at the counter of the bait shop. She had just sold six cases of "special shrimp" to a man in New Mexico. She was arranging for their shipment when the door banged open and J.B. rushed at her.

"What are you playing at, girl?"

"I'm not playing at anything," she said.

"Why's your teacher saying you need to see a doctor? What's that about?"

"I don't know what you're talking about. I feel fine."

"Well, she says we have to take you to a psychologist if you don't pep up. That's not happening. You snap out of this funk you're in, and I mean now. No more sulking around. This life gives you everything, and you need to stop pouting and be thankful."

"I'm not pouting. Besides, all I ever do is work and go to school. That and wash up after you beat on people. Why do I have to do all this? Why can't I just be a kid?"

"Listen here, I put my trust in you. You're my daughter and you do as I say. Just be happy, you hear me? Don't make me do anything I don't want to do."

"Yes, sir." Merley seethed inside but held her tongue, knowing he would only get louder and angrier if she provoked him.

You're not my father. You're nothing to me but a monster.

"One more thing."

"Yes, sir?"

"You're going with me tonight on the boat. I need your help with something."

Merley cringed inside. She hated going out on the boat with him. That usually meant he had someone or something he needed to get rid of and she had to help. She couldn't stop a groan from escaping.

"You have something to say?"

"No, sir." Defeated, she hung her head.

❖

She had to get away from here. And fast. The boat trip that night had been the worst one yet. *What could a kid that young have done to piss him off?* The boy couldn't have been much older than her. She'd helped J.B. lift his stiffening form over the edge of the cruiser's gunwale. There wasn't as much blood as usual, just some streaks on his face. J.B. was awful sketchy too. He kept glaring out at the Gulf like someone was watching him.

"Why'd you kill him, Papa?"

"Never you mind why. He's dead and now he's gone."

"But he's just a kid."

"Not too young to steal drugs. Just shut up and let me think."

He was all twitchy, like he was scared or something. What could scare him? Merley couldn't help picking up on his tension and started glancing out to sea too. *What am I looking for?*

"What has you all spooked? You're scaring me," she said.

"Nothing has me spooked. Just watch him and make sure he stays down. I want to make a stop before we head home."

They'd tied cinder blocks to his ankles and waist, as usual. He wouldn't be back. It was weird that J.B. asked her to watch him. Something about this was off.

"He's gone, and he's not coming back up unless the chains rust. Can we just go home now? I have school tomorrow," she said.

"We will, after our stop. We've got a long ride ahead. Get some sleep if you want."

"What? Where are we going?"

"Just out to one of the rigs," he said.

"Are you crazy? That'll take forever. I have school, you know."

"I know. Don't worry. It'll only be an hour or so out and back. It's a jack-up rig and it's not that far out. Besides, I told you, go get some sleep in the cabin. It's probably better if they don't see you."

"If who don't see me? What's going on?"

"Dammit, I said go in the cabin and get some sleep. I mean it," he said.

Merley slid off the seat and headed to the cabin.

Why's he acting so weird? Why're we going to an oil rig in the middle of the night? She shucked off her shoes and climbed into the narrow berth. She didn't plan on sleeping, but before long, she was out.

The clunking of the boat against something woke her. She slid out of the bunk and crept up the ladder to see where they were. When her eyes were level with the deck, she stopped. If J.B. saw her he was sure to lose his temper. She could hear his voice but couldn't see him.

"It's not my fault, Chupa. The idiot took too much of the stuff. By the time I'd found him he was already gone. You have to explain it to him. It's not my fault."

"Okay, Mr. Nerbass, but you know El Mayo. He's going to want his nephew returned to him."

"It's too late for that. I had to get rid of him. If anybody saw him this whole operation could've been busted wide open."

"This isn't good, señor. He is not going to be happy. Now he can only rely on your word of what happened. I suggest you go home and wait to hear from us."

"Now, that's not fair. I give you good service. I'm never late, you always get your cut, I've proven my loyalty. My business shouldn't suffer because he sent a boy to do a man's work."

"Mr. Nerbass, you forget yourself. It is by his grace you continue to exist. I wouldn't trifle with that, were I you. I'll talk to him. We will see how he responds. If he gives me the go-ahead, I'll get more product to you by the weekend. For now, we wait and see."

Merley slid the hatch door further back, hoping to catch a glimpse of the man speaking. It was stuck and she had to pull harder than she expected. When it finally came loose, it banged back into the housing. The voices above her stilled.

She winced and froze. *Uh oh. Now I'm in for it.*

"Who's there? Nerbass, if you are trying to double-cross us—"

"No double-cross. It's just my kid. Hold on. Put that thing away." Merely could hear nervousness in his voice.

"Merley, come out on the deck."

She pulled herself up the rest of the ladder and stood in the open. J.B. and the other man were standing on top of the cabin. The oil rig loomed above them, its lights illuminating the boat. She looked at the man who had been speaking. His face was in shadow, but she could see he was a big man. Tall and broad, with dark skin, like chicory coffee with milk. She clearly saw the gun he was holding. She hoped he would stay up there.

"Come on up here, girl. I want to see you," he said.

Dread tightened her stomach, but she did as she was told. The man gripped her face in his massive hand and turned it this way and that. It wasn't painful, just awkward and uncomfortable. He stared at her for what seemed like forever. She stuck out her chest and stared back.

"This man your daddy?"

"No, sir. He's my stepfather. My daddy is dead." She tilted her face up defiantly. *Take that, J.B.*

The man laughed a huge bear of a laugh that startled her. Light glinted off his front tooth. It was golden, creepy. His breath washed over her, acrid and bitter. *God, get me out of here, please.*

"Is that so? How he died? Mr. Nerbass have a talk with him?"

"Now just a minute—" J.B. said.

"Quiet. I'm talking to this girl, not you. So, how did he die, your father?"

"He died in a shrimping accident a long time ago. He didn't even know J.B."

"Is that right? Okay, little girl. Is there anybody else down there with you?"

"No, sir."

"Can I believe you? I'm not sure I can believe your stepfather."

"Go look for your ownself. There's nobody here but me and him."

He looked at her for a long time. She refused to let her eyes drop, vowing not to show her fear. Apparently, her stubbornness impressed him, because he smiled and seemed to relax.

"Okay, I'm going to believe you, little one. Your daddy here, he's lucky he's got such a strong child. If you ever want to come to work for me, I've got a place for you, you hear? Remember my name, Juan Rodriguez. That's me. If you ever get into trouble, use my name."

Merley nodded, though she knew using his name was the last thing she'd ever want to do. He signaled to her to go back below decks, and before long, she heard the motor kick to life. She nestled under the thin blanket and tried to get back to sleep, but the whole experience of the night weighed on her.

J.B. is a bad man. What he does is wrong, and I'm just as wrong by staying here and not saying anything. And those people, the ones he killed and the ones he beat beyond recognition? What about them? What about their families? If I stay here much longer I'm going to die, I know it. I can feel life ebbing out of me a little bit each day. If he doesn't just haul off and kill me, I'll waste down to nothing soon. A soul isn't meant to live like this. Please help me, God. If you can hear me, please help me get away from this place.

Sleep over took her, finally, and she slept fitfully, wrestling with bloated, water-soaked bodies she had helped send to the deep. When

J.B. shook her awake, she could see the sky was already lightening toward sunrise.

"Listen up, you ever contradict me again and I'll tan your hide. Get on up to the house and see about breakfast. You got school in an hour, so get."

"I'm getting. Give me a minute, will ya? Besides, you're not my father and you need to stop saying that. My father was a good man who never hurt nobody. I ain't no part of you."

The suddenness of his movement caught her off guard, and before she knew it she was slammed into the bulkhead, her face flaming from the sting of his slap.

"Don't talk that way. You're every bit of me. I made your life what it is. You respect me, girl, or you'll pay."

"I am paying! This life is hell. God don't want me to be helping you with your drugs or with your beating and killing. I'm not meant to be here."

"Well, how about if I fix that for you? How about if I take you right out of it? Your mamma don't care at all for you. I could drop you in the swamp tomorrow and nobody'd cry a tear. Hear me? Shut this complaining off now, or I might just do it."

"I hate you. I hate everything about you."

Another slap, this one much harder, left her head spinning. She wanted to keep fighting with him, to prove that she was stronger, but she gave in. It was too hard. She squeezed past him and raced up to the house. Heck if he'd get any more help from her, that was for sure. He might be able to make her keep quiet about his business, but she didn't have to work for him. She'd run away. That's what she'd do.

She started planning her escape. Merley Addison Nerbass, the killer and drug runner, would disappear and she'd just be Addison Bergeron. She'd take back her real daddy's name and build a new life he would be proud of. She'd forget old rotten J.B. was ever a part of her. She would leave as soon as she could and he'd see he couldn't hold her here. But she'd make sure she was well out of his reach when she left. Those hands were heavy, and she'd had enough of them. If he ever found her, he'd kill her. She knew that, so she'd have to be careful.

❖

The next few months were hard. She and J.B. fought almost constantly. Her mamma was no help at all; in fact, she seemed to enjoy the strife. By the time summer rolled around, Merley was ready to make her move. J.B. had burst into her room that night, spitting mad. She'd held fast to not working for him as much as she could. He'd get mad like this from time to time, and she'd have to give in a little. *Not this time, though. I'm out of here and you can't stop me.*

"You'll be at the damn bait shop at three tomorrow afternoon, girl. I mean it. No more lollygagging for you. This is my last warning. I've got to go meet with my buddy Ramon, and I need you to take care of the shop. You better show up if you know what's good for you."

She wanted to scream at him that she'd be gone tomorrow and he could take care of his own damn shop, but she bit her tongue. She had to have as much time as possible before he started looking for her. And he'd look. She knew that. As much as she'd seen him do and had done for him, he'd kill her before letting her get away. Once she ran, she'd have to keep running until she was sure he wasn't behind her. It'd be better to kill herself than to let him find her.

She had been happy to see her mamma throwing back glass after glass of red wine at dinner. No worries about her waking up when it was time to take off. She just had to wait until she heard J.B.'s truck leaving the house. He spent his time Lord knew where, but he was always gone from midnight until just after seven in the morning. *Maybe he goes out to that rig every night.* It wouldn't surprise her. The last time he met with Mr. Ramon he'd been gone until nearly supper time the next day. This was her best chance to get away.

She finally heard his truck spinning gravel in the driveway. *Time to go.* She toed open her door and listened. The sonorous sound of her mamma's snoring gave her clearance. As quietly as possible, she slid open the bureau drawer where the important family papers were. *I need to have something that proves who I am, even if I don't want to be me anymore.* She found her birth certificate and slid it out of the envelope. Merley Addison Bergeron. The name her real papa had chosen for her. Merley for her mamma's aunt, and Addison after his grandfather.

Well, lots of people go by their middle names. I doubt J.B. even knows what my real name is. His head's too big, making me go by Nerbass. I ain't no Nerbass.

She tucked the form back into the envelope and pocketed it. Noiselessly, she left the house. The sharp tang of salt drifted in the fog. It would be a good six hours before the sun was high enough to burn it off. By that time, she planned to be far from this place. There was nothing for her here. It was the empty husk of a life eaten from inside out. The taste of it on her palate was as bitter as chicory. Determination, a hard knot in her stomach, pushed her out into the darkness. Without a backward glance at the cypress-shrouded cabin, she opened the shed door and maneuvered her bike out to the hard-packed dirt road leading to her new life.

CHAPTER ONE

"Hey, Dink! Bring me some fresh boudin out here! This crap 'bout to crawl off on its own!"

Adi cringed at the guttural sound of Bertie's shouted order and her use of the diminutive nickname. She really needed to talk to her about that. Adi was anything but "dinky." Sure, when she'd shaken the mud of Terrebonne Parish, Louisiana, off her boots, she wasn't nearly the size she was now. *It's amazing what a regular diet and the lack of fear can do for you.* Bertie had been a lifesaver. She'd driven her rusty old Ford up to the back lot of Michaud's Boiling Point and practically stumbled over Adi's sleeping form near the Dumpster. If it had been T'Claude who'd found her, she'd have had a cold shower from the hose as a wake-up call. But luck, for once, had been with her and Bertie had been the one to find her. She hadn't asked many questions, just poked her with her walking stick and said, "Well, Dink, if you gonna sleep out here with the raccoons, people gonna think you ain't got no sense. Best get up now and come on in with me."

Adi had been "Dink" to Bertie ever since, never mind that she'd shot up a good four inches in the past eight years. Eight years of living in the warm embrace of a woman who cared not a whit where she originated. A woman who loved her the way she vaguely remembered her father loving her. A woman who never even questioned whether Adi needed or wanted a place to land. No, Bertie had simply provided one. She had brought Adi into the restaurant, fed her the first proper meal in as long as she could remember, and tossed her a stained, but clean, white apron.

Adi grinned as she remembered Bertie's most famous speech, one she'd given countless times. *"Listen here, Dink, ain't nobody gonna give you what you need in life, you hear? You got to take a hold of this life and give her a good shake. Scare the daylights outta her, till she drops what you need. Then you pick it up and run with it. Right? Don't you be lying around waiting neither. Get yourself up and get a hold of life. Now, look here, you go on over to that big pot there and I'm gonna tell you what to drop in it. You do like I say and we gonna be all right."*

And Adi had done just that. She had chopped and peeled and stirred just as Bertie dictated. In the end, she felt good about what she produced. Maybe it wasn't the best oyster gumbo ever served, but it was her first, and with Bertie's tutelage, she improved with every batch. Now Bertie trusted Adi to handle not only the gumbo, but the boudin, étouffée, creole, and maque choux.

Adi shook her head in resignation. There would be no changing Bertie's mind about her name. She turned back to the task at hand, making fresh boudin. She pulled the boiled ground pork from the cooler and put it beside the commercial grinder on the butcher block counter. She mixed in the blend of onion, celery, bell pepper, and garlic she had prepared earlier. Chopped scallions, parsley, and rice followed. She topped the concoction off with fresh ground black pepper, salt, cayenne pepper, ground thyme, and ground oregano. Nothing made Adi feel better than the scent of fresh spice. She loved making good food with her own hands. She would never be in a position again to rely on someone else to prepare food for her. As long as she could breathe, she could cook. That was another lesson she learned from Bertie. *"Listen up, Dink. Never wait around for somebody to fix you something to eat. You hear me? You get over to the stove and fix it up for yourself. Cooking is from inside, Dink. You got it, I got it, durn near everybody's got cooking in 'em. Problem is, most folks just too durn lazy or been kept from the knowing. All you got to do is do."*

Adi smiled, thinking what a great gift Bertie was in her life. When she thought about where she might have ended up, she shuddered. Somehow, she'd picked the right Dumpster to crawl behind. For that, she would always be thankful. She filled sausage casings with the mixture, pumping it through the grinder. She twisted each segment closed as she went. Water was already steaming in the skillet, waiting for her creation. She dropped the finished boudin in the water to allow the steam to marry the flavors inside. While it steamed, she prepared a plate with saltine crackers and a crusty baguette. She slid a bowl of melted garlic butter on as well, knowing Bertie's fondness for the treat. Nothing pleased her more than cooking for Bertie. She felt it was the best way she could thank the woman who'd saved her life.

As she placed the piping hot boudin onto the plate, she caught the metallic creak of the kitchen screen door. T'Claude lumbered into the room, taking up far too much space in the small kitchen.

"What you got there, Dinky?"

"This isn't for you, T. It's for Bertie. And my name is Adi, not Dinky."

"Heck, Bertie calls you Dinky all the time."

"Yeah, well, that's Bertie, not you. You call me by my name, or you won't be getting any boudin, or étouffée, for that matter."

"Well, dang, Adi, okay. No problem. So, how about a taste of that?" He grinned at her, showing his trademark dimples.

Adi smiled back at him. "Okay, but save some for the paying customers." She couldn't deny T'Claude his taste of boudin. He did own the place, after all. T'Claude Michaud was the son of Claude Michaud Sr., a man who had earned his living as a Louisiana politician in the days when that was a "paying" position. Michaud had owned a piece of every business in the parish by the time God saw fit to remove him from office. A powerful heart attack had ended his life in its prime, leaving T'Claude quite a nice sized bank account, and had given him the opportunity to open the restaurant he'd always dreamed of. T'Claude left the restaurant in Bertie's capable hands for the most part, but he did like to come by from time to time and sample the wares. He was an easy boss except for those days when he met with Jack Daniels before coming to visit. He had a mean temper when in his cups. Only Bertie's voice could stop him then. Something about the woman just forced sense into your head, whether you wanted it or not. But today appeared to be a good day. *Thank goodness.*

"What have you been up to T'Claude? Have you been up to the casino lately?"

"Ah, chère, they robbed me blind up there. Them casino folks just love to see ole T'boy coming. They figure I'm going to make their week and set about to empty my pockets as quick as they can!" They laughed together, knowing that T rarely carried much cash into the casino and usually left with more than his fair share. He had a knack for cards that served him well. Adi had often tried to get him to show her how he was so successful, but he insisted it was pure luck.

"T'Claude! You come on outta that kitchen and let that girl be. She got work to do, you know!" Bertie yelled.

Adi smiled as T made his way ponderously through the small room into the dining area. He might be lucky with cards, but she was the really lucky one at Michaud's.

She scooped up Bertie's plate and followed him out the door. "Here you go, Bertie. Careful now, it's fresh out of the pot. Don't burn your mouth." She slid the plate onto the polished cypress bar where Bertie waited.

"When you ever known me to be burning my mouth, Dinky? You know I got more than a lick a sense about hot food."

"Course I know that, but you know if I forgot to say something you'd tell me I was trying to kill you."

Bertie laughed her deep rumbling laugh and threw her hand up. "Yeah, you right there. How's the gumbo coming for tonight?"

Abruptly, the door to the restaurant opened and the sound of voices raised in argument preceded the first guests of the day. "I cannot believe you, Bill. Seriously? How hard can it be to find one small town in Louisiana? You act as if you've never heard of GPS!" The scowl on the face that went with those words marred what was otherwise attractive features.

The woman was average height, had dark hair, almost black, and skin so pale it looked as if she'd never seen the sun. Adi took in her outfit. She was wearing creamy white slacks and a cream and brown top that buttoned at an odd angle. Her shoes were about the highest Adi had seen, matched the cream color perfectly and showed off delicate feet with pale pink toenails. The man behind her looked harried and unkempt, in fancy blue jeans, a button-down shirt, and a tweed blazer. He was visibly upset, his tanned face red and drawn.

"It is not my fault the place is so small it's not on a map! You navigate if you think you can do a better job, Dawn." With that, he glared at Adi and added, "How about a table? We're starving."

"Oh, sure thing, mister, just take any one you like. I'll get you some menus." Adi turned to grab them, wanting nothing more than to get these two fed and out the door. Bertie and T'Claude turned so they were leaning back on the bar.

"Where are you folks coming from?" Bertie called. "Not many folks find their way to New Iberia without planning on getting here."

The new arrivals glanced up at her, but neither answered. "Well, we don't cotton much to folks as won't state their business around here. You got some reason you don't want to say?" Bertie raised a skeptical eyebrow as she narrowed her eyes on her prey.

Tweed jacket cleared his throat. "No, ma'am. Not at all. We drove down from New Orleans. We're trying to find the town of Carencro, but it seems we're a little turned around." Cream pantsuit looked at him sharply.

Adi wondered what their story was. They sure were acting strange. "Here you are,'" she said, handing them the menus. "There's fresh hot boudin in the kitchen if you'd like an appetizer." She turned away from the table, but took only a half-step before the woman spoke up.

"That would be nice. Yes, please. And what drink would you recommend to go with that?"

Looking back, Adi said, "Well, about the best thing to drink with boudin is a nice cold beer. I'd say either a Hopitoulas or a Jockamo."

"A what or a who?"

"They're both IPAs made here in Louisiana."

"Okay, I'll have the Hopitoulas and he'll have the Jockamo."

Adi nodded and moved off to get their order. When she returned, Bertie and T were sitting at an adjoining table engaged in a spirited conversation with their customers. She shook her head. These two used this place as their own gossip central. They had a knack for making strangers feel welcome. She was sure by the time she got them fed these poor folks wouldn't have a secret between them. That's just how it was at Michaud's. The Boiling Pot was a pot full of other folks' business. Bertie and T just kept stirring it.

"Here you are, folks. Y'all figure out what you'd like for dinner?"

"Thank you. I'll have an oyster gumbo, a crawfish étouffée, some collard greens with ham hocks, and the cornbread dressing please. He'll have the shrimp creole, the garlic stuffed pork roast, the maque choux, and the stuffed crab. Please add the bread pudding, the mud pie, the crème brulee, and the sock-it-to-me cake for dessert."

Adi looked at the woman, taken aback. She had just about ordered everything on the menu. "You sure? That's a whole lot of food, ma'am."

"Quite sure. Thank you." She flicked the menu back to Adi with a quick turn of wrist. The man followed suit. Adi looked at Bertie and T. Bertie's eyebrows had all but disappeared into her hairline, and T's mouth was standing open. He snapped it closed like a fish gulping air.

"I'll pull another table over for you folks. Adi, be sure you bring each dish out as it's ready. No reason to let it get cold."

Shaking her head at the vagaries of strangers, Adi elbowed the kitchen door open and started preparing the meal.

Bertie followed hot on her heels. "So, Dink, what should I do to help you out?"

"Grab the greens and get them going, Bert. I'd just like to know where they think they're going to put all this food. This is going to be enough to feed the road crew after a hard day on the highway."

"Can't figure what some people can eat, though, Adi. You know that's the truth."

"That I do. We best get going."

They worked in quiet synchronicity, the usual atmosphere in their kitchen. As each dish was ready, Adi calmly carried it to the table. It wasn't easy to hide her disgust at the plates she returned with, barely sampled. "Well, I sure don't get ordering to feed a herd of cattle then eating like a little bird. Just don't make sense to me."

"Maybe they just don't know what they ordered, so they's having a hard time deciding what to dig into."

"Maybe. I'll just be glad to see the door swinging closed behind 'em."

"T'Claude sure is having a good ole time chatting them up though. Think he's going to be downright sorry to see them leave."

"Too bad for him. This cake is the last of it. I sure hate seeing all that food go to waste. Durn foolish folks." She made the last trip from kitchen to table, waving at Jacques Fontenot and his family arriving for their customary Sunday dinner. At least Jacques's family would appreciate the cooking enough to clean their plates. Adi remembered the burning ache of hunger in her belly before Bertie found her. She knew how precious food was. Waste made her stomach turn.

Settling the final dish in front of the woman, Adi said, "There you are, ma'am. That's the last dish. I sure hope y'all enjoyed it." She had turned back toward the kitchen when the woman called out to her.

"Excuse me? Would you mind if we take a second of your time?"

Adi looked longingly at the kitchen door. If only she'd sent Bertie out with the final dish. She was going to be hard-pressed to stay civil with these people. "Sure thing. What can I do for you?"

"I was wondering who the chef is here. Would you mind asking them to come to our table please?"

"You're looking at the cook. So what can I do for you?"

"Oh." The woman seemed startled. "I was expecting someone more mature."

"Age doesn't make you mature, ma'am, only experience. I'm plenty old enough to handle my job here at the Pot, and take any complaints headed my way. So go ahead and say your piece. I have other folks to cook for."

The woman held out a pale, slender hand. "My name is Dawn Chapman. I work for *Epicuriosity*. Have you heard of us?"

"Can't say that I have, ma'am."

"Please call me Dawn. We're a national food magazine. We feature foods from different regions that might be unknown to our readers. Our goal is to broaden the palate of folks across the country and interest them in the cuisines that most strongly represent the featured state. Louisiana is our state of focus for our January issue."

Adi wasn't sure what response the woman was looking for. She had no idea or desire to know about any magazine. She just wanted this Dawn and tweed jacket to pay their bill and hit the door.

"Listen, we were looking for a chef to feature from South Louisiana. Our plan was to dine at a restaurant in Carencro, but as you see, we didn't make it there. I have to say though, the experience we have had here has been exceptional! You're an accomplished chef, Ms...?"

"Adi, Addison Bergeron."

"Ms. Bergeron. We would like to feature you as our south Louisiana chef. Would that interest you?"

Adi felt a knot of dread settle inside her. "No. Thanks very much, but I'm not—"

"Of course she's interested!" T'Claude practically shouted. "The Boiling Pot would love being featured in your article." He eyed Adi. "Let me handle the arrangements. Adi, go on back and take care of dinner service."

Adi's shoulders ached and her stomach roiled with the buildup of tension. She had to think about the movement required to get back into the kitchen. *National magazine.* Not at all something Adi wanted to be a part of. She not only liked her life just fine as it was, she needed it that way. She needed the security of Bertie's house and the peaceful obscurity of her simple life at the Boiling Pot. National magazine meant possible recognition. That would never do. She had to figure a way out of this, and she had to figure it out fast. T'Claude was like a dog with a bone though, and she knew changing his mind would be difficult to say the least. She didn't have long to wait. By the time she'd finished serving the Fontenot family, T was in the kitchen, practically bouncing.

"Adi, listen here. I got all the information from those magazine folks. They'll be sending the reporter next week. I wrote the name down somewhere...just a sec...Oh. Here it is, Griffith McNaulty. Ms. Chapman said she's the best in the business. I can't tell you how important this could be for the Pot. This is going to give us national exposure, hon. We'll be drawing folks down from all over to taste your cooking! Aren't you excited?"

How can I tell him? There simply wasn't any way she could have her face pasted on some flashy magazine cover. She'd never heard of *Epicuriosity*, but that didn't mean much, since she avoided places such magazines might be. If J.B. Nerbass happened upon anything that led him to her, her life was over. She had done her best to forget the cabin in Dulac and what her life there had been. She wasn't that girl anymore, and no way was she giving J.B. any chance at finding her. She had to make T'Claude understand.

"T'Claude, you know I'm not the reason folks come to the Boiling Pot. I just cook the way Bertie taught me. She's the great secret here. Those folks need to feature her, not me. I'm just a simple cook, and you know it."

"Simple cook? Bertie taught you? Heck, Dinky, Bertie sure enough cooks good, but what you do to that food is like some kind of magic, girl. She gave you a start, but no, you're the chef here. You're the one they're coming to see, so get used to it."

"I'm not doing it, T. I just can't. Forget it. It's Bertie or it's nothing. I mean it." Adi's voice rose as she spoke, drawing Bertie out of the kitchen.

"What in tarnation is going on out here? Why y'all shouting at each other?"

"Bertie, talk some sense into this girl. You hear me? She's going on about not doing this interview. You and I both know she's the reason folks come back for more once they've tasted her cooking. She needs to snap out of it and get with the program. I'm going for a smoke. You settle this." He stomped outside.

"Dink?"

Adi studied her shoes, avoiding Bertie's gaze. "I can't do it, Bertie. You know I can't. Just explain it so T can understand. I can't do this."

Bertie wrapped her arms around Adi, holding her close. "It's going to be okay, baby, you hear me? We aren't going to let nothing or nobody do you any harm. If you can't do this thing, you can't. But before you decide for sure, in one way or the other, let's just think on it a while. Maybe you aren't clearly seeing as how this could be to your advantage. What's the worst thing that could happen? Huh?"

Adi couldn't stop the hot tears rolling down her cheeks. "You know, Bertie. He could find me, that's what. You know where and what I came from. You know I can't let him find me."

"Let's see. It's been eight years since you came here. Seems to me if he was looking for you, he'd have found you by now. Besides that, girl, you're not the child who rode up here that day. You're a grown woman. You don't hardly look at all like that dinky skinny little thing curled up by the Dumpster. This here is a chance for you, Dink. It's your time to shine, baby, and shine you must. You just need to sit with the idea a bit. Let it fill you up and look good and hard at how it could make your life better. Don't you dwell on the bad thoughts. They scare you because you was a child then. Ain't nobody on this earth got the power to make you do or go anywhere you don't want to go. T and I won't let that happen. You know this."

"I'm scared, Bertie." Adi crumbled into her warm, comforting body. "I'm so scared."

"I know you are, baby. I know. But there ain't no need for that fear no more. You just got to realize that. Okay? We're going to sit on my porch, you and me, and we're going to look at all sides of this thing. After that, if you don't want to do it, well, I suppose you won't."

"You got this, Miss Bertie?" T'Claude asked, standing in the doorway.

"I sure do, T, I sure do."

CHAPTER TWO

G riffith noted the change in light as they left the interstate and entered the two-lane highway. *It was silly of Dawn to send a driver. I could've found my way here without a problem.* Still, it was nice not having to worry about anything. She'd have the driver drop her at the restaurant and either get a cab or a ride to her room. The rental car would be dropped off for her at her hotel in the morning. The road was bordered by centuries old live oaks hung with a curtain of Spanish moss. She appreciated the difference in her surroundings, while remaining skeptical of her current assignment. Her career had taken a nosedive in the past year. Jobs like this one would rebuild her battered credibility, though slowly. The familiar fist of anger squeezed her gut, her throat filled with the bitter taste of bile.

She shook off the memory. There was nothing she could do to rewrite her history. *Leave it alone; let it go.* She should be thankful she had friends like Dawn Chapman, people who believed in her and turned a deaf ear to the innuendos and rumor. *Focus. Give Dawn your best.* With a sigh, she thought about her current subject, Michaud's Boiling Pot and its unknown chef, Adi Bergeron. She had to find a way to make this more than a fluff piece. She needed to get back to hard-edged journalism, and a bit on food in a backwater joint wasn't going to do it.

Her first glimpse of the Boiling Pot left Griffith wondering what could possibly have brought Dawn to the location. It looked more like a glorified gas station than a restaurant. *The parking lot's pretty full. That's a good sign.* The peeling gray paint wore a fine coating of dust from the dirt of the lot. The neon sign flashed and clicked on its last leg. Shaking her head, she pushed through the glass front door and knew instantly what had caught her foodie friend's attention. The place smelled like heaven. So many rich scents wafted through the air that Griffith had to swallow as her salivary glands reacted.

"Grab any table and we'll be right with you," called a voice from the back area.

Griffith looked around at the other patrons, who were clearly very happy with the fare. She found a table near the window and dropped her bag onto the open seat across from her. She rolled her shoulders to ease the tension of her long journey.

The place was definitely unique. The walls were decorated with vintage advertising signs, some of which looked original. There were all manner of items hung from the ceiling beams. There wasn't any order to it, more like someone just tacked up whatever odd bits and pieces they came across. The strong south Louisiana accent of her fellow diners was soothing in an odd way, their speech melodious and rolling. Regardless of the story, Griffith was going to enjoy the experience of this culture.

A young woman hurried across the room and stopped in front of her table.

"Hey there. Your first time at the Pot?" She held out a plastic covered menu.

Griffith looked into eyes as deep as night, and nearly as black. The woman's skin was deep bronze, set off by a fringe of coal black hair. *She must have indigenous blood. Gorgeous. She asked me something; what was it? Oh, right.*

"Yes, it is."

"Well, you're in for a treat, then. We got all kind of good things for you to eat. What can I get you to drink?"

"Just water, please."

"You got it. Be right back."

"Wait, miss? I'm here to meet with someone. The owner, Mr. Michaud? Is he here?"

"Aw, no, ma'am. T'Claude doesn't usually make it in till around four. You got a good two hours to wait him out. Does he know you're coming?"

"He knew to expect me today, but I made better time than I thought I would on the drive. Thanks. I'll give him a call."

Griffith watched the woman walk away as she pulled out her phone. Something about her commanded attention. She was attractive, sure, but it was more than that. She just had something that set Griffith at ease. *Must be the Southern hospitality thing. Whatever.* It was nice to feel comfortable in a strange place.

Michaud was happy to hear from her and promised he would be there shortly. He recommended crawfish étouffée for lunch. Griffith looked around for the waitress, but didn't see her. She stretched her legs out under the table and sipped her water.

"So you decide what you'd like to eat?" The woman had appeared so quickly Griffith missed her approach.

"Actually, yes. The étouffée, please."

"Coming right up." As she said this, she slid a saucer with a pale, steaming sausage link across the table and then placed a basket of saltines beside it. "This is just a little teaser for your taste buds. Have you had boudin before?"

Griffith eyed the strange dish. "No, I don't think I have."

"Well, trust me, you'll love it. Just cut it open and scoop up the filling with a cracker. I'll be back to see what you think."

Griffith did as instructed, and though she was prepared to jettison the hot meat and rice mixture, the taste was unbelievable. She quickly helped herself to more. As she took her last bite, the waitress picked up the empty plate and replaced it with a wide shallow bowl filled with a golden brown liquid dotted with bright red and white crawfish tails. In the center was a generous mound of white rice finished with chopped green onions. The aroma billowing up from the plate wrapped around Griffith's senses like a warm blanket.

"Oh my God, that smells so good."

"Well, thanks. I think you'll be happy with it. Go on; dig in. I'll be back."

This time Griffith watched her walk across the room and into what she presumed was the kitchen. She wondered what her story was. She was a great server and very friendly, although most people she'd come across in Louisiana had been incredibly friendly so far. Maybe Michaud would have a similar attitude. That would make the interview process so much easier.

She lost herself in the divine taste of her meal, each bite better than the one before. Whoever this Adi Bergeron turned out to be, she sure could cook. The lunch crowd began to thin out as Griffith savored her final spoonful of deliciousness. The sounds of laughter and banging pots echoed from the back room. She glanced at her watch. It had been forty minutes since she had spoken to Michaud. Hopefully, he would make an appearance soon.

The waitress who had served her was coming through the back door again, but this time she was calling to someone over her shoulder. "Yeah, you're right, Bertie. I didn't think he had it in him. Go on, Jose, get on home. I'll finish up for you." She turned toward the room and looked right at Griffith. She smiled and Griffith had to smile back. *Such a looker, but way too young.* Just as well. She had come to get a story and needed to focus on that alone.

"Looks like you didn't like that étouffée one bit, huh?"

"Nope, not at all." Griffith ran her spoon across the empty surface of the bowl. "Could you just pack this up to go?"

They both laughed. "So what brings you to New Iberia besides meeting T? Are you here to tour the plantations? Avery Island?"

"No, I'm not exactly a tourist. I'm here to write about this restaurant for *Epicuriosity* magazine."

Griffith watched as the waitress visibly recoiled from her. *What's that about?*

"Oh. Here's your check. I'll take these dishes." She hurried from the table as if she were being chased. Obviously, not everyone at the Boiling Pot was happy about the article.

The door opened and a large man walked in. "Hey there, Adi. I sure hope you took good care of Ms. McNaulty."

The waitress stopped for a moment and looked back at her, then quickly went into the back area. The man walked toward Griffith with his hand held out.

"Hey there, Ms. McNaulty. I'm T'Claude Michaud. Call me T."

She shook his hand, expecting a fierce grip, but was surprised by the lightness of his touch. Truly a gentleman, then. "Hello, you can call me Griff."

"All right, Griff, how was your lunch?"

"It was absolutely delicious. I can see why Dawn was captivated by this place."

"You're too kind. We just make simple food for simple folks. Nothing fancy. What did you think of Adi, there?"

"The waitress?"

"Ah, well, I guess. Among other things. She's our chef, you know."

Griffith leaned forward, her interest piqued. "Really? She seems so young to be so accomplished."

"She is young, but she's been with us since she was fourteen. She learned a lot from Bertie about how to make food that sits right up there in your heart when you eat it. People just love her. We feel real lucky that she found us."

"Found you? In what way?"

"Oh, she was a runaway. Bertie found her curled up by the Dumpster some years back, looking like a little raggedy kitten pushed from the gutter. All she had with her was a rusty old bike and the clothes on her back. She must have had a hard life before then. Won't say a word about where she comes from, though. At least not to me. Bertie may know, but hey, you girls talk to each other more than to us guys."

"So she's been here since then? No one ever came looking for her?"

"Nah. You know how it is with some folks. They think their kid running off is the best thing that ever happened. It's a shame some folks are allowed to have kids. Bertie's raised her up from fourteen. She's a fine young woman now, and an excellent cook."

Griffith thought about the runaway angle. Hard luck stories with happy endings always sold well. She could turn this into a real human interest story and sell the article to the *Times* or a news mag. *Please give me more to work with.*

"I plan to make her the focus of the article. Maybe she'll open up a bit."

"You can try. I've already told her I expect her to answer any of your questions. She knows it's important. For now though, what can I tell you about our little slice of heaven?"

Griffith pulled out her recorder and proceeded with her original interview plan, which was to get background first, then talk to the chef and whoever else could fill in the cracks later. The history of the

Michaud family was colorful, and she was pleased with the interview. She asked her final set of questions.

"So, T, who are the people behind the Boiling Pot's success? Who makes things run smoothly here in your restaurant?"

"There's Adi, of course. And Bertie Durall, our first cook, and Jose, who is basically the busman and dishwasher. They make it smooth as glass. On Sundays and special days, I have little Ellen Robichaux come over to help with seating and taking orders. She's fifteen, so she only works on weekends."

"Great. Thank you. Would you be willing to sit down with me again if I need clarification on anything?"

"Sure I would. Am I going to get a preview of the story? You know, like to approve it or something?"

"Well, we don't generally ask for approval, but you'll be more than welcome to read the article before publication."

"All right, then. Fantastic. Can I get you a drink or anything?"

"No, I think I'm going to find my room at the hotel and rest a bit before I start working our interview into notes. I'd like to get contact information for your staff, though."

"You got it. I'll be right back. Do you need a ride to your hotel?"

"That would be nice, thanks."

He left the room briefly and returned with a paper in hand.

"Here you are. Adi's going to drop you off at the hotel on her way to the market. Now, don't worry if she clams up. She's really nervous about being interviewed."

Griffith nodded. "I understand. No worries."

A few minutes later, Adi came out of the back room. Gone was the open friendliness of earlier, replaced by guarded curtness. "Come on. Let's go. I have to get the chicory and get back here after I drop you off."

"Fine by me. Lead the way." Griffith followed her out to a rusty old Ford pickup, probably from the sixties. She wondered if she was better off walking, but when Adi turned the key, it started right up with no hesitation. Adi must have picked up on her concern. She rubbed a gentle hand across the worn dashboard.

"No worries with Pete. He's totally dependable. Me and Jose just finished giving him a full tune-up."

"Good to know. So, I hear you aren't so sure you want to talk with me. Is that right?"

Adi dropped the truck into drive and started onto the highway. Griffith wondered if she was going to ignore the question.

"I guess. I'm just not that interesting is all. Bertie and T are who you should write about. They both have amazing stories to tell."

"And I will. I want to talk to all of you, Jose too. I want people to know how you guys work together to make the Boiling Pot so wonderful. I'm not here to hurt anyone, Adi. Just to do my job."

Adi didn't answer right away. She just stared straight ahead. "If it's all the same to you, I'd rather you just talk to them."

What is she so afraid of? "I wish I could do that, but we both know who cooks the food at the Pot. You are a focal point in the success of that place. People are going to want to know about you. I can promise you'll be happy with the article I write." Adi grunted in reply as they pulled into the hotel driveway. "Thanks for the ride. I'll be calling to set up a time to talk."

"Okay."

Griffith climbed out of the truck and grabbed her bag. She watched as the pickup headed out, wondering what was up with Adi. Was she trying to avoid the interview because she was nervous, or was there more to it? Just where did she come from? The way she went from warm and friendly to completely guarded concerned Griffith. *Time to dig up some background information on the taciturn chef.*

CHAPTER THREE

G riffith stretched as she moved away from her laptop. She'd done her best to research Adi Bergeron, but had hit dead ends at every turn. She hadn't found a single link to her anywhere. She had no social media pages, nothing. It was hard to fathom a twenty-two-year-old with no Internet presence.

What's her story? There's no way I'm blindly writing about this woman. I'm not going to get burned again. I'll have a full and accurate picture of Adi Bergeron before my byline gets attached to any story about her. Too bad if she doesn't like it. My integrity is nonnegotiable.

She ran her hands through her tangle of curls and leaned back against the chair. She had to rely on her instincts. Right now, that meant caution. She would do the interview, and if she didn't get a sense of candid integrity from Adi, she'd be on the plane back to Los Angeles in a flash. Her career couldn't take another knock, even if it was just about some backwater chef with a shady history. But first things first, she needed to find out what the good people of New Iberia thought about the Boiling Pot and its staff. Sometimes the best angle on a story came from the oblique. In her experience, people always had an opinion when she said she was writing an article. The best place to find background would be the local grocery store, the churches, and the salons and barber shops. It was Sunday, so she would make the rounds at the churches first. Hopefully, she would get something useful. She pulled up her maps application and searched for churches near her. There were six to choose from, and this being

South Louisiana, she elected to try Our Lady of Perpetual Help Catholic Church.

The service was in full force when she arrived, so she slipped into the back row. The sanctuary was about half full, mostly with older folks. The rhythm of the priest's voice and the answering congregation lulled her. She caught herself nodding and bit the inside of her cheek to stay awake. *I'm so glad my parents didn't attend church regularly. I'd have made a poor penitent.* When the priest finished the Mass, he invited all to the hall for community time. *Perfect.* She wandered out the big wooden door and drifted to the parish hall with the other churchgoers.

She found a table and sipped the dreck that was passed off as coffee. She was patient as she waited for an opportunity to chat.

"Hello, I don't recognize you. You must be new to the parish. I'm Ina Dupré."

Griffith smiled at the elderly lady with bright white teeth and hair in an old-fashioned bouffant. "Hi, I'm Griffith McNaulty. It's nice to meet you."

"Well, you aren't from here, that's for sure. That accent is distinctly un-Cajun. Where are you from and what brings you here?"

"Actually, I'm a reporter. I'm doing a human interest story on one of your local restaurants."

"You don't say? That's pretty neat. Which place are you writing about?"

"The Boiling Pot."

"Oh, we love the Boiling Pot. They have THE best gumbo, hands down."

Griffith laughed. "That's good to know. I thought their étouffée was quite remarkable yesterday."

"Well, nobody can beat my étouffée. Not even Adi Bergeron."

"Funny you should mention her. She's going to be the focus of my article. What do you know about her?"

"Oh, she's a mystery that girl. Just showed up here a while back. She sure is a sweetheart, though. Just about the nicest young woman in town. Always has a kind word and a smile. On your best day you couldn't find a friendlier soul, I guarantee."

"So she's a kind person and a good cook, huh? Any dark secrets?"

"Well, I don't know about that. She sure doesn't talk about her past much. Never speaks of family and such, but she's a good girl. That's all that matters. Around here, we don't judge people on what they done, just what they do."

"She's not right with the Lord, and you know it, Ina Dupré."

A different woman walked over to them, this one with thin lips pressed into what looked like a perpetual moue of distaste.

"I declare, I don't know what you mean, Grace La Blanc. She's right with the Lord. I know it in my heart."

"She lays with women. That, my dear, is a sin."

"Hush now! You don't know what you're talking about. And it's none of our business."

"It's what my Charlie says. I believe my boy. If he says she's queer, she is. He asked her to prom and she refused him. Said she wasn't interested. Hasn't shown much interest in anyone else, for that matter."

"And that makes her a sinner? Just because she doesn't like your boy? I think not. You go on about your business, hear? This doesn't concern you anyway."

The two women bickered back and forth a while, and Griffith wondered if Adi's sexuality might be behind her guardedness. Griffith had been an out lesbian all her life, but it was probably much harder in a small town like this, and in the Deep South, than it was for her in LA. She would broach the subject with her later. Maybe this wouldn't be as hard as she predicted. *And that doesn't make for a headliner story.* She swallowed her disappointment and returned to the bickering church ladies.

❖

Adi tensed as the car rolled to a stop in front of the Boiling Pot. She watched as the reporter slid out from behind the wheel. She flipped her golden curls out of her face and straightened. While not much more than five feet tall, she moved with a confidence Adi envied. After locking her door, she turned and surveyed the restaurant. Adi quickly ducked away from the window. *I'm not ready. I can't do this.* She scrambled back into the kitchen, heading for the back door.

"What you think you're doing?" Bertie called. "You know you can't just run off without meeting this gal. You agreed to sit down and talk with her. Just hang on, now."

Adi made herself stop, one hand on the screen door. She hung her head. "Well, maybe I made a mistake saying that."

"Too late to run now, girl. You got to at least meet with the woman. She ain't going to eat you, you know."

Adi swung back toward Bertie. "I don't know. That's the problem, Bertie. I don't know a darn thing about what I'm supposed to be doing. Why do they want me to do this, anyway? What does anyone care about some Cajun off the bayou? So what? I can cook, throw stuff into a pot that comes out edible? That doesn't make me news, Bertie."

"What you yelling at me for, you big chicken? Get yourself back out there and say hello to that gal, you hear me?"

Adi choked back another smart comment and inched toward the front door. "I'm going, but I'm not happy about it." Bertie just shook her head and looked pointedly at the door.

Adi turned and pushed through. She inhaled sharply as she collided with the reporter. The impact shook her, though she towered above the smaller woman. It was like running into a brick wall. She thrust her arms out defensively and managed to unbalance the reporter, causing her to stumble backward.

"Oof...hey, slow down there. You're going to hurt someone rushing around like that."

"Sorry, I'm sorry. I didn't know you were here."

"Yeah? That's odd, because I swear I saw you ogling me from the front window a second ago."

Adi felt her face heat and looked away. "Well, um, yeah, but I didn't realize you'd come inside yet. I was on my way out to meet you."

The woman smiled and Adi found herself caught by the play of blue and green in her eyes. Her smile lit her entire face, and Adi felt an answering smile of her own. *She's beautiful. Her nose is all pushed up and small. And those freckles.* The warmth of her embarrassment turned into something new, a different kind of heat that confused her. She shook free of the awkward moment and stuck out her hand.

"No hard feelings?"

"None taken."

"So, Ms. McNaulty, how do we do this?"

"My mother is Ms. McNaulty. You can call me Griffith, or Griff. Let's grab a table and go over the ground rules. That sound good?"

"Okay, Ms—Griff. Can I get you something to drink first?"

"Coke. No ice."

"You got it. Pick any table and I'll meet you there."

When Adi returned, she noticed that Griffith had placed a small recording device on the table and had her tablet computer open in front of her with a flat keyboard attached. The light on the recorder was dark, so she felt comfortable speaking her mind.

"I'm not really sure what you need from me. Do you want recipes and stuff? How does this work?"

"Let's just talk for a bit first. I'd like to get to know you, so I can help the readers feel a connection with you."

"Okay."

"So, tell me a little about yourself. What kind of things do you spend your off time doing?"

Adi tried to think of an answer. She felt all tangled up inside, like she used to when her mom was in a mood. She grabbed her soda to hide her discomfort, and in her haste to drink, ended up coughing and choking as it went down the wrong pipe.

"Are you okay? Here, take this." Griffith held out her napkin.

Tears running down her cheeks and still coughing, Adi gratefully took it and wiped her face.

"Thank you. I'm sorry." She fell back into a coughing fit.

"No problem. Let's start over. My job is to capture who you are and how cooking has influenced your life. We want to draw people in with the human side of you, you know, your backstory. I'm only here to help you tell your story, so relax."

Adi nodded, her throat spasms finally clearing. The words were a comfort. She could do this. She just had to avoid talking about anything before landing at the Pot.

"There isn't much to tell, really," Adi said.

"What? No hobbies? You know, knitting, carpentry? Video gaming?"

"No. None of that."

Adi sensed Griffith's frustration and knew she needed to get the ball rolling. Glancing around the brightly lit room, she saw the old child's pedal car hanging from a ceiling beam.

"See that pedal car? Want to know why it's hanging there? That's a good story for sure. You see, the owner of this place is T'Claude Michaud—"

"T. Claude? What does the T stand for?"

"Oh no, not like that. T stands for little. You know, petite? T'Claude is for little Claude, since his daddy was Big Claude Michaud."

"Got it. So, the car?"

"Yeah, well as I heard it, when T'Claude's daddy was a congressman, he bought T'Claude that little car to make up for being away from home so much. When he was in town, Big Claude was out pressing the flesh, always sitting over at the gazebo in the town square. One afternoon as he was about to get a commitment for a campaign donation, up rides little T'Claude. He had pedaled his little car nearly half a mile to find his daddy. They say he climbed out of that car and walked over to his dad and said, "You said you was going to take me fishing. So, come on. Get in the car and let's go.

"The donor thought that was so funny he ended up giving Big Claude twice as much as he expected. So when he went back to Baton Rouge he took T's little car and kept it in his office. It stayed there until he died. It was the first thing T'Claude put in the restaurant. He says it's his daddy's good luck charm."

"That's a great story. So do you think it's brought good luck to the Boiling Pot?"

"I guess. Seems like things have gone well for him."

"And how about things for you? Do you feel lucky to be at the Boiling Pot?"

"I sure do. This place is my home, you know? I feel like myself here. If it weren't for Bertie and T, I don't know where I'd be."

"How long have you been working here?"

"I started about eight years ago. Bertie taught me everything she knows about cooking. I learned some from reading old cookbooks too. I love to cook. When I cook, I lose myself. I only connect with what my hands are doing and how everything I put into my dish is going to marry. I love the way one little pinch can change a whole dish. It gives me freedom, you know?"

"It sounds very spiritual for you. I know that the end result is divine. So when you're cooking you feel free? How does cooking free you?"

"Oh, it's like, I'm there, but I'm not at the same time. I feel free to be all I am and nothing less. When I'm cooking, I don't have to worry about anything. Well, nothing but the food in front of me. I can let go of everything else, not worry about anything or anyone. I love that."

"It sounds amazing. How did you end up here? Does your family like your cooking?"

Adi went on alert and her breathing tightened. "Bertie is my family. I suppose she likes my cooking, but probably because it's really her, cooking through me."

"Her cooking through you?"

"Yeah, because she's the one who taught me to cook. When I cook, I hear her in my head, reminding me of what to add and how much. She's always a part of my cooking."

"So you say Bertie is your family. How are you related? Is she your mother?"

"Well, no. Bertie's…she's my foster mom, I guess. We aren't blood kin, but we are soul kin, if you know what I mean."

"So not truly family, then?"

"Yes, we're family. Just a different sort family. She raised me."

"What happened to your parents?"

"I don't want to talk about that. It's personal."

"I can respect that, for now. I'm not saying we won't revisit it later, but for now, I understand."

"Good. Thank you."

"So how about your life outside of the restaurant? Do you have a special someone to spend your off hours with?"

"No, just Bertie. We're here from around eight in the morning till about eleven most nights. We just drag ourselves home at the day's end and rest until we get up and come back the next morning."

"That sounds like a grueling schedule. Does the restaurant ever close?"

"Oh sure. We're closed on Mondays, and we take off for Christmas and New Year's, along with the other major holidays."

"But no vacation time other than that?"

"Not really. Well, Jose takes two weeks every August to go see his family in Guatemala. And Bertie goes to see her brother around his birthday in April."

"And you? Do you take any time other than those holidays?"

"No, not me. I have to be here to cook. Besides, Bertie is here almost all the time and she's my family."

"Okay. Well, I think that's enough for now. I want to talk with Bertie next, and then Jose. Could I get back with you later this week for a follow-up?"

"I guess so."

"I do have one last question."

"Shoot."

"Where can I go to have a drink and you know, a little company, in this town?"

Adi considered the question. She hadn't taken Griffith for the fun night type. "Well, there's Boudreaux Icehouse. It's pretty much a beer and pool hall. I guess there's guys there for company."

"Oh, no. I'm not into guys, if you know what I mean. I'd rather have the company of a friendly woman."

Adi swallowed hard. "Um. I'm not sure. I mean… I, uh. I don't know."

"You don't huh? Would you like to help me find out?"

Adi's throat was suddenly drier than a stale saltine. Her abdomen tensed, but she didn't know if it was from fear or excitement. *This is crazy. How can she know?* She'd always been careful not to let on that she liked women. It wasn't safe to feel that way here. She cleared her throat. "No. Thank you. No."

"You're sure?"

Griffith looked sincere, but Adi couldn't afford to let that part of herself out just yet. She didn't need another reason to be afraid. One day, she'd be in a place where she could be herself, but for now, until Bertie was ready to retire, she lived here, and she wasn't about to go making waves.

"Yes."

Griffith reached out and rested her hand on Adi's forearm. She felt the touch all the way through her. It was like an electrical shock. *It's just because I know she knows. That's all.*

"Okay. Let me know if you change your mind."

She picked up her bag and walked to the door. Before she pushed it open, she looked back at Adi.

"You're sure? Really sure?"

Adi felt her whole body heat with the glance. She wanted to change her mind. Take a wild chance and feel, but her answer was out of her mouth before her body had time to catch up. She'd been hiding so long it was automatic.

"I'm sure."

Chapter Four

I sure am happy you got our Adi to talk to you a bit," Bertie said.

Griffith looked into Bertie's warm, honey-colored eyes. A smile creased her ginger brown face, welcoming and open. *This is a strong woman.* She needed to be tactful asking about Adi. It was evident that the fierce loyalty Adi had for her was equally returned.

"Me too. It wasn't easy. She doesn't like talking about herself."

"I know that's right. Adi can hold on to words tighter than a gator to a snapping turtle. But you got her to talk, so you should feel mighty happy about that. Now, what do you want me to talk about?"

Griffith considered how to continue. What she wanted was to know everything she could about Adi, but the other members of the Boiling Pot crew were also important. She needed to flesh out all of the characters here.

"Well, let's see. First, tell me about how you came to work at the Boiling Pot. How long have you been here?" Griffith said.

Bertie shook her head and laughed. "Lord, I been here so long! I was here the day T'Claude looked at this shop and decided he wanted to buy it and make it a restaurant. I been here since day one."

"So how did you meet Mr. Michaud? What made you want to work for him?"

"Heavens now, I been knowing T since he was in diapers. My mamma used to work for his folks. I would help her out when I was home from school. Mr. Big Claude, he paid my tuition. I got my degree in education from Grambling thanks to that man."

"Really? So did you use your teaching degree?"

"I sure did. I taught fifth grade for seventeen years. I was good too. Only reason I stopped teaching was because I came back to New Iberia to care for my mamma before she passed. Mr. Claude then hired me to teach that rascal, T'Claude. Lord, he was a handful that one. Couldn't get that boy to sit still to save my life. But he learned. He truly did. Mr. Big Claude was afraid he'd never get into LSU, but he did just fine."

Griffith could see how proud Bertie was of Michaud. Clearly, the working relationship in this place was more like a family than a business. That would make a great addition to her story. The way the team connected was unique.

"So why a restaurant? What motivated the decision to open the Boiling Pot?"

"It was like this, T'Claude wanted my cooking. Sometimes when I was teaching him, we'd stop for lunch and I'd make him something special. When he was grown, he wanted me to work for him as his own cook, but I found the idea of that demeaning. I mean, I'm college educated, and I like making my way on my own terms. So I had to tell him no. But he wouldn't have it. He said then we would just have to open a restaurant, him and me, so he could have my food and I could have my self-respect."

"So you opened the Pot together?"

"Absolutely. I'm the silent partner. We let folks believe it's all T'Claude's place, but I own fifty percent. And when my time comes, that will pass to Adi. She's like my own daughter, so she'll inherit my share."

Griffith was impressed. Leaving your legacy to someone outside your immediate family meant a lot. *I wonder if Bertie has any children of her own?*

"That's a big gift. Will your family support your idea? I mean, when the time comes? Why is it that you've chosen her? How did Adi come to mean so much to you?"

"That girl nearly scared the life out of me. One morning I parked my car and headed inside when I heard a rustling by the Dumpster. I was sure it was some ornery raccoon or something. I walked over there, big as life, to chase it away when up pops this skinny stick of a girl. Lord, I thought I was going to have a heart attack. Only thing that saved me screaming was the complete look of terror in her eyes. She looked like a colt about to jump out of her skin. And dirty, mmm, mmm. Couldn't tell what color she was from all the road dust. I didn't say much more than 'Come on, let's get you cleaned up and fed.' And she followed me right into the Pot."

"Did she say anything about where she had been? What had happened to her?"

"Look here, in this place we know better than to ask questions we aren't going to like the answers to. I knew she had come from trouble. I knew we could help her find her way. That was what mattered."

"But weren't you curious? Didn't you ever wonder what had become of her family? Worry that they'd be missing her?"

"Well, sure, I worried. I can't imagine someone having a child and not worrying for them every day that they breathe on this earth. Oh, I did my civic duty. I looked in all the papers and called around to the sheriff asking about missing kids, but got nothing. It was like she grew up out of the dirt under that Dumpster. Nobody looked for her. Never."

"The sheriff didn't take her to social services? Foster care or something?"

"He would've if I told him she was with me. No, I just said I'd seen a strange child out on the highway near Carencro. He never came to check my story. Couldn't be bothered, I guess."

"So you just sort of adopted her?"

"That's right. We adopted each other."

"What did you do about school?"

"Well, I taught her. Just as I had taught T'Claude. Some kids are meant for proper school, and some need something different. I tried talking her into going to the local high school, just so she could have friends and such, but she wouldn't have it. Instead she made friends through church. Not too many, but good ones."

"Does she keep in touch with them?"

"Oh, some I guess. They all went off to college after graduation, but Adi didn't want to try for it. I know she could've gotten a scholarship, smart as a whip, that one. But the idea of leaving here scared her. It still scares her. She's carrying something heavy in her soul. Something that makes her feel she doesn't deserve what other folks take for granted."

"That's a shame. That kind of fear can be so debilitating."

"Lord, yes. I was hoping that being recognized as the fine chef she is would bring out the brash in her, make her want to step out into life, you know? But no, if I didn't practically force her, she wouldn't have talked with you."

"I'm easy to talk to, or so I've been told. I'm not giving up, either. I wish I knew what it is that she's afraid of."

Bertie just smiled and shook her head. "You got your work cut out for you, then. She ain't likely to tell that story. The hurt it caused runs deep. " Bertie tilted her head and gave her a serious look. "But listen here. If you hurt my girl digging around in her past just because you're curious, you going to answer to me. Some people don't need their past brought up just to satisfy other folk's gossip needs. You be careful what you do, now. I want Adi to get free, but only if it ain't going to hurt her. You might be just the ticket. I get a sense that she's about done out on hiding and almost ready to swing it loose. Make sure it's her wanting to tell you, not you worrying at something that can bust open and drown her. You hear me?"

"I do. I'll be careful. Thanks. And thanks for letting me talk with you, Bertie. You have a pretty amazing story yourself."

"Nah, just a bunch of nothing."

Griffith laughed. Being around people so self-effacing, so humble and kind, was a far cry from her life in LA. *I'd forgotten what the rest of the world can be like.*

❖

"Not that. That's cumin. We want the coriander. It's in the aluminum can to your right."

"This can?" Griffith asked.

"Yes, that's it," Adi said.

"How much do you want?"

"We need half a teaspoon. That will do these two fillets."

"You mix the spices for one order at a time? Isn't that hard to stay on top of? Why not make a batch of the seasonings?"

"You would think that would make it easier, right? But no, what that does is make for mistakes, under seasoned or over seasoned red fish isn't what we're serving. I do individual orders, because the individuals who ordered them want the best I can give them. It's how I work."

"Hmm, there might be something to that."

"You think?"

Griffith's breath caught at Adi's rakish grin. She was unbelievably sexy when she teased. *I'd like to get her teasing me in a completely different way. Does she know what she's doing to me?*

Griffith moved her hand closer to the cutting board where the red fish was being dressed. As she hoped, Adi's quick movements caused an accidental brushing of their hands. Her body reacted to the touch with a tensing of her nipples. *I can imagine those strong hands playing across my abdomen.* She pictured the dark bronze skin on her white belly, working magic. Griffith moaned low in her throat at the image.

"I like watching you cook. It's really magical. You're like a painter or something. And so serious! This is the first smile I've seen on your face tonight."

"I'm sorry. I get kind of lost when I cook, disconnected. I hope I didn't offend you."

"Oh, no. It's fascinating. Go on, keep doing your thing."

Adi smiled again before turning back to her work. Griffith enjoyed watching her in her element. She was completely absorbed in her work. She would ask for certain ingredients to keep Griffith involved, but truly, she was somewhere else entirely, and that was okay with Griffith. It gave her the freedom to imagine all sorts of scenarios with spices and skin and heat.

So far they had prepared meals for over sixty diners. Each meal was a work of art and created individually. Watching Adi move efficiently and gracefully around the nicely equipped kitchen was a real turn-on. *I've never imagined wanting to be a piece of meat, but to have those hands on me...* A sharp noise behind her brought her back to where she was, a busy, working kitchen. Bertie was plating sides on dishes Adi had handed her way. She was the bass to Adi's treble, weaving her own style of magic at the neighboring stove.

Watching them in tandem was amazing. Griffith leaned back and enjoyed the show.

Watching Adi, you would never guess what a skittish person she was in reality. She was confident and secure in her knowledge of cooking, and she made a point of going out to the tables to deliver about half of the meals in person. *Jovial and friendly. Really well suited to her craft.* Griffith felt especially lucky that she had dined late on Sunday, allowing Adi time to spend with her at her first meal. It colored the whole experience. She knew the diners who received that special level of attention would find their food even more delicious. Her article was practically writing itself. On the surface, anyway.

She watched a while longer before heading out into the dining room. The noise level was higher than it had been earlier. Many of the diners were finishing their entrees and getting comfortable in preparation for dessert. She pushed through the entry door and turned, heading to the porch she had discovered on the north side of the building. It was a charming space, wooden clapboards painted dove gray, a full railing, and the ceiling painted baby blue to ward off wasps.

She slipped into the wicker rocking chair and watched the night drift by. This was such a peaceful place. No wonder a scared runaway girl would choose this as the place to land. She imagined what that must have felt like to a young, frightened Adi. To come across an unlikely sanctuary that gave her all she needed to grow into such a fine person. *If I can get her to talk about her fear, what she's hiding from, I'll feel better about this article. But is that true? Do I want to know out of professional integrity or is it something else?* Griffith wasn't sure if her motivation to find Adi's past had to do with her need to be accurate or her curiosity about Adi. Did she really need that background to stand by the story? Probably not.

Her determination not to be tricked into writing Adi into a person she wasn't came from her experience with Tabitha. But Tabitha had been a criminal and had deliberately subverted the truth. The article she'd written had cost innocent people their life savings and her, her reputation. The stakes were different here. No one would be bankrupted by her not revealing Adi's history. The one at risk was Adi. *So why am I so hungry to know? Is it just instinct, the journalist in me wanting more? Is that a valid reason to dig into her past?*

When she had written the in-depth article about Tabitha Moore for the *Wall Street Journal*, she had failed. She had allowed her personal feelings to cloud her professional judgment. Her backside was still bruised from the beating she had taken from her profession. She had completely bought Tabitha's line that she had been a pawn in the Ponzi scheme at Trenton, Bigelow, and Culp. Griff had derided the CFO of that corporation, slandering his name in Tabitha's defense, writing things Tabitha had told her as information from a "source." Lies, most of them, and when the crap storm hit, Tabitha was nowhere to be found. She'd gone missing with over thirty million dollars that belonged to the workers' 401k plan.

Not only did her peers vilify Tabitha, but Griffith along with her. If she had been more impartial, she wouldn't have created the doubt that gave Tabitha her chance to run. She couldn't be any more penitent for her part in the escape and misinformation, but she had been duped as well. Tabitha wasn't paying for her crime; Griffith was. She was persona non grata in the world of serious print journalism. Complicit through stupidity.

Fact checking wasn't optional and half-truths weren't going to cut it. She would be subtle, but she would get to the truth, no matter how painful. It might be just an article on a chef for a magazine about food, but if she wanted her career back, she had to build it carefully and as strongly as she could at every step. And if her instincts were right, there was more to the story that might mean a step back toward the kind of writing she'd built her life around.

She pushed herself up from the deep-seated rocker and headed back inside. *No time like the present.* She was fairly certain Bertie would back her up if needed. She walked into the kitchen just in time to see the quick caramelization of sugar on a crème brûlée. It looked yummy, making her wish she had one of her own.

"You're back. Perfect timing. I have two more crèmes to do, then Bertie and I were going to have a little bread pudding. You want?"

"Um, yes!"

That smile again, it just changed Adi's whole demeanor. "Good. I'll be done in a sec. Bertie's making the Jack Daniels sauce now. Go watch."

Griffith walked up behind Bertie and watched as she deftly whipped in the whiskey. The sauce was a beautiful golden brown and smelled divine. "Hey there, get those mitts on and pull three ramekins out of the lower oven."

Griffith did as she was told, her stomach growling in anticipation. The puddings had a fine golden crust, and brown hints of raisin poked through. She knew the ultimate touch would be the addition of the sauce, but she could've eaten the pudding as is. Bertie slid the tray onto the counter. She pulled out three saucers and upended the puddings as quick as you please.

"The trick is the turning. If you turn them when they're nice and fresh from the oven, they want to let go of the bowl a lot easier. Let 'em cool and forget about it."

She lifted the ramekins and each plate now held a perfect little castle of golden deliciousness. Bertie scooped a generous amount of sauce on each and handed one to Griffith.

"Now, it won't be good unless you burn your mouth. Go on and take a bite."

The incredible taste and velvety texture of the pudding was unlike anything Griffith had ever eaten. It wrapped around her tongue and sent waves of happiness through her. *Amazing.* The sauce was fantastic, just the right accent for the mélange of custard, bread, butter, and bourbon soaked raisins. She could die happy now. There was no way that dish could be topped. She had hands down had the best dessert of her lifetime.

Adi leaned on the counter next to her, enjoying her own pudding. Griffith watched the play of the muscles in her arm as she scooped a fresh spoon of heaven.

"How is it that you keep so fit with all this good food around? If I worked here I'd have a hard time not indulging."

"I've pretty much grown up here in this kitchen, so I guess I just adapted to the menu. I like walking too. When I get a break I usually walk down to City Park and walk the trails. Sometimes I take a canoe out on the Teche too. That probably helps."

"Canoeing? Seriously? I haven't been in a canoe since Girl Scouts."

Adi hesitated, then looked directly into Griff's eyes. Griffith felt a jolt of energy, not knowing what Adi was looking for, but hoping she saw it in her.

"You're welcome to come along. If you haven't ever been out on the bayou, it's pretty awesome. Give you a feel for what make this place special."

Griffith knew instinctively the value of the invitation. This was something Adi cherished, and she wanted to share it with her. *She wants me to know her. It's only a matter of time until she opens up to me. If I can just be honest with myself and Adi, we'll be fine.*

"I'd like that. When would we be able to go? What's your schedule?"

"I suppose we could go tomorrow. We're closed, so we can take as long as we like. I just have to run a few errands in the morning."

"That would be great. Thank you. Where and when should I plan to meet you?"

"Let's say ten thirty. We can meet up here and drive down to Jeanerette."

"Perfect. I'm looking forward to seeing the bayou. I've seen pictures, and it looks beautiful." *Keep it casual, McNaulty. Don't lose this chance.*

"Just wait until you see it up close. Be sure and bring a long-sleeved shirt and pants. The sun can be fierce, not to mention the mosquitoes. Oh, and sunscreen. I'll take care of provisions."

Griffith was excited about the prospect of spending the day with Adi. *She's starting to trust me. I've just got to make sure that trust isn't misplaced.*

"Great. I really appreciate you giving me the tour."

"It's my pleasure."

"Okay, on that note, I'm going to call it a night."

"What, you aren't going to help with the dishes?" Bertie said.

"Umm..."

"Aw, I'm just pulling your leg. It's Adi's turn to help Jose. You and me, we can just slip on out." She grabbed Griffith's hand and led her out the back door to the parking lot.

"Which rattle trap is yours?"

"I don't think you can see it from here. I parked on the other side of Adi's truck."

"Well. All right then. I'm in that Impala, there, so I'll say good night."

"Good night, Bertie. Be careful getting home."

"You too. Oh, before you go, I just want to say you sure have a good way about you. I was all kinds of worried about how Dink was going to react having a stranger in her business, but you calm her down. I've seen more smiles on that girl today than I have in a month of Sundays. Be sure you don't mess that up, now. You go spooking her with too many questions and she's going pull herself all in like a big old turtle. Don't you let that happen, you hear?"

"I hear you. I'll be careful."

"Good, see that you are."

"Night, Bertie."

"Good night."

CHAPTER FIVE

*F*ool. *What made me go and invite her canoeing? She's*
a reporter, for heaven's sake. Idiot. Adi punched the seat
next to her in frustration. *I'm never going to be a normal person. I'll*
always be tied to J.B. He killed me long ago and I'm still just figuring
that out. She'd helped Jose close up and headed to her car about an
hour after Bertie and Griffith left. She'd had nothing but regret over
her casual invitation to Griff. The knot in her belly was tighter than
a Baptist's purse at happy hour. *I need to call her and tell her I'm*
sick or something. I can't do this. She kicked herself, realizing the
only thing she knew about contacting Griffith was the hotel she was
staying in.

Should *I just drive over there and start knocking on doors? No,*
that's crazy. I just have to suck it up and get through tomorrow. I'll
be okay. I just need to forget about who she is and enjoy being on the
bayou. If I just have fun, I can keep her questions away. The thought
of being on the bayou with Griffith was pretty appealing, all in all. She
liked her, enjoyed spending time with her. Heck, when their hands
had touched tonight, it was like she'd put her hand on a live wire.
The electric feeling that washed through her had been all she thought
about until now. *I'd like to touch more of her.* Knowing Griffith might
feel the same way was distracting. That's how the invitation had
slipped out. She kept imagining what it would be like to be floating
on the quiet waters with Griffith in the boat ahead of her. She'd be
able to watch the wind play across Griff's tangle of soft golden curls,
the subtle play of muscles in her arms and back as she rowed.

I'll be able to imagine all sorts of things. But it's not my imagination that she's a danger to me. She could destroy me with the slip of a pen. And the fantasies I create in my mind around her could destroy me in this community if I ever acted on them. I have to protect myself, my life. I have to do whatever it takes to stay hidden.

She tried to shake off her fear and relax about the canoe trip, but it was harder than she thought. Bertie was asleep in her chair when she got home, but the creak of the door hinge had her sitting up and looking around.

"Hey, Dinky. How you doing?"

"Aw, Bertie. I don't know how I'm doing. I'm getting myself in all kinds of trouble with my big mouth."

"Honey, you got a nice mouth. Not too big, not too small. Just right, in fact. What's worrying at you? You look like a dog circling a treed raccoon. Set on down there and tell me what's the matter," Bertie said.

"It's Griffith. Why'd I go and invite her to spend the day with me tomorrow? What was I thinking?"

"Seems to me you were thinking of having a nice time with a beautiful woman. Nothing wrong with that."

"Everything's wrong with that. I can't be spending hours and hours with her. You know that. You know what made me who I am, Bertie. You know she can't be getting into all of that."

"Shucks, girl. You hold on to that secret any harder and that coal's gonna turn to a diamond. I'm telling you. I know you lived hard times, harder than most. Things you seen and done, well, they ain't good things. But that's the past, child. You don't even know that that man is still alive, much less looking for you. This gal may be able to help you find out. She's got connections and credentials to find out a lot more than you or me. If you can find it in your heart to trust her, maybe she can find out if he's out there looking. Maybe she can help you get free of him for good."

"But what if she writes about me and J.B.? What if her story brings all of his hate and anger down on us here at the Pot? I can't risk that. I can't put you and T and Jose in that kind of danger," Adi said.

"Seems to me, the danger is in not speaking up. If folks knew about him, they'd find a way to put a stop to him, don't you think?"

"I don't. He owned the local police when I was a kid. Probably owns even more now. He's a scary man, Bertie."

"He can't own all the police. There has to be a way to bring him to reckoning. Lord knows you've suffered long enough hiding here. You deserve a life. You deserve to be the woman I raised you to be. Free, proud, and happy."

Adi hunched her shoulders, knowing what Bertie said made sense. But Bertie didn't know J.B. She hadn't watched the cold, calculated look in his eye when he killed someone. She hadn't seen the bodies, bloodied and bruised, that she'd helped him consign to the deep. Most of all, she didn't know about Ransom Prejean. Adi'd never been able to bring herself to tell Bertie about the man whose life she took. She knew that she really hadn't had a choice, but she'd never forget his face. Never forget his kids. Bertie had something there with the thought of using Griffith to find out more about J.B., but she still thought the risk was far too high. It might cost her the only happiness she could remember. *Heck, it could even send me to prison.*

"I'll think on it, Bertie. I promise. I know you want me to shake free of his hold. Maybe I can figure out some way to make that happen. Maybe Griffith can help, but for now, I just have to keep holding my secret."

"Well, I hope you'll see the sense in what I'm saying and take a chance. You got to know you can't live your whole life this way. It's been eight years of hiding. Eight years of sticking to the shadows and watching life go by. I'm not going to be here forever, Adi. I'm seventy-four years old. You got to figure a way to build a life for yourself. One that fills you up and pushes all that darkness out," Bertie said softly, staring into space.

"Don't talk that way. You aren't going anywhere for a long time. I'll do it, I promise. I just have to do it in my own time, in my own way," Adi said.

"See that you do. Best get on to bed now, since you got you a date tomorrow. Want to be looking well rested for that pretty gal."

"Bertie. It's not a date, I mean…we're just going canoeing." It wasn't surprising that Bertie knew. She always knew things before Adi did.

"Umm-hmm. Tell yourself whatever makes you feel good, but I know a date when I see one. You and her got date written all over yourselves."

Adi walked back to her room, wondering how Bertie felt about her possibly wanting to date women. It didn't seem to faze her. She shook her head. Strange things going on these days. *I don't even know some things about myself, and everybody around me wants to tell me who I am.*

There was no way she'd be able to sleep. Too many thoughts bounced around in her head, crashed into each other, and kept her all keyed up. By the time she showered and climbed into bed she'd half convinced herself to tell Griffith everything and ask for her help. She'd played out so many scenes in her head. How Griffith would be disgusted with the idea of her past and call the law down on her. How she'd spend the rest of her life in an orange jumpsuit, watching reruns and eating gruel.

Or that Griffith would be on her side and try to ferret J.B. out of his liar's nest and bring him to justice. How she'd stand in front of Adi and call him out on the things he'd made her do. Her two-page spread of his inglorious history as a drug dealer open in front of them while they dined on the finest food Adi could prepare. His angry, red face as he was taken into police custody.

But none of that would happen. It couldn't. She didn't trust the situation with Griffith enough to give her the truth. She needed the security of her deception. Even more, she needed to sleep. She finally gave up and switched on her radio, letting the music carry her out of her head and into sleep.

She was skipping up the pier, looking forward to seeing Rachel at the store. Papa had promised to take her this afternoon, and she knew she should be happy, but something was sitting on her chest, making her feel like crying instead of laughing. Something she couldn't explain, but it got stronger and stronger the closer she got to the bait shop.

When she was six feet away, her feet seemed to stick to the worn wooden boards of the pier. She looked down in panic to see why it felt that way. Her feet were melted into the wood, her shoes now one with the planks below them. When she pulled to loosen them, they stretched and elongated, making her legs look like the giraffe she'd seen on TV. Finally, she pulled hard enough to pop one foot up. It snapped back into shape without any pain but stuck fast when she set it back down.

Seized by terror at what was happening to her, she screamed, cried out for Papa to come help her. She pleaded with God to send him out of the bait shop. She watched the door, hoping to see him coming. When it finally began to open, relief flooded through her. But there was something wrong. The door, which normally swung freely open, was sticking to the frame, stretching just like her feet. She saw someone on the other side, pushing with their back to the door.

"Papa, Papa, help me," she cried.

The door opened fully, but the person pushing it stretched out and exploded. A mist of red wafted toward her, bathing her in its sticky brilliance. Blood. Everywhere she looked, bright rivers of red blood all cascaded toward her. She felt the first wave of blood touch her and shrank back from it. But it was no use. It flowed up her legs, swarming around her knees and into the bottom of her shorts. Soon she was covered from the waist down in the cloying, sticky mess.

"It's going to strangle me. If that blood reaches my neck, it's going to suffocate me."

She screamed again, calling for her papa. He was there, coming through the door. He put his foot into the cavity that had been the other person's chest and walked quickly toward her. He would save her. Now he would save her.

He walked toward her, raising his hand. A gun? Why does papa have a gun? The blood was almost to her neck. "Papa, please!"

There was a flash and she flew backward, pain slicing through her.

Adi sat up clutching her chest, sweat making her shirt cling to her. Her pulse raced, and she tried to calm herself by taking deep breaths.

That didn't happen. It was a dream. She felt wetness on her cheeks and knew she'd been crying in her sleep. *I can't let him find me.*

CHAPTER SIX

Griffith walked out onto the dock at the Jeanerette Canal landing a little after ten. It was already hot, and the bayou made the air steamy with humidity. She wiped at the sweat trickling down her forehead and looked back at Adi, near the truck. She'd been quiet on the ride here, not saying more than a few words. Her eyes were puffy and bruised looking. *I guess she's not a morning person. I'm not going to let it ruin this glorious day. She'll perk up.*

Griffith looked out at the water. This place was surreal; the bayou looked like a scene from a campy "alligators are going to eat you" horror flick. There were trees in the waterway, their bases covered in green lichen. The classic Spanish moss hung so low on the limbs it brushed the water's surface in places. Cypress knees poked above the water here and there.

It was just a little eerie, and it couldn't have been any further from her life in LA than if she were on the moon. If it weren't such a beautiful sunny day, she would've turned around and headed back to her hotel room in New Iberia. Sighing, she walked back to the truck to help unload the boat.

"Wow, canoes have changed since the nineties. This thing looks pretty high-tech."

Adi laughed. "Not really. It's just borrowed some old ideas from kayaking to make it lighter and easier to maneuver. Come on, let's get her in the water."

Griffith and Adi off-loaded the canoe. It was nice how easily they worked together. No communication necessary, just easy. They slid the long shell into the still water. It barely disturbed the surface.

Adi steadied the hull as Griffith climbed in. She was happy it went as smoothly as it did, since she really didn't want to be gator bait. She hadn't been in a small boat in years. The bright purple hull was solid and the molded seat was comfortable enough.

Adi leaned forward and handed her an oar. "Here you go. I usually paddle up to Lake Fausse Point. It's about a two-hour paddle. That's what you're going to want to see. We can relax there for a while and then make the paddle back in about an hour and twenty minutes, with the tide. Does that sound okay?"

"Sure. It will feel good to get a workout."

"Great. Let's go."

As they glided along the bayou, Adi pointed out various landmarks to Griffith. Some were manmade, others purely natural. It was abundantly clear to Griffith that Adi loved the bayou.

"You know what the Chitimacha say about the Teche?"

"The Chitimacha?"

"The native people that originally inhabited this area. They're still here, and very much a part of what makes this area unique."

"Really? What do they say about the Teche?"

"In their folklore, when the tribe was strong, there was a huge venomous snake. It was so long they measured it in days it took to walk its length. The snake was an enemy of the people because it was swallowing their way of life. One day their chief called together the warriors and bid them to kill the snake. They had only clubs, spears, and arrows to kill it, but swore they would succeed. It took them days and the snake twisted and turned in the fight. During its last death throes, it slowed and flattened, lying still at last. The Great Spirit flooded the place of its death with life-giving water, and the tribe flourished. The bayou Teche is proof of the snake's exact position when it breathed its last breath."

"That was some snake, huh?"

"Yeah. I love those old folk tales. My dad used to tell me all sorts of tales when I was a kid."

This was the first time Adi had mentioned her father. Griffith carefully navigated around the casual slip. "Did he? My dad was always at work when I was a kid. I don't remember him being around much at all."

"That's too bad. My dad was a shrimper. He took me out with him on the Gulf as often as he could. Those were good days."

"Sounds like it. My mother was always there for me growing up. I could count on her, no matter what."

"That must have been nice. It's that way with me and Bertie. I know she's always in my corner. She's all the family I'll ever need."

"What about your mom? Was she in your corner?"

Griffith sensed the stillness her casual question created. *Damn. You pushed a little too hard, McNaulty.* Hoping to break the tension she said, "Wow, what kind of bird is that? It's huge."

Adi rewarded her effort by looking where Griffith pointed. "Oh, that's a blue heron. Aren't they beautiful? You'll see plenty of them while you're here."

"I'm glad. I like them. What do you think about when you travel the bayou? When you're alone, I mean?"

"All sorts of things, I guess. Sometimes I think about the restaurant, or something new to try on the menu. Sometimes I think about things I can do to thank Bertie. Mostly, I just think about how peaceful it is here. How I don't have to worry about things."

"Do you worry a lot?"

"Some. Not as much as I used to. When I was younger, I always worried that someone might try to take me away from Bertie. Make me go live with strangers or something. Now those worries are behind me."

"Bertie is pretty amazing, huh?"

"Heck yeah. She's a truly wonderful person."

"Hmm."

They paddled along silently, watching the wildlife and listening to the unbelievably loud croaking of the bullfrogs. Before long, the bayou widened out into Lake Fausse. Here the trees were incredible. They could paddle right up to their trunks. All sorts of birds were everywhere.

"Look, over there." Adi was pointing to the east. At the top of a cypress tree was a large nest. "That's a bald eagle nest."

"How can you tell?"

"By the size and location. If we're lucky we might catch sight of the nesting birds."

"That would be amazing."

They stilled their paddles and drifted between two large tree trunks, watching the nest. As they watched, an eagle flew gracefully across the waterway and landed on the nest. Griffith's arms broke out in goose bumps and she caught her breath. Again, she was reminded just how far she was from LA. It was such an elegant bird, in such a serene place.

"Here, let's have a bite to eat and rest a while. I didn't bring anything too fancy, just sandwiches and trail mix. Oh, and water."

Adi passed her a sandwich and a water bottle. The setting, the food, and the company were all so perfect. She enjoyed being around Adi, around the calm she projected and the way she made such a simple life look so inviting. *What is it she's hiding? Why can't this simple life be her story?*

Griffith shook her head. It didn't matter how nice this was, how nice Adi was. What mattered was the truth. She owed it to herself, and to Dawn, to find out what Adi's issues were before they printed a big feature piece. The hard questions were still ahead, and with a little luck, she could get the answers without losing this connection. Adi could be a real friend if they could get past the hard stuff.

"Adi?"

"Huh?"

"Tell me about when you first met Bertie. What was it about her that made you trust her?"

Adi was quiet for a long moment as she thought. "I was just a kid, you know? I didn't think about whether or not I could trust her. She saw me, she got me up, fed me. I don't know. I just knew I was safe."

"Why? Why did you need someone to make you safe? What was chasing you?"

"I don't want to talk about that. I already told you."

Griff decided to lay her cards on the table. Around here, that seemed to be the way to go. "I know what you told me, but I still have to ask. It's what I do. I need to know, for me. I have to be sure that when we print your story, Dawn's magazine can stand behind it."

"I don't care what you need for your story. I don't talk about that time. That's not me anymore. I'm done talking about it now. Let's talk about something else."

Griffith could hear the anger in Adi's voice and wished she could see her expression to know just how upset she was. If she wasn't careful, she could get her California butt dropped into the swamp.

"Okay. Fine. Let's talk about something else. What do you want to talk about?"

"Let's talk about you for a change."

Griffith laughed out loud. "Me? Okay. What would you like to know?"

"What made you want to be a reporter?"

"That's a fair question. I guess I've always loved people's stories. Even as a kid, I wanted to know about other people. What made them who they were. I loved asking the questions that got them talking, maybe because I didn't have stories of my own. My life was pretty classic Americana. No drama, typical family. Maybe I was looking for heroic people to fill my subconscious, I don't know."

She took a chance on upsetting the canoe, and shifted to look back at Adi. The intensity she felt talking about herself was reflected in Adi's eyes. "One thing I do know, I'm good at my job. I'm good at it because I care. I want to know everything because I genuinely care about the people I write about. It has come back to bite my ass, but I care. I think people's stories should be heard. Not just the big names, or the stuff everyone gets to hear about. The real stuff, the things that matter, the parts that make someone who they are. What makes you who you are, Adi?"

"What do you mean?"

"Well, I mean you're probably the only twenty-two-year-old in the world who doesn't have a vibrant life on social media. When I Googled you before coming here, I couldn't find a single thing about you. That's unusual."

"Oh, well, I don't really have a lot of time to spend on the Internet. We don't even have a computer at home. I like to spend my free time like this. Living real, not virtual."

"No computer at home? Wow, I have my computer with me most of the time, and if not, I have my smartphone. It's essential for me to be connected."

"I'm connected, just not with electronics. I'm connected to this place, to other places I've explored. I don't know. I just don't feel compelled to be online. It's not what's important to me."

Griff thought about that. It was refreshing to think of life without constant information overload. Refreshing, and maybe a little bit scary. "I've had friends in LA go on technology vacations. You know, no Internet, no TV for periods of time, but I've never known anyone who just wasn't connected. It's so different."

"It works for me. I think if I did all of that, I'd be stressed out all the time. I like the pace of things here. I've got everything I need."

"Interesting," Griff said. She turned back around and slipped her paddle into the still water. "Let's go. I'm ready to see more of this beautiful place."

Adi dug in as well and the craft began to move across the lake. When they neared the eastern edge of the lake, the marsh grass thickened and only a narrow strip of water cut through.

"This looks like fun. Is it navigable?"

"Most of the time it is. It leads back into Bayou L'Embarras. We could go, but we won't be able to turn back until it widens out. That will be a bit of a haul."

"But it looks like so much fun."

"Looks can be deceiving. I got stuck in a weed row like that so bad once I had to back paddle for almost an hour. Believe me, we don't want to do that. We could head up to the state park, though. The waterway narrows down there, but not quite so much. There will be gators up that way, if you want to see them."

"Okay, that sounds like fun."

They headed north and west to the park and saw about a dozen alligators along the way. It made Griffith nervous the way they sat in the water with just their eyes and nostrils showing. Adi assured her they had nothing to worry about.

By the time they made it back to the canal landing, Griffith could feel the ache of a good workout in her shoulders and arms. She'd be sore tomorrow, but she wouldn't have missed this adventure for the world.

"Isn't it going to be hard to be on your feet cooking all day tomorrow?"

"Oh, I'll feel it, but it will pass. I do this pretty regularly, you know."

"Well, I know I'm not picking up a single thing tomorrow. Thank you for this day, Adi. I really had a great time."

"You're welcome. I'm usually on my own out there. It was nice to have company. I...I'm sorry about earlier. I know you're just doing your job. I hope we can be friends?"

"Sure we can. I hope you'll trust me enough to tell me your story someday. I get that you can't right now, but let's not close the door on that. Please?"

Adi nodded but didn't say anything else. It was something, anyway. Griff didn't have a ton of time, and she got the feeling it was going to be slow and steady movement with Adi. *Toe the line. We'll get there.*

❖

Adi stretched her achy shoulders before getting out of bed. The trip with Griffith yesterday had been a lot of fun, but she would be paying the price for it today. At least she didn't have sore legs to go with her arms. She wondered how Griffith was feeling this morning. She would check in with her later. It was nice to have Griffith around. She was surprised at how comfortable she felt around her. The invitation to go canoeing had slipped out without her thinking about it, and she'd desperately wanted to back out. But when Griff had shown up, all smiles and light, the doubts vanished. Instead, she'd been filled with nervous excitement and had wanted to make sure Griff had a good time.

The idea of a reporter following her around and prying into her life had been so unappealing, but the reality wasn't so bad. If only she could trust Griffith not to write about her past and at the same time, get her help finding out about J.B., she might just get the freedom she wanted. She felt so disconnected to the child she had been, and she realized that being around Griffith had made her aware of how far she'd come. But the risk to her loved ones was real. Too real to disregard. She'd have to make sure there was no chance they'd be hurt.

Consciously, she knew she wasn't really responsible for Ransom's death. That was on J.B. It would be his word against hers if it ever came down to it. But running away and hiding for all this time would reflect poorly on her. And if the truth came out, J.B. wouldn't stop until she was dead. Until they all were. No, there was no way she could ever let anyone find out what she'd done. As much as she wanted to see if Griff could help, it wasn't worth the risk.

Time to get moving. The day won't wait forever. She hopped up and hit the shower. She would put all thoughts of that time out of her head and just be in the present. She dressed in her jeans and a T-shirt and went into the kitchen.

"Yum. It smells good in here," she said.

"It should. There are hot biscuits in the oven and grits on the stove. Get yourself a plate and have some breakfast," Bertie said.

"Thanks."

Adi loaded her plate, poured some coffee, and sat at the table with Bertie.

"So what did you do with your day off? Did you go to the community center and play some bridge?"

"Nah. Those old folks make me tired. I went down to Louis's house and watched his grandbaby for a couple of hours. He had a doctor's appointment and you know how his girl relies on him to watch little Clayton."

"He must be getting pretty big now, huh?"

"Aw, he's just about the perfect age. Old enough to get around on his own, but too young to talk back. He's pretty easy to take care of. How was your boat ride with the reporter?"

"It was fun. She's awfully easy to be around too."

"That's good. Did she ask you too many questions?"

"No, just a couple I couldn't answer."

"What do you mean you couldn't answer? What you mean is you *wouldn't* answer. You're going to have to let go of the past, sometime. There's a thing about hard history, the letting go is almost as painful as the living of it. I know you regret the things you were made to see and do. We all got regrets. Thing is, you can't live on them. I worry about you keeping all that nasty stuff bottled up. Griffith is here to tell your story, and the restaurant's, of course, but your story even more. This is your chance, girl. Time to take a hold of the rest of your life. You know there was a reason those folks ended up at the Pot. A higher hand directed them to our door. You can't ignore that."

"Maybe. Maybe not. I don't know. I just can't talk about that time. You're the only one I've ever told. It's just too complicated."

"Well, at least think about it, Dink. It would be good for you to not carry that weight on your own. Maybe she could help you. I know you're worried about what your father's going to do. You're scared he's going to come up here and hurt you, me, everybody. He might. He sure might, but isn't he hurting you now? Isn't he keeping you small when you're meant to be so much more? Thing is, by not speaking up, you're leaving other innocent people in danger. You just have to find a way to bring the whole sorry mess to light. Griffith might know the way. That might be why she was led here."

"It's too risky."

"Risk is the backside of happiness. You can't have one without the other. I know one thing for sure. You are gonna bust open if you don't let that stuff go. I can see it bending your soul, plain as day. If you don't figure out some way to come to grips with it and resolve it, you're going to regret it. It will break you."

"Bertie..."

"Bertie, what? What? I'm telling you the truth, Dink. It's getting worse every day. You have to do something. You need to find a way to be in the world, girl, not just on it."

Adi swallowed the last of her bitter coffee, savoring the chicory tang. She rinsed her dishes and put them in the dishwasher.

"I don't want to talk about this. I'm off to Johnson's to get the crawfish. I'll see you at the Pot."

"All right. If that's how you want it. I'll see you later."

CHAPTER SEVEN

G riffith looked at her computer screen. *Am I doing the right thing? I know there's something in her past that Adi is afraid of.* It could be abuse, but her instincts said there was more to it than that. She felt like she was betraying the fragile trust Adi had shown her by even thinking about running a search, but she hadn't lied. She'd told Adi that she had to have the facts, for Dawn, for the magazine. It still felt wrong. If only Griffith could get Adi to tell her where she had been before she landed at the Boiling Pot. If she knew, she'd be able to decide if it was appropriate to write about it. They could talk about it. As things stood, Griffith was handicapped by Adi's reticence.

A simple computer search might help her piece together Adi's childhood. She now knew that Adi's father had been a shrimper. That limited her search to over 100,000 commercial shrimpers along the Louisiana coast. Adi arrived at the Boiling Pot on a bicycle, making it more likely that she came from one of the communities due south of New Iberia. She'd probably taken the coastal road, which meant the most likely towns would be the ones back south, toward the Gulf.

Griffith pulled up a map of the area on her laptop. *Where did you come from?* There were several possibilities along Highway 90. Morgan City had a fairly large shrimping community, and Berwick and Patterson also had active shrimping communities, though smaller. If she kept going down the coast, eventually Highway 90 led to some much smaller communities. Should she start looking? Griffith had never hesitated researching her subjects. Not even with Tabitha.

She'd been stymied by Tabitha's machinations, but she did her best to get the truth. *Why am I feeling so conflicted? I'm just doing my job.*

Griffith typed in Morgan City. After a minute's hesitation, she hit the enter key. She searched *missing teenagers/Louisiana* and found a registry of missing persons. It would be tedious, but this was the kind of research she was built for. Finding the connections that led to her story took time and effort. Griffith was determined not to shirk her responsibility to get it right this time. She read through the entries, narrowing the window for disappearance to late 2007 to early 2008.

Inputting her parameters brought her twenty-seven pages of results. It would probably take her a week to go through the list just once. Questioning whether it was worth her time, Griffith grabbed a notebook and got down to work. After three hours, she leaned back and rubbed her aching eyes. Her list of possibilities was short, only a handful of girls the right age and description for Adi so far. She needed a break, and something to eat.

She contemplated going back to the Boiling Pot, but she wanted something different tonight. She opted for a hibachi joint down the street from her hotel.

The restaurant was cozy but clean. The shared tables were mostly busy, which she took as a good sign. She put her name on the list then headed to the tiny bar for a beer. She had taken one sip when someone placed a gentle hand on her shoulder. T'Claude Michaud was standing beside her.

"Hey there. You aren't scouting a new place for your story, are you?"

"No, not at all. Just having dinner. How are you, Mr. Michaud?"

"Now, come on, call me T. I'm good. This is a good little place to eat too. Can I buy you dinner?"

Griffith looked at him, gauging his motivation. Was he interested in her or just being considerate? If it was the former, she would have to be clear that he wasn't her type. His warm smile alluded only to friendship.

"Well, that depends."

"Oh?"

"Yes. If you're thinking to influence my writing, I can't be bought. If you're thinking to share a pleasant dinner, I'm all yours."

He laughed heartily. "No influence peddling here. My dad took care of that for the family. I would just enjoy talking with you over dinner."

"You're on, then."

The hostess called them to be seated, and they crossed the bar to the dining room. The other diners at their table were involved in conversation, so they were able to talk uninterrupted.

"So, what do you think of the Pot? Is everyone treating you nice?"

"Oh yes, everyone has been wonderful. Adi's my primary focus, of course. She's very intriguing."

"Adi? Really? I find her about as exciting as watching paint dry."

"Oh come on, you know she has a story. She's hiding something and that's what I want to unlock. Her secret. I think the human interest potential of a runaway turned professional chef will really appeal to the masses. Her relationship with Bertie and you defines her. I want the backstory, the root. What motivated her to leave home and how she ended up here."

"You looking for pearls among the cockles, girl. Adi is as plain as plain gets. She isn't hiding anything. You want her to dredge up her past for your story? What if her past is hurtful to her? That just ain't right to be pulling at someone for something they let go of so long ago. Look here, now, if you hurt that girl, you're going to have me to deal with, you hear?"

"I don't want to hurt her. That's the furthest thing from my mind. I just want to have all the facts. If there is something in her past that could damage you, or your business, wouldn't you want to know?"

"Aw, you can't be serious. Adi was practically a baby when she landed at the Pot. She grew up right here. We know all we need to know about her. She's a good person with a good heart. And it don't hurt that she's an amazing cook."

"You have to wonder what it is that keeps her so tense all the time, though."

"She's not tense all the time. That's just special for you. Most of the time she's laid back and easygoing. I don't think you get just how shy she is."

"I don't find her shy at all. She's hiding something, and she knows it's my job to find out what it is."

"Now see, that's where you're wrong. Your job is to write about the restaurant. Whatever Adi isn't telling you has nothing to do with the Pot."

"How can you say that? How can you even know? Has she told you what it is?"

"No."

"Then you really have no way of knowing how it could impact your business. This article is going to bring all sorts of attention to you and your place. If there is a time bomb ticking in the kitchen, it's likely to blow once we publish."

"Whatever happens, happens. Just give Adi the space she needs. She's special, that girl, and she's the reason my restaurant is so damn good. Her past don't affect the present."

"I can't give her space. It's part of my job. If I don't get all the information I need to feel secure with the article's veracity, I can't put my byline on it."

"You can't be serious. Something that happened, or didn't happen, to a fourteen-year-old kid is going to keep you from writing your story?"

"It all depends on what that something is, T'Claude. That's why I have to keep asking until I get the truth."

"Whatever. Good luck with that." He stood and dropped a couple of twenties on the table. "Dinner's on me. Take care."

Griffith sat back and blew out a frustrated breath. She felt out of sorts. The need for background on Adi was imperative, but talking to people about it made her feel sullied. Dirty. She had to get Adi to open up to her on her own. There wasn't a clean way around it. *In LA there wouldn't be any question about the need to know what was in someone's closet. The people here are so...private.*

She pulled out her cell phone and dialed the number she had for Adi.

"It's your dime, best be talking."

"Hello?"

"Yeah, what you want?"

"Um...this is Griffith McNaulty. I'm trying to reach Adi Bergeron?"

"Well, why didn't you say so? This is Bertie. Adi's still working. She won't be leaving the restaurant for a few more hours. You can call the main line there if you need her. I doubt she'll be able to take a call, though."

"What time does she usually finish on a Tuesday night?"

"It'll be eleven if it's a typical night. If it's busy, it'll be closer to midnight."

Griffith checked the time. Eight forty-five. Two or three hours to go. She could go back to her room and search more missing persons reports.

"Okay. I'll catch up with her later then. Thanks."

"You're welcome. If you want, you can come on over to my place and wait for her here. I don't have much going on. Just watching my programs on television."

"Thank you, Bertie. I might just do that. I didn't realize she lived with you. I guess I just assumed she lived on her own. Would it be okay to come over around ten thirty?"

"Sure, honey. You come on when you feel like it. I'll be up. I don't go to bed until I know my girl is home safe."

"Great. Thanks again."

"Well, all right. Bye now."

Griffith said her good-byes and left for the hotel. She put in another hour studying old missing persons notices before grabbing a quick shower and heading over to Bertie's house.

It struck her that she didn't exactly know where Bertie's house was, but the feeling she knew them had made her forget that fact. She called again and got directions. The house was charming, a little Victorian cottage, probably dating from the early 1900s. There was a nice wraparound elevated porch with a wicker swing.

Griffith rang the bell and waited. Bertie opened the door in a quilted robe covered in small pink roses.

"Hi, Griffith. Come on in and make yourself at home."

"Hi, Bertie. I really appreciate your invitation to wait here for Adi. I hope it's not an inconvenience."

"Not a bit. How about a little something to wet your whistle? I'm having my little sip o' hooch. Puts me right to sleep."

"That sounds great. What exactly is hooch?"

"Heh, heh, it's called a Dark 'N Stormy. Just a little rum and a little ginger beer."

"Yum. I'd love to try one."

"Coming right up. You sit yourself down on the couch and put your feet up. Don't tell me your feet are fine. Everybody puts their feet up after ten in this house. It's a rule."

"Got it. Couch. Feet."

"You learn quick for a foreigner. I might get used to you hanging 'round here."

"I do my best to assimilate. You make it pretty easy."

Bertie returned, drinks in hand, and sat beside Griffith on the comfy couch.

"Ooh Lord, I'm telling ya, my feet need this time. It's harder on the feet than anything else to work the restaurant all day."

"I'm sure it is. How old are you, Bertie? If you don't mind me asking."

"Girl, just when I thought you were about civilized, you going to go and ask an old woman her age? Didn't your mamma teach you better than that?"

"I'm sorry. I didn't—"

"I'm just pulling your leg. It's no secret around here. I'm going to be seventy-five on my next birthday. Which, if you were wondering, is coming up next month."

"That young, huh? I'm just amazed you're still working every day. Are you ever planning to retire?"

"Retire for what? I'll retire when the good Lord sees fit to retire me. We were put here on this earth to do, not to sit. I take my day of rest on Monday. What am I gonna do if I'm not working? Sit around here and grow mold? No, that's not for me. I'm pretty happy with my life. You sound like Adi with that talk."

"So Adi has talked to you about retiring?"

"Oh yes. She has made it her personal mission to get me to quit. Ain't going to happen. Not for her, not for anyone. Besides, who's gonna look after her if I'm not up at the Pot every day?"

"Does she need someone to look after her?"

"Don't we all?"

Griffith thought about it. She hadn't had anyone looking after her since she left home at eighteen to attend the University of Southern California. She hadn't thought she was missing anything by being independent. In fact, she had always felt it made her better at her job. Nothing tying her down. She was able to go where the stories were at a moment's notice. She had built quite a reputation as a freelance journalist precisely because she had no one looking out for her.

"I plead the fifth. I'm here to find out about you all, not to fill your time with my life story."

"Aw, now. We Southerners love to hear people's stories. Makes you look suspicious if you don't share."

"Well, what's Adi's excuse then? She's a Southerner. Why does she get a pass on sharing her life story?"

Bertie stared at Griffith for a long while before answering. "You trying to trip me up, huh? She has her reasons, and they're good enough for me. I'm not going to be the one who tells you what she's put behind her. She has to do that herself. I expect if she comes to trust you enough, she'll tell you."

"I hope you're right. God knows I'm doing my best."

"That's all you can do, then. Come on. You have got to see what happened on *General Hospital*. You're not going to believe it."

Chapter Eight

Adi slid out of the truck and kicked the door closed behind her, cradling her injured hand. She couldn't believe how stupid she had been. She knew better than anyone to avoid the sharp end of a knife. She could've lost her finger. As it was, she wouldn't be cooking for the next few days. Thank goodness T'Claude had stopped by at the end of the night. He had arrived just in time to rush Adi to the emergency room.

She had been deboning chicken for tomorrow's special when she lost her focus. She couldn't get Griffith out of her head. It surprised her that it wasn't fear of being discovered she was thinking about, but the way Griffith looked sitting in front of her in the canoe. The sound of her happy laughter over the water. The kiss of sunlight on her cheek as she turned to ask about the gators. The play of the muscles in her arms as she pulled on her oar. *So beautiful.* The sharp sting of the knife pulled her back into the present.

She was lucky she had missed any major tendons in her index finger. The doctor washed the incision thoroughly before stitching it up and sending her home with a prescription and warnings to keep the wound dry and clean.

"You know, Adi, you could've just told me you wanted some time off. You didn't have to cut your finger off," T'Claude said as they walked back to his car. "At least you didn't bleed on my leather seats."

"I'm sorry. I don't know what happened. I could pretty much debone a chicken in my sleep."

"You think? I don't agree. Clearly, you need to be a little more awake to work with a sharp blade. I guess we can shut down for a couple of days. I don't want Bertie trying to handle the place on her own."

Adi felt terrible. Jose was learning the ropes of the kitchen, but he sure wasn't ready to run the place yet. "I'm really sorry, T."

"Aw heck, it will be the perfect opportunity to repaint the bathrooms. Lord knows they need it. Don't worry about it. Let's reopen on Friday. You can sit back in the kitchen and talk Jose through the meal prep. Bertie can help out, but she won't be overwhelmed."

"You know she isn't going to be happy about us closing down."

"I know, but that's tough. She'll get over it. And like I said, we can do some work on the place."

They pulled into the dark parking lot. T'Claude parked next to Adi's truck. "You going to be okay to drive?"

"Sure. No problem. I'll see you in a couple of days."

T nodded as she climbed out of his car and got behind the wheel of the Ford.

The drive to the house was uneventful, if a little challenging. Suddenly wiped out, she couldn't wait to lie down. She unlocked the door and opened it as quietly as possible. She knew Bertie would've waited up and was probably asleep in her chair. She should have called her so she could've gone to bed.

She stopped short after gently closing the door. Yes, Bertie was sound asleep in her chair, but Griffith was asleep on the couch. She looked so adorable, one hand curled under her chin, an errant strand of golden brown hair fluttering with each breath. Adi stood frozen, watching the almost-stranger sleep. A warm tenderness swept through her and the desire to walk over and tuck that strand of hair behind Griffith's ear was almost too strong to resist.

What the hell is the matter with me? Why did seeing Griffith, or even thinking about her, make her feel this way? She had done serious damage to herself as a result of this distraction tonight. It had to stop. Adi didn't appreciate the way Griffith's being here was interfering with her life. She liked her life, loved it, in fact. She didn't want this. She hadn't asked for it, and it was time for it to end.

Adi reached back and pulled the door open, then closed it with a little more force than needed to wake the sleepers. Griffith sat up quickly, on guard almost immediately. Bertie opened her eyes and grimaced.

"What in the world is wrong with you, Adi? That ain't the way to come in the door after midnight and you know it. You're not too big for me to take over my knee, now. You best be apologizing for that rude awakening."

"What happened to your hand? Are you okay?" Griffith said.

"Lord. What happened?" Bertie got up and moved over to inspect her hand.

"It's nothing. Knife just slipped. It'll be okay in a few days."

"The knife just slipped? How did that happen? You haven't cut yourself in the kitchen since you were fifteen."

"Well, I have now. I'm sorry I woke you both. I'm pretty tired. I think I'm going to go to bed."

"Griffith has been here waiting to see you since ten thirty. You be polite now and sit here and talk for a while. I'm going to bed. Griffith, I don't want you driving around this late. It's not safe. Adi will show you the guest room after your visit. I expect you at the breakfast table in the morning. Don't disappoint me."

"Yes, ma'am. Have a good sleep."

"Good night."

"Good night, Bertie"

"I'll look forward to the story of your hand in the morning. Sleep well."

Tension filled the room as Bertie left. Adi didn't know what she should do. She knew what Bertie expected. But Griffith felt more like an intruder than a guest. She didn't want to make nice right now.

Griffith broke the ice. "I'm sorry to surprise you by being here. It wasn't my intention to impose myself."

"It's okay. I'm just really tired. Was there something important you needed to talk to me about tonight?"

"It doesn't seem important now. It can wait. Why don't we just call it a night?"

Suddenly, Adi felt bad. Griffith was such a puzzle. She made her feel things she didn't want to feel. She wanted to hear things Adi didn't want to say. But really, she was a nice person and didn't deserve to be treated rudely. Griffith didn't know she was throwing Adi into chaos. She sighed and dropped onto the couch next to Griffith.

"I'm sorry."

"You said that. I think you said it twice, even. Don't sweat it. I'm not that thin-skinned. I ambushed you by showing up at your house. You have every right to be a little peeved. We can talk in the morning."

"No, it's okay. What can I help you with?"

"We're friends, right?"

"I guess. I mean, I hardly know you. So, I don't know…"

"Okay, well we have the potential to be friends, then? I mean, I really enjoyed our time together on Monday. I feel comfortable around you. I think we could be good friends."

"So you came over here at ten thirty to ask me if we could be friends? I have to admit, I think that's kind of weird." Griffith laughed that darn laugh, the one that made Adi feel like a school of mullet were swimming around in her belly.

"It sounds strange now, but when the idea hit me, it made perfect sense."

"Okay, if you say so."

"I wanted to say, let's get to know each other. I want to spend time with you, off the record. You hardly know me. I hardly know you. Let's change that. Does that sound reasonable?"

"Look, you're here for a reason. You're here to write a story, of which I am the subject. That kind of limits the scope of our association. You'll be wheels up back to LA once your work is done, right? Why would you want to invest in a friendship with me? It's not like you're sticking around."

"Because I like you, Adi. I really like you. I want to be your friend…and maybe, something more?"

"Huh?"

"Come on. You get that I'm attracted to you, right?"

"Uh—"

"Wait. You do like women, don't you?"

Adi felt her face go hot and knew she was bright red. She knew she was a lesbian; she just didn't think anyone else knew. She certainly hadn't advertised it. She had known since she was eleven years old and kissed Rachel Comeaux, but she hadn't kissed anyone since then. She had educated herself about her sexuality thanks to the Internet, and the youth group at the community center. But she had never acted on her desire. She just felt she wasn't ready, and it wasn't like the little town she lived in was crawling with options. Her plan had been to move to New Orleans when Bertie was finally ready to retire. To find a job cooking and to explore her sexuality in a larger, safer place. Granted, Bertie didn't seem to be in any hurry to retire, and it was getting harder not to break out, but Adi had learned patience at an early age. How did Griffith know?

"It's okay, you know? To be gay. It's perfectly natural," Griffith said. "I mean, if you are a lesbian, it's nothing to be ashamed of."

"Are you a lesbian?"

"I am. Have been all my life."

"So...you've kissed women before?"

"I have. Have you ever kissed a woman?"

"No. I mean, not a woman."

"No?"

"Well, not a woman. I kissed a girl when I was a kid."

"Okay. Have you ever kissed a guy?"

"Yeah. I kissed Josh Babin. When I was fifteen. Or really, he kissed me."

"And who did you like kissing more?"

"Aw heck, Griffith. I know I'm a lesbian. I just didn't know you knew that. How exactly did you know? I haven't even talked to Bertie about it, not really."

"I guess it takes one to know one. I hope I haven't made you uncomfortable."

"No, I'm just surprised. Is it that obvious? I mean, do you think other folks might guess?"

"Some might wonder, but if you haven't talked about it, it's all speculation at this point."

Adi's chest tightened and she felt light-headed. The prospect of something that personal being talked about by other folks made her feel sicker than when she'd sliced her finger. "You're not going to write this in your article, are you? I'm not sure I want that out there just yet."

"Heavens no. Adi, what I write about will focus on your cooking, what inspired you to be a chef and, I hope, the story of how you ended up at the Boiling Pot. That's it. Nothing about your sexuality needs to be included. I was just curious for myself."

The relief was almost overwhelming, and she wondered if the pain medication was giving her the light-headed feeling, or if it was Griffith's proximity. *Both.* "Good, thank you. If they heard about it back home...I mean if they knew. Oh, I don't know what I mean. I'm not a part of my past any more. I never belonged there. This is my home, for now. When Bertie is ready to retire, I'll move somewhere even bigger, New Orleans or Houston, somewhere I can be myself. The small minds of Dulac won't matter a bit."

"Of course they won't. They don't, in fact. People who can't or won't accept folks like us are fewer and fewer these days. You can have a full, free life, Adi. It's out there right now. Trust me; I live it every day. Being a lesbian is just like having brown eyes. It's a part of who you are and you can't change it."

"You make it sound so simple. You have no idea the kind of hate that lives in these bayous. Nope. No one will know about me until I am so far from South Louisiana you can't even remember the echo of what I was. Please, Griffith. Please be careful not to say anything to anyone."

"You don't have to worry about me, Adi. I'm here to talk to you, not about you. So, back to my original question. Would it be okay for you and me to get to know each other a little better? To build a friendship? An open, honest friendship? You can't have too many friends, right?"

Adi laughed in relief. "Yeah, I guess that would be okay. I'd like to be friends, but I'm not sure about anything more."

"If that happens, it happens. Let's just play it by ear, okay?"

"Okay."

"Sounds like you're going to have a few days off. How about you show me some more of the unique things in New Iberia?"

"That sounds good. We can go to Avery Island. That's where they make Tabasco sauce. And we can go crawfishing too. Have you ever been?"

"No, I can't say that I have. Do I need a license or something?"

"I've got that covered. Let's see what tomorrow's weather is going to be. If it's a nice day, we'll do tourist stuff. If not, as long as it isn't raining, we can crawfish. I have to warn you, it's messy and you'll be doing most of the work, thanks to my hand. You still want to try it?"

"Sure I do."

"Great. Let's get some rest and make plans over breakfast. Come on, the guest room is this way."

Adi lent Griffith an oversized T-shirt to sleep in and showed her where the bathroom was. She even found a new toothbrush in a cupboard.

"Okay, I think you're set. See you in the morning," Adi said. The medication was making her woozy and she was desperate to lie down.

"Good night," Griffith said.

Adi slid into her bed, wondering about her unexpected guest and their conversation. *What was that about? I planned to stop this and now I've gone and opened myself up to her even more. Do I want this? Can I trust her?* Adi wanted to trust her. She liked Griffith, the way she made her feel. When Griffith smiled at her a warm rush of delicious tension washed over her. She liked that feeling, craved it. If she could just keep Griffith out of her past and here in the present, she'd get more of that.

What would it be like to kiss her? Adi imagined pulling Griffith against her and looking into her green eyes. So green they were like those times out on the bayou when the sun hit just right and light cascaded through the water. The depth of the water, and those eyes, seemed endless. If she leaned her head, just so, she'd meet those full red lips. Would they be as soft as they looked? *I bet they'd be softer than a kitten's belly after a nap. And warm. They'd be warm, for sure.*

Adi knew the kiss wouldn't be the childish pecking she'd done with Rachel. It would be full and deep. A real kiss. One that could open so many possibilities. Her body flushed with anticipation of the imagined kiss. She ran her hand up her belly to her hard nipples and teased them. *When I kiss her, it's going to be a beginning and I won't stop it. I'll let it come. She'll kiss me back and she'll press into me with her whole body. I'll feel her full breasts against mine. Then I'll slide my hand down her back, to the top of her jeans, then over the round curves of her ass and pull her harder to me.* Adi let her other hand slip into her pajama pants. She felt Griffith touching her, and she touched herself as she imagined it. She bit her lip to stop the sounds that wanted to slip out as she crested the wave of passion the images evoked. She stilled her hand and drifted in the haze that followed. *I have to kiss her.*

Griff's reason for being there resurfaced, and the pleasure drained away in an instant. *She's not going to let it go. It's what she does for a living. I can't be mad at her for that, but she's dangerous. If only the past didn't exist. Shoot, if she doesn't like that I won't tell her about my life, too bad. I'll just keep us both in the here and now.* Adi tried her best to push away the doubts, but they were hard upon her. She tossed and turned for a long time before finally falling into an exhausted sleep.

❖

Adi stumbled blurry-eyed into the kitchen the next morning, the smell of homemade biscuits a siren's song. She saw Bertie had gone all out today, as grits and sausage fought for space on the table.

"Morning, sunshine. Don't you look all bright-eyed and bushy-tailed today," Bertie said. She was standing at the stove with a hot skillet ready for eggs.

"Morning. Is the coffee done?"

"Just about. Go on and pour us out a cup. Best get the sugar down and the cream. Lord knows that city gal ain't going to be set for chicory. We gots to sweeten it up for her, you know? You want sunny-side up or blindfolded?"

"Blindfolded, please. Why don't you sit down and let me do that?"

"No, ma'am. Not with that hand all bandaged up. I cooked breakfast all my life. Won't hurt me none to cook a couple more. What's the story with that hand?"

"I don't know. The knife just slipped," Adi said.

"Slipped? All by itself? That's as true as the sky is purple. What really happened?"

"I was distracted. I don't know why, but I can't get Griffith out of my head. She takes up all my thinking space these days."

"For real?" Bertie clicked her tongue. "Mm, mm, mm. That sure enough is a shame. Seems like she's a mighty nice gal to be cluttering up your mind and making you hurt yourself. Why do you suppose that is?"

"That's just it. I don't know. I mean, she makes me all quivery. Like a hound dog's found a squirrel in my gut and isn't giving up the chase. Plus, she scares the living tarnation out of me, cause she wants to crack open my past."

"So the hound dog? He ain't a part of the fear? He some other kinda thing?"

"I guess so. He's more about how it feels when she's close to me. How I feel, you know?"

"Praise the Lord, I know. I ain't had that feeling in a month of summers, but I remember it like it was yesterday. Sure enough. So, who's gonna win? The hound dog? Or that big ole gator from the bayou whose been living in your closet all your life? You going to let the gator swallow you up this time? You're all grown up now, and if that man comes around here trying to make trouble for you, he won't get nothing but trouble back," Bertie said.

"You say that, Bertie, but you don't know him. You don't know what he'd do. He's pure evil. I can't lead him here. I can't ever let him find me."

They heard noise in the hall and stopped their conversation.

"Good morning. What smells so good?" Griffith asked.

Adi wondered if she'd overheard anything. *I hope not.*

"Just a little bit of breakfast to start out the day. Good morning. Sit on down and tell me how you like your eggs."

"Wow. I don't usually eat breakfast, maybe just a piece of fruit on the way out the door. I guess I'll have them the way Adi is having them," she said.

"I'll pour you some coffee. Cream is on the table. Sugar?" Adi said.

"Oh, I'll take it black."

"You sure? This is coffee and chicory. It's an acquired taste."

"Let me acquire it, then," Griffith said.

Adi shrugged and poured her half a cup. She figured that would leave plenty of room when Griffith decided to add the cream and sugar. She watched as Griffith inhaled the potent fragrance and sipped. When she took a deeper pull and then sighed in contentment, Adi was surprised.

"This is delicious," Griffith said.

"Not many folks have that reaction the first time they take chicory black. You must have had lots of strong coffee before."

"Well, truth is, I've had coffee all over the world. This isn't nearly as strong as Turkish coffee, but the chicory adds a nice bitterness."

"Really? Where'd you have Turkish coffee? In LA?"

"Actually, in Marrakech. I was interviewing the owner of a textile mill there a few years ago. *That* was strong coffee."

"I guess. Want me to fill you up?" Adi felt her face flush as she thought about what she'd just said.

Griffith gave her a long, slow smile before answering, dimples highlighting each cheek. "Sure, thanks."

"Don't hold back now. Them grits won't eat themselves, and Adi will eat it all if you don't jump in," Bertie said. She slid a plate with two perfectly cooked eggs in front of her.

Griffith took a modest amount of each item and grinned when she saw Bertie eyeing her plate with a frown.

"That isn't enough to feed a crow. It's no skin off my nose, but I'm not making more, so I hope you took your fill."

"I did, I promise. I'm not much of a breakfast person. This looks so good, though."

"Hmm."

"You two have big plans today?"

"T's closing the Pot today. He's getting the bathrooms painted and doing some repairs, so I'm going to take Griffith to the Tabasco factory. She ought to get a kick out of it."

"Yeah, she will. So now I just have to figure out what I'm gonna do with my day off. Maybe I'll get Jose to come help me get the garden turned so we can plant next weekend."

"I could do that for you," Adi said. "That's always been my job."

"No, not with that hand you can't, and Jose is going to need something to do. You just have a fun day with Griffith, and me and Jose will take care of things around here. He's a good man."

"He'll want to be paid, you know."

"And? You don't think I can afford him? What do you think he'll charge me?"

"Aw, I don't know, Bertie. I just feel bad not doing it for you."

"Never you mind feeling bad. I'm going to pay him with the peaches we put up last summer. That and the promise of his share of fresh vegetables. I'm sure he'll be happy with that. He's almost like a son to me. Don't you worry none."

"Okay, but the fall garden is all mine."

"Deal."

"Well, I'll earn my night's keep by doing these breakfast dishes. Any tricks to your machine?" Griffith said.

"That's nice of you, Griffith. No, the machine is pretty straightforward. I'll leave you to it. Time for me to take my morning pills. You girls have a good time today."

"Thank you."

Bertie left the room as Adi and Griffith cleared the table. Adi scraped the plates into the trash while Griffith rinsed them and loaded them into the dishwasher.

"What about the pots?" Griffith said.

"Bertie likes to do those herself. She's always afraid I'll mess up their seasoning."

"But if they're clean, what seasoning...no, never mind. I probably wouldn't understand. I guess we're done here. I'll go back to the hotel and shower and change. Should I come back here after?"

"No. I'll come by in about forty minutes. If you aren't ready, I'll wait in the lobby."

"Okay. See you in a bit."

Adi watched Griffith walk out to her car. She liked the way the sun glinted on her hair. She wanted nothing more than to run her fingers through the mass of curls and feel their weight. As Griff opened the door she looked back at Adi, her heart-shaped face broken by her dimples.

"See you soon," she said.

"Bye," Adi said. She was starting to really enjoy having her around. Last night's conversation was weighing heavily on her mind, though. How could she keep Griffith from discovering her past? She needed to figure that out. Would she get that kiss today? Her heart raced and her palms began to sweat. *Can I do this? Can I start something with her that might end up destroying me and everyone I love? Is it worth it? Maybe I need to find out.*

She turned back to the house, thinking critically about what she'd said last night. She had sounded so naïve and juvenile, asking her to keep her secret. That must have taken her down a few notches in Griffith's book, who clearly made no excuses for her sexuality. She hadn't even flinched when she brought up her attraction to Adi. And... wait. Damn. In her medication-induced state, had she mentioned Dulac?

Panic hit like a Mack truck, knocking Adi on her tail. She grabbed the porch rail to steady herself. What had she done? If Griffith connected the dots and found out about Dulac and J.B., Adi would have no choice but to run, as far and as fast as her money would take her. J.B could *not* find out where she was. *That was a stupid mistake.* She felt weak, her stomach turning sour at the thought of what might happen. She had to hope Griffith had missed her comment. She slumped against the wall. *I don't want to run.*

CHAPTER NINE

When Adi arrived at the hotel, Griffith walked out to meet her.

"Hey, great timing," she said. "It's only about a half an hour to the island. I checked and the factory is bottling today."

"Awesome. I was hoping to see that."

"Are you a Tabasco fan?"

"I pretty much like all hot sauce, but I've never seen it made before. I saw on their website there's a Jungle Garden as well. Why are you laughing?"

"I wouldn't get your hopes up. The garden is pretty nice, but not very exotic. It's mostly live oaks and egrets."

"But they said there's a sacred Buddha."

"Oh, he's there. Don't know how sacred he is, but you'll get to see him. Maybe more gators too. Don't get me wrong, it's really lovely and all, but not very jungle-y."

"So no tigers in the bamboo?"

"Ah, no."

"Shoot. Now I'm disappointed."

"You'll get to see lots of pepper plants and some great old buildings. The country store is cool too."

"Well, okay, but I'm still bummed about the tigers."

"Yeah, me too. We could see a black bear, so there's that. You can find something to listen to on the radio if you want."

"I'd rather just talk."

"Okay. What shall we talk about?"

"Let's talk about why you're afraid of your past. Could we do that?"

"Griffith—"

"What? I'm serious, Adi. What is it in your past that has you so tense? Why did you run away? What were you running from?"

Adi sighed, and Griffith worried she would turn the truck around and take her back to the hotel.

I'm just doing my job. I'm not going to give up, no matter how long it takes. I need to get her to open up without breaking the tenuous friendship we're developing. And if we can't have a friendship because of my job, so be it.

"Look, I don't have anything to hide. It's just old stuff. Stuff that damaged me as a kid. It took me a long time to get past those hurts, and I just don't feel ready to reopen the wounds. Do you understand?"

Griffith felt there was more to it than that. She had learned a long time ago to follow her instincts. The best stories came from asking the big picture questions, and she needed to know the root of Adi's fear. Every nerve in her body was tingling with that familiar sensation that came with a complex story. *This is something real. Something deeper. I can't give up. If I can just get her to see that, I can help her put her demons to rest.* Kids ran away all the time. There wasn't anything new in that. But if Adi's reason had been simply having shit parents, she would have said so. The fact that she didn't say so meant there was more to the story.

"Kind of. I understand what damage abuse does. I've dealt with survivors before. You can trust me. I don't want to bring anything to the surface that's going to hurt you. That's not why I'm asking. I feel like there's something holding you back, and that makes me uneasy. I want to understand why you have to hide, but I can't if you don't give me information to work with."

"You say I can trust you, but I have to know that I can trust you. Not just today or next week, but trust you forever. This doesn't have anything to do with the story you're writing, but everything to do with who I am. Before I would ever tell you, I'd have to be sure you won't let something slip that ends up hurting the people I love."

What in the world could be that terrible? What could cause that level of fear and paranoia? Whatever it is, is big. This is what I was picking up on. Do I really want to know? Is a story worth it?

"What is it? Why does my knowing about it threaten your loved ones?"

"It just does, okay? Just trust me on that. You're a journalist, and you're here to write a story. When I'm sure about you, when I know you see me as a friend and not just some story you want to write, I'll tell you everything. Nothing held back."

"Promise?"

"Yes, I promise."

"In that case, what do you want to listen to? Top forty? Country?"

"How about oldies?"

"How old? Your oldies might be my current playlist."

"You're not that much older than me."

"You'd be surprised."

"I'll be twenty-three in July. How old are you?"

"Older than anyone you went to high school with. I'm thirty."

"That's not old. Hey, seven years is nothing around here. My dad was twelve years older than my mom."

"Really? How old was she when they first met?"

"She was twenty-one, he was thirty-three, when they had their first date. But Mamma looked older than she was, and Daddy never grew up."

"You mentioned your dad was a shrimper, right?"

"Yeah. He worked for an old man, running his boat. Dad loved his work. He was so much in his element on the open water. I think he died happy, because he died at sea, you know?"

"I can understand that. They say the sea is a harsh mistress. How did he die, if you don't mind my asking?"

"No, I don't mind talking about him. He was caught in a tropical storm offshore. The boat capsized and all hands were lost. Six men went down that night, my dad among them."

"How old were you when that happened?"

"I was seven. I went out every morning to meet his boat on the dock. That morning, he just didn't show up. Mamma called the coast guard. We didn't know about the storm. It went south and we didn't even get any rain. Mamma tried real hard to act broken up about it, but I knew she was happy to be free of him. She wasn't a very nice woman."

"No?"

"No."

"Is she gone too?"

"I hope so."

Griffith pondered the information, tucking it away to put through a search engine.

"Did I shock you?" Adi asked.

"No, not really. So you didn't get along with your mother?"

"Uh, that would be an understatement. She'd as soon smack me as look at me. We were like oil and water. I think she resented me. I always thought, if not for me, she would've never married my dad. I think she pictured a different life for herself. One without me or my dad. After the accident, it was only me keeping her down. I paid for that crime on a daily basis."

"So is that the reason? Why you ran away?"

"In some ways. Hey, smell that? That's the Tabasco peppers. We don't have much farther to go."

Griffith caught the scent of the peppers, an almost tickling sensation more than a smell, really. It sat right at the top of her nasal passage and made her want to sneeze. It grew stronger the closer they got. A cute little house appeared on the right side of the road with a barrier arm just in front.

"What is this? A guard post?"

"It's the toll booth."

"This is a toll road?"

"No, but it's a private road onto the island, so we stop here and pay the toll. This lets the island officials know how many visitors are on the island."

"Hmm."

They arrived at the visitors center soon after. It was a charming old brick structure, a factory straight out of the 1920s. They went in and were greeted by a local, describing the history of Tabasco. The bottling plant was fun to watch, especially the large wooden mixing barrel. They were given sample bottles of sauce.

"I never knew there was more than the red sauce," Griffith said as they exited into the store.

"Oh yeah, they have seven varieties. Here, this is the tasting bar. We can try all of them."

"Wow, they have Tabasco ice cream?"

"Yep, and Tabasco Coke too. But let's try the sauces first."

They dipped bread and chips into the individual sauce cups they were given to try each variety. Griffith skipped the habanero, but Adi indulged.

"Man, that's hot-hot. But good."

"You're sweating and your face is red."

"Hey, at least I'm not crying. Pass me some of that bread. A lot of that bread." Adi wiped sweat from her brow.

"I have a better idea. Let's get the ice cream now."

"There you go, but bread too, please?"

Griffith handed her last slice of French bread over to Adi. Their fingers touched during the exchange and Griffith felt a jolt of electricity go through her. Judging by Adi's reaction, she felt it too. She grinned and led the way to the ice cream bar. She ordered them each a scoop of the Tabasco vanilla. Griffith scooped up a tiny spoonful and held it to Adi's wide, sensual mouth. She met Adi's eyes, challenging her to taste.

"Here, you take the first bite."

Adi's cheeks flushed as she opened her mouth. Griffith slid the spoon inside and held it while Adi sampled. She could feel the movement of Adi's tongue on the plastic spoon. It was almost erotic, this game of tasting. *I wonder if cayenne peppers are an aphrodisiac.*

"Let's take this out to the patio to eat. There are some tables out there," Adi said.

They pushed through the door to the outdoor area. There were tables and vendors selling even more food items with Tabasco as an ingredient. Griffith looked around, surprised by the array.

"I had no idea pepper sauce could be so versatile. I think it's pretty amazing what they've done here."

"I think you're pretty amazing. Here, your turn for a bite."

Griffith turned to the spoon Adi held up. She took it into her mouth, savoring the sweet taste and sharp bite of pepper. She bit down on the spoon, pulling it from Adi's hand.

"Hey now, you've got your own spoon. Give me mine back."

"Make me."

"I'll make you." Adi pulled Griffith toward her and Griffith prepared to be kissed. She was surprised when Adi's hand sneaked under her T-shirt and tickled her side. She laughed and tried to pull away, but Adi held her fast.

"Stop, stop, I give up!" She laughed. Adi's tickle turned into a warm embrace that felt so right it shook Griffith to the core.

"You know, they have a new food tour you can take. It goes to all sorts of eateries in Iberia Parish. They asked T'Claude if they could add the Pot to the tour, but he didn't want to commit to always having something with Tabasco on the menu. I'd sign us up to take the tour, but I'd rather make fresh food for you instead."

Griffith smiled and reached for Adi's hand. She doubted Adi realized just how sweet she was. She felt Adi squeeze her back and was pleased when she didn't shake off the affectionate grasp.

I really like her. She's so genuine, and unjaded. So different from the women in LA. Is that why I'm so attracted to her? I've been with women around the world, but no one like her...Adi is just so...real.

Whatever she was running from hadn't taken that from her. *I could destroy that in her. I've got to be so careful. No story is worth that. Not at any price.*

"How about you take me to see the jungle gardens now?"

"Okay, we can do that. Just remember, I told you it's not very tropical."

"That's okay with me. I'll enjoy it regardless."

As they drove to the jungle area, Adi pointed out various birds and plants. "There's really just a dirt road that goes through the gardens. We can stop and get out if we want to. There are a couple of fenced ponds that probably have gators. Then there's Bird City. It should be impressive this time of year. The egrets should be nesting now."

"Bird City?"

"Yeah, that's the place old Mr. Ned made for the egrets to roost. Back in the late 1800s the fashionable ladies all had hats with exotic plumage. The egrets around here were almost eradicated through over hunting. Mr. Ned McIlhenny founded Bird City to save them. It worked too. He brought eight young egrets here and raised them in captivity. He released them in the fall for migration to Mexico. They sure enough returned the following spring and brought some friends with them. Now there are thousands of them who return every year."

"Wow. That's amazing. It's great that he was a conservationist. That surely wasn't the fashion back then."

"No, it wasn't. Mr. Ned didn't care what people thought of him. He did things that pleased him for his own reasons. Wait until you see the bamboo he cultivated. Oh, and Buddha, of course."

"Tell me about Buddha."

"Well, this Buddha is supposed to be from the twelfth century. It was sent from China to New York in nineteen twenty when two warlords were fighting over territory. The one who owned the Buddha didn't want it damaged or looted. Unfortunately, he never reclaimed the statue and it sat in a warehouse for nineteen years. One day, two friends of Mr. Ned heard about the unclaimed Buddha and bought it for him as a gift. They sent it down via rail car. Mr. Ned built the whole Chinese garden around the Buddha."

"I've never heard of it. Is it large?"

"It's larger than life-size, but not too big. He built a pagoda around it, and later, they glassed it in to protect it."

"I definitely want to see that."

"You will. Trust me."

The gardens were beautiful to Griffith. The variety of flowering plants was astounding. Adi pointed out that she was lucky that she was there during the spring. Most of the year there weren't nearly as many flowers. The timber bamboo had to be four inches in diameter and more than fifty feet tall.

"You said it wouldn't be tropical, but this...this is spectacular. Can we get out and walk around?"

"Yes, I guess so. We just have to be careful. There may be snakes in there."

"Awesome. Let's go." Griffith jumped down from the cab of the truck and headed straight into the bamboo stand. It was otherworldly walking among the towering grass. Griffith felt connected to the earth here, in this spot. There was energy here, a moist, sultry heat that danced along her limbs and ran through her, out and up. She looked at Adi, hurrying over from the truck, and wanted to send this primal wave of heat out to meet her. *If I touch her right now, we'll be swallowed up by this energy.*

"Wait up, Griffith." Adi hurried to catch up.

Griffith reached out and took her hand. She drew her into the grove, and they stared up at the towering grass stalks. "Makes you feel kind of small and insignificant, don't they?"

"Yeah, they do. It kind of creeps me out being in here."

"Really? Why? Are you scared?" Griffith felt alive here. Nothing about it scared her. Adi's reluctance puzzled her.

"No. Just not comfortable."

How could she not feel the energy? Maybe she did, but it frightened her because she didn't have an experience to connect it to. *I need to turn that around. This is good energy and she should know it.*

"Well, I can fix that. Come here," Griffith said. She pulled Adi close to her. It was steamy hot in the bamboo and sweat coated her forearms and her face.

"Hey, don't do that. Let me go."

"I don't think so. I've been waiting for just the right moment to do this." And with that, she stretched up and kissed Adi. It was a soft kiss, almost tentative at first, but when Adi didn't jerk back, Griffith deepened the kiss. She felt tingling to her toes as Adi parted her lips and allowed access to her warm, sultry mouth. Every nerve ending fired with the emotions the kiss stirred in her. *God, she's so sweet.*

They finally parted, though they stayed close to one another. Griffith gazed up at Adi, hoping to discern what Adi was feeling. *We definitely have chemistry. There's no doubt. Will it go anywhere? Do I want it to? Will Adi be okay with something simple, temporary, like most of the other women who've filtered through my life?* Except Tabitha. That had been a real mistake. One that cut so deep it took a year to get over it.

I can't repeat that. I have to keep this simple. Just good, honest fun. She's never even been with a woman, with anyone. I'd be her first. Well, I'd make it memorable. I just have to figure out if that's what she wants.

Adi would have to come clean about her past for there to be something even momentary, though. Griffith would dig up the bones of the story in Dulac and then it would be up to Adi to own up. She would find out to protect herself, and her career, but she wouldn't confront Adi with the truth if she didn't need to. She thought about what T had said about hurting Adi with the past, and she wondered just how important the article was. Maybe it really could just be about the restaurant and the great food. Adi as a person now was pretty amazing. There would always be another article to get her career back on track. *It doesn't have to be this one, right?* Adi would have to open up on her own, and Griffith hoped she would.

"That was nice. Thank you."

"Thank you, you mean. You're the one who kissed me, Griffith. I would've never—"

"Never say never, kiddo. I learned that a long time ago. Your gorgeous lips have been asking me to kiss them. So, I gave in. I'm glad I did."

"Me too."

"Oh yeah? So you want to do that again sometime?"

"Sure I do. I want to do that again right now."

"Ah, ah, ah. Save some for later. It makes it all the better to savor it. Let's go see some more of this wonderland. And then you can take me home. Maybe I'll let you kiss me good night."

"Maybe?"

"Well, it all depends on how the rest of the day goes."

The rest of the day was extraordinary. Griffith marveled at how easy it was to be with Adi. If she didn't know better, she would say Adi was the singularly most open and honest person she had ever encountered. *Unless we're talking about her past.* Her ease at describing the island's features and the candid expression on her face as she told Griffith about the McIlhenny family legacy warmed her through and through.

It really felt like a date, like her very first date, actually. Pins and needles of excitement raced through her, and the casual brush of Adi's arm against hers sent a rush of goose bumps down her arm. She felt the easy laughter and silliness that went with first dates. She felt young, like a kid again. She felt her jaded, LA exterior flake away with Adi's gentle banter. She wanted this feeling to last, to hold on to it. She could tell Adi was feeling it too.

What a shame that the truth would come calling, exacting its pay in whatever form it took. Whether Adi was running from abuse or something worse, she had to know the truth. It was just who she was, and being involved with someone meant knowing everything about them. Maybe it wasn't fair; maybe it was too much for some people. The journalist in her never slept, and once she had questions, she had to find answers. And if Adi was running from something, maybe she could help. And that way she'd also know what she was getting into if they got involved. *Am I rationalizing?* Griffith struggled against the knowledge that this blissful moment was a façade. That reality would come knocking, and soon. She pushed the thought back and walled it off. She would enjoy today and let tomorrow worry about itself.

When they pulled up in front of Griffith's hotel, Adi turned off the truck.

"So? Do I get to kiss you?"

Griffith smiled at the shy way Adi asked. "Yes, please kiss me."

Adi leaned over and wrapped Griffith in her arms. She put her cheek against Griffith's and inhaled deeply. "You smell so good."

Griffith chuckled. "You mean I smell like sweat and peppers, right?"

"No, I mean, yes, but you smell like sunshine and rain. You smell like all the good things. I could breathe you in forever."

"Adi, that's beautiful. Thank you."

"I mean it."

"Just kiss me, already."

Adi's lips touched hers so gently at first that Griffith wanted to push out and capture them, but she waited, letting Adi set the pace. The pressure deepened, and she felt Adi tasting her. Griffith parted her lips, beckoning, and Adi complied. The warmth that washed through Griffith with the touch of Adi's tongue on her own was electric. She couldn't restrain herself any longer and pulled Adi deeper into her mouth. The kiss went on and on, never fevered or reckless. Just deeper and deeper until Griffith felt that it would consume her. She pushed against Adi gently.

They broke apart, both struggling to catch her breath.

"Good night, Adi."

"Good night."

Griffith stumbled out of the cab and closed the door behind her. That kiss had nearly undone her. She walked to the hotel entrance without looking back. She finally turned as she pulled open the door. Adi's gaze was so intense it was as though she could feel her hands sliding over her. She felt heat race through her as they looked at one another. Adi waved once. Griffith waved back and entered the hotel.

What am I doing?

CHAPTER TEN

The morning sun streamed in the window of Griffith's hotel room. She rolled to her side to avoid the piercing rays. Morning came early here. In LA, she could easily sleep until ten, her apartment suitably dark until she chose to open the blinds. *The light here comes right through the walls.* She could still smell the faint scent of peppers in her room and smiled, thinking of the day before. She had really enjoyed spending the day with Adi. And the kisses... oh, the kisses. They were just about as perfect as kisses could be.

Griffith tensed. *What are you thinking? This isn't high school, and Adi isn't your first girl crush. Get a grip.* She needed to focus on her reason for being in this place. It wasn't to steal kisses and get all hung up on a woman. It was to tell a damn story.

She sat up and slapped her hands on the mattress. *Snap out of it. Yes, she's gorgeous and different from any woman you've known. So what? And this place, it's like some kind of Neverland, where things drift at the pace of slow-moving clouds.* Not at all the hectic, busy world Griffith lived in. She needed to shake off the heavy, hazy state she found herself in and get busy. She needed to be far more LA, and far less down-home.

She had more than enough to write the article Dawn wanted, and she knew it would be a hit. Her prospects for her next job were thinner than spider silk, but she could pick up a lead and find something that would sell. She needed to get this done and move on. But moving on meant her connection to Adi would be lost. *What about the itch Adi's hidden past has started that won't stop? Should I follow my gut and get to the story behind that story? What would that mean for Adi? Does it matter? Damn you, Tabitha. I don't even trust myself, now. You've ruined me.*

Her phone rang, pulling her out of her head and into the present. *Who calls someone at the crack of dawn?*

She grabbed at the offending phone, ready to rip the caller a new one. "Hello?"

"Hi, um, hi," Adi said.

The irritation slipped away as Adi's voice soothed her. *She's so innocent. I wonder if she's ever called a woman before?*

"Hi, Adi. How's it going?"

"Good, it's good. So I was wondering, did you want to go crawfishing? It's going to be hot, but not so hot we won't find some."

Griffith tensed. *Damn, should I spend another day with her? Am I getting in too deep? How can I stay objective if all I really want to do is run my hands down her gorgeous arms and kiss her? How is this going to help me? Crap. To hell with it.* "Sure I do. What should I wear? And what do I need to bring? I don't have a fishing pole."

"Huh? Oh, no poles are needed. I have traps. You should wear something you don't mind getting dirty. And boots if you have them. Something that can take mud. Sunscreen and bug spray are a must."

"I don't have any bug spray. And my boots aren't really made for mud."

"That's okay. Just wear your oldest clothes. I'll be there in half an hour. We want to get out on the paddy before it heats up too much."

"The paddy?"

"Yeah, the rice paddy. That's where we catch the crawfish."

"Okay…"

"Trust me, I've been doing this all my life."

"So half an hour?"

"There about. That going to work for you?"

"Sure…"

"Great, see you soon."

Crawfishing? In Maine, they trapped lobsters in little wire or wood cages. Weren't crawfish essentially small lobsters? *This isn't Maine. I'd better do some quick research. The closest I've ever been to catching a lobster is picking out the one I want for dinner in a tank.*

Adi had said something the other day about it being messy and her doing most of the work. She pulled up a webpage dedicated to the craft on her smartphone. WikiHow showed worms, a pole, and string. Not too difficult, but Adi said no poles. Then there was a trap that looked like a clothes hamper on its side. Strange, but okay. The last suggestion was to simply reach into the water and grab the little buggers as they walked by. None of these looked messy or difficult, except the hand method. *No way I'm going to use my hand to catch them.*

She headed for the shower. *Get clean, then, presumably, get dirty.* She relished the effect of the hot spray on her back. Waking up was always a challenge, but a shower went a long way toward coherence. And caffeine. Coffee was the next order of business. The little room pot did nothing for her, but there was a coffee shop in the lobby. She quickly dried and dressed in her comfy jeans and an old SC sweatshirt. Pulling on a baseball cap, she made her way to the lobby and the promise of caffeine. When she met Adi outside, she was surprised by the small trailer she had attached to the truck. It was carrying a covered vehicle of some sort. She walked over for a closer look. Adi got out and wrapped her arms around her from behind. Griffith felt a flash of heat as their skin connected. *How does she do this to me? I'm not a pushover, and she's got me all frazzled. It has to be her innocence. Shake it off.*

"What's that under the tarp?"

"Oh, that's a four-wheeler. Best way to get to the rice field. Too muddy for the truck." Adi kissed the back of her neck and moved away.

Griffith missed the embrace as soon as it was gone. *I wish I'd turned around.* "Muddy?"

"Yep. That's why they call crawfish mudbugs. They build their holes in wet mud in the creeks and rice fields. Even in the swamps, but I like the rice fields best. You can predict the depth of the mud before you step in."

"So you weren't kidding when you said this was going to be messy."

"Not at all, but it'll be a mess of fun too. I brought you some hip waders to keep your feet dry. Are you wearing a belt?"

"No, just my jeans."

"That's okay. I have some belts that should work in my kit. Let's go."

They rode down to the rice field, talking about the trip to Avery Island, but avoiding any talk of the kisses.

When they reached the rice farm, Adi drove right out toward the field, stopping about a hundred yards away.

"Okay, now the fun begins. Let's get the bike off the trailer and load up."

Adi lowered the ramp while Griffith took the tarp off the four-wheeler. It was bright blue and larger than Griffith had imagined. There was a wire and steel tray welded to the front and another in the back. The saddle area looked like it would hold them both, but it would be a tight fit. *Excellent.*

Once Adi had the bike on the ground, she reloaded the ramp and locked it with a padlock. She tossed Griffith some heavy rubber waders from the truck bed. "Try these. They look like they'll fit."

Griffith looked at the boots with their long rubber legs and the loop of canvas at the top. She cautiously slid one shoe down into the boot. The fit was fine, if unusual. She looked over at Adi, who had her own set of waders on, hooked into a canvas belt slung low around her hips. *Sexy, pure Louisiana swamp goddess sexy. That's what she is.* Griffith looked down at her own overly large boots, sagging around her knees. *I am so out of my element. I wasn't designed for this. I must look like a clown.*

Adi had a rakish grin on her face and Griffith flushed with embarrassment.

"Here, catch." Adi tossed a belt to Griffith. The buckle was just like a military belt. Adi bent over the tailgate of the truck and tossed things onto the ground, giving Griffith a perfect view of her sweet round backside. The humidity level kicked up a notch where Griffith stood. *If this were LA, I'd have you bent over that tailgate and it wouldn't be for unloading a damn thing. You have no clue what you're doing to me.*

Griffith looked at the assortment of things on the ground. There was a five-gallon bucket, two sets of heavy rubber gloves, a small ice chest, twine, and some strange wire and net things that must be the traps.

"Could you use those bungee cords to strap the bucket down? Here, take these first." She handed over one pair of gloves, a helmet, and some goggles.

Griffith pulled on the gloves, then attempted to fasten the bucket to the front tray. The gloves made it quite a challenge. She stretched the cord around the ungainly thing and tried hooking it to the tray. The metal end barely missed her cheek as it snapped back. "Crap. I don't think this is my forte."

Adi was busy attaching things in the back, but she looked up at Griffith. "Oh, hold on. I'll give you a hand."

She made quick work of the bucket and slid into the wide saddle. "Okay, let's go. You climb on behind me and hold on. Put on your helmet and goggles first."

Griffith did as requested, feeling like a kid dressed for Halloween. She slid into place behind Adi, enjoying the way her thighs snugged tight against Adi's and the feel of her chest pressed to Adi's back. The big bike roared to life and they took off across the field. At first, Griffith had a death grip around Adi's middle, but as she got used to the feeling of the bike she eased back and began to enjoy the ride. It was over all too quick as they stopped beside the first flooded field.

"We'll set out traps in each paddy as we go along, then circle back to start collecting. Here, watch how I set this up."

Adi pulled the wire and net traps off the back of the bike and shook them open. The wires crossed in the middle, locking in place and forming a little wire tent over a square of netting. She pointed to the center of the net. "We tie the bait right here. And a couple of weights too."

She demonstrated, tying the weights and a chicken neck into the center of the net. "We'll set four traps in each paddy. So you set up two more traps here and I'll do another."

Griffith gritted her teeth. *Tie a chicken neck here, she says. Right.* Griff had traveled the world for her work; she'd eaten things in other countries they'd never serve in California. She could do this. She reached cautiously into the Ziploc of chicken parts. They were warm and fragrant, not in a good way. *Gotta do it.* She pushed her forearm against her nose, trying to tame the stench. Her stomach was about to flip and make her lose her coffee. *Good thing I'm not a breakfast eater.* She finally nabbed a slippery piece of meat and dropped it unceremoniously onto the net. *Tie it.* She grabbed the two bits of string in each hand, but tying them was virtually impossible with the cumbersome gloves. *She made it look so easy. It's anything but.*

Just then, a gust of wind blew one of Griffith's curls across her cheek, where it promptly stuck to the sweat accumulated there. Without thinking, she started to sweep it away with her finger. Her chicken gut dripping, glove wearing, stinky finger. She gagged.

"Time out. I don't think I can do this," she said.

Adi looked over at her. She wasn't sure what it was, but Adi found something particularly funny about the situation. She started belly laughing so hard she doubled over.

"What's so funny?"

"Your face. Oh my God, the look on your face is hysterical. Hang on. I'll do the chicken if you set up the traps. Deal?"

"Deal. How do I get this funk off my glove?"

That set Adi off on another round of guffaws. "Just go rinse them off with the water in the cooler. Oh, Lord, you're killing me."

"I'm happy to amuse you, but I'm going to throw up if this stuff isn't gone, like yesterday."

"I'll help," Adi said.

She had streaks of tears on her face, but hurried over with a cup of melted ice water. She poured it over the gloves as Griffith vigorously rubbed them together. Then Adi tenderly wiped the crud on Griff's cheek away with her thumb.

"Thanks, I'll let you do the chicken. All I do is open the wires and slip them into place?"

"Yeah, it's simple."

"Right." Griffith was doubtful, but it really was as easy as Adi said. They made quick work of setting up the traps. Then Adi directed Griff out into the flooded field to set the traps down. She had to make sure they were as flat on the ground as possible. The mud sucked at her waders as she walked from spot to spot. It made Griffith think of the sanitation workers who went into the sewers back home. *What manner of filth is this? It feels like it wants to suck me right down. Just don't fall down. Don't fall. The Internet didn't say shit about the mud factor. I'll add some blazing editing to that damn Wiki page.*

It seemed like it took forever, but they finished the first paddy and moved through the succession of fields until they had no more traps. There were twenty-four in all.

"Now comes the fun part," Adi said, "collecting our little friends. Come on."

They climbed on the bike and Adi kicked it into life. Then she ran it full throttle back to the first paddy. Mud was flying out on either side of the bike, slapping into Griffith's legs. *Charming. I managed not to fall, but now I'm getting the full mud bath at no extra charge. People pay for this crap in LA.* She was happy to have the helmet and goggles. Luckily, Adi was a sensible driver and didn't attempt any tricks. Griffith didn't relish the idea of flying off the bike into the rice field.

"Come on, let's go get them." Adi grabbed the bucket and handed it to Griffith. "I'll haul them up and you collect them in the bucket."

They walked slowly out into the field to the first trap. Adi put her good hand gently on the top that stuck out well above the water line. She quickly lifted the whole thing clear of the water. The net dipped deeply in the middle as it was raised, and in the bottom, several angry red crustaceans flapped their tails and waved their claws.

"You want me to touch that? Are you kidding?"

"No, just hold one corner and put the opposite corner in the bucket. Then we'll shake them loose."

They did just that with the first and all the other traps. When they were done, the bucket was more than half full of crawfish. They rode back to the truck and dumped the bucket into the big ice chest. As they rode between fields, Griffith's job was to steady the bucket now perched on the back tray. When they finished, she couldn't believe how tired she felt. The time seemed to fly by. Her waders were caked in mud from the ankle down, and she knew she looked a sight. *If my friends could see me now.* She had mud in her hair, on her face, and flaking off both forearms. She looked at Adi. Her waders had mud around the ankles, but the rest of her was basically clean. *How did she manage that?* She reached down and grabbed a fistful of mud.

"Don't," Adi said, backing away.

"Don't what?" Griffith moved closer to her, mud dripping out of her tight fist.

"Don't even think about it."

"I don't know what you mean." She slapped her hand onto Adi's back, slinging mud from her shoulder to her hip.

"Hey. That wasn't very nice. I didn't even make you tie the chicken necks."

"Ugh." She wrapped both muddy hands around Adi's waist and held her.

"You sure are a cute little swamp rat. Makes me want to kiss the breath out of you."

"Yeah?"

"Yeah, but only after you take a shower," Adi said.

Adi dumped the last haul into the ice chest and tossed the empty bucket into the back.

"Peel off your waders and gloves and toss them in the truck bed. We can go hose down at the house and boil up these babies."

"Sounds good. Did you happen to bring anything to drink?"

"Oh, sure. There's water and beer in the small cooler in the cab. Help yourself."

Griffith went straight to the cooler, desperate to wet her parched throat. She took an icy cold bottle of Abita and popped the top.

"Can I grab something for you?" she asked, looking back at Adi. She was bent over, detaching the chicken necks from the nets, her dark hair falling over the side of her face. The muscles in her arms bunched and relaxed with the effort. She was gorgeous. Griffith leaned against the truck and watched unashamedly.

Adi must have noted the still silence. She looked up quickly from her work and caught Griffith watching. She blushed a deep red and smiled. "You like what you see?"

"You know, I kind of do. Even the big line of mud down your shoulder."

Adi tried looking to see behind her shoulder, but just ended up twisting and showing more of her long, lean body to Griffith.

"I like this game. But seriously, can I grab you something to drink?"

Adi stood up and smiled again. "Sure, I'll have what you're having. Looks good."

"It is. Strawberry, no less."

"My favorite."

"I think it's going to be mine too. Can we sit in the shade somewhere?"

"Yeah, but just for a sec. We'll need to get the catch back pretty quick. Come on."

They walked to a nearby live oak and sat down. The breeze began to kick up, which Griffith was grateful for. That had been hot, physical work, something she hadn't done outside a gym in a long time. She leaned back against the rough bark of the tree and watched Adi. She was leaning forward with her head on her knees.

"Whatcha thinking, Lincoln?"

"Nothing really. I was just thinking about how easy it is to be with you. I feel happy spending time with you."

"I like spending time with you too. Thanks for cutting your hand. You've made the last two days really special."

"Good. I'm glad they've been special. I'm not glad about the cut though. It stings like a mother right now."

"You didn't reinjure it, did you?"

"No, it's just all the movement and sweat. It will be fine in a few minutes." She tipped her bottle back and finished the beer. "You almost done? We have to get those crawfish into a nice pot of boiling water before too long," she said.

"Yeah, I'm nearly done."

"You do like to eat crawfish, right?"

Griffith swallowed her last sip. "Um, sure. I guess. They were great in the étouffée. I'm sure they'll be just as good boiled."

"Better. They'll be so good you won't believe it."

"I can't wait. This is hungry work."

"Yeah, it is. Let's head back."

They loaded up the bike and drove back to Bertie's house. They enjoyed a comfortable silence, both worn out from the adventure. Bertie was sitting out on the porch as if she were waiting for them.

"Is she expecting us?"

"Well, sure. She's probably got the water all ready for the crawfish. She knew we'd be bringing back a mess of them. I always do. Let's take them around the back and clean them before we hose down. Then you can shower first while I help Bertie get the other stuff in the boil."

"Okay."

They rinsed the crawfish and then left them near the huge pot Bertie had boiling on a propane burner in the back driveway. Adi poured in seasonings from a nearby box. Griffith saw potatoes and onion slices in the roiling water. The scent was rich and spicy, and Griffith heard her stomach growl at the thought of the deliciousness to come.

"Here. I'll hose you down first, then you do me," Adi said, aiming the hose her way.

Griffith held up a hand. "Wait. Hold on a second." Then she screamed as the stream of cold water pelted her side. She ran up the porch steps. "Let me get my shoes off."

"Okay, but hurry. I need to get the corn ready to go in."

Griffith kicked off her sneakers and jumped down into the grass. She tensed, waiting for the cold water. When it hit, it still shook her, but she managed not to cry out. She dutifully turned and allowed Adi to wash the bigger patches of mud off her clothes.

When she was finished spraying her down, Adi tossed Griffith a towel from a box near the stairs. She kicked off her shoes and handed over the hose. "Okay, now you do me."

Griffith squeezed the handle and sent a stream of water directly into her chest. The white T-shirt did little to hide Adi's nipples as they reacted to the water. They were on the large side and incredibly distracting. Griffith imagined slipping one into her mouth and…"Turn around. I want to get your shoulder."

Adi dutifully turned, unaware of what her body was doing to Griffith. But it didn't help. When the water hit the well-defined muscles of her back and shoulders, Griffith nearly lost it. She loosened her grip on the hose until the water was barely a trickle. Adi looked back at her, puzzled.

"I'm freezing. I'm going to hit the shower." Griffith dropped the hose and practically ran through the house to the sanctuary of the bathroom. She peeled off her soaked clothes and jumped into the shower. The warm water helped her clear her head and get a grip. *What do you think you're doing here? This isn't the time or place to be fantasizing. And what am I supposed to put on after my shower? I'm not going to be walking around in a towel.*

Just then there was a knock on the door. "Here are some sweats for you to wear while the clothes wash. I'm going to leave them just by the door. Don't worry, Bertie and I will be out back. The house is yours for now."

"Thanks. I'll be out in a few minutes."

"No rush. We'll be busy with the crawfish."

Griffith felt a rush of relief. Maybe she hadn't completely made a fool of herself out there. Adi seemed perfectly fine, and she was incredibly grateful for the dry clothes. She finished her shower and dressed in the comfortable, if large, sweats. *Sweats. I haven't worn sweats since high school. I feel like an overgrown toddler.* She checked her reflection in the mirror. *Yes, indeed, a thirtysomething, two-year-old. I wonder if this look will get Adi's attention?* Knowing she didn't have a choice in attire, she gathered up her clothes and wrapped them in her towel, then went in search of the washing machine. When she found it she saw that Adi had left the lid up and her clothes were already inside. She dumped her load in and started the wash.

When she made it to the back drive, the smell of the boil permeated the air, making her stomach grumble. "That smells fantastic. When do we get to eat?"

"It won't be long now. The vegetables are done. They're in that ice chest. Now we add the crawfish."

Adi added lemons and more seasonings to the water. When it returned to a boil, she dumped the crawfish, flipping and fighting, into a wire basket and lowered them into the water. She put the lid on and sat down near the cooking pot.

"This is the tricky part. I have to watch for the boil to come back up. Then we wait two minutes and kill the heat. Could you bring me that bucket of water?" She pointed to a bucket near the porch.

Griffith collected the bucket, noting that the water was cold. When the time was right, Adi turned off the propane and opened the pot. She slowly poured in the cold water.

"Now I'm going to need your help. Open that second ice chest and help us pour in the crawfish. Bertie, time to season."

Bertie grabbed the box of seasoning while Griffith opened the ice chest and Adi lifted the wire basket. "Get that big paddle now and stir as Bertie seasons."

As Adi slowly poured in the crawfish, Bertie sprinkled in the seasoning and Griffith stirred the whole mess. It was like clockwork. Clearly, they had done this many times before, and Griffith appreciated having a part in the process.

When they were finished, Adi closed the ice chest and smiled at Griffith. "Now you can say you've done a crawfish boil. Bertie? Who's coming by to eat?"

"T'Claude said he'd be by, and Jose and his girl too. Go on and get the table spread. I'll get the trash can lined and ready."

"Can I do something? Shall I get plates?"

They turned and stared at her.

"Ah, no, no plates. We're going to spread the table with newspaper. When folks get here we'll put out paper plates and folks can fill them. You just put your trash on the newspaper. When dinner is over, we'll roll it up and put it in the trash can. You know us Cajuns, very efficient. No reason to waste clean plates on a crawfish boil. Come on, let's get the table."

Adi led them to the garage and a large round table with a hole in the center the size of a garbage can. They carefully rolled it out to the driveway and set it up. They piled the top with open sheets of newspaper, tucking an edge into the trash can Adi slid below the hole.

"Now when we're done, everyone rolls together and cleanup is a cinch. There are folding chairs in the garage too."

They placed six chairs around the table and sat while they waited for the others to arrive.

"Well, city gal, whatcha make of crawfishing?" Bertie smiled.

"I think it was hard work. Lots of stink and mud."

Adi and Bertie laughed.

"Yeah, you right about that. Lots of mud, for sure. But it was fun too, no?"

Griffith thought about the day. It had been fun riding the four-wheeler with her body pressed against Adi. It had been fun to work together and catch so many crawfish. And cleaning up? That would have been more fun if Adi had slipped into the shower with her.

"It was fun. Not something I want to do on a regular basis, but fun."

There was a loud scraping sound as T'Claude pushed through the gate.

"Hey, y'all. I brought the beer." T'Claude held up a cooler. "Nice and cold. Who's ready?" He handed a dripping bottle to each of them. "Allow me." He popped the caps with his church key.

Griffith was sure she'd had a Rolling Rock before, but it had never tasted so good. Jose walked up the driveway with a lovely young woman. She waved and smiled.

"Hi, Ms. McNaulty, Adi. This is Rosa."

"Hi, Rosa, it's nice to meet you."

"Grab a couple of beers, Jose. I'll go get plates." Adi went up the stairs and into the kitchen. T'Claude began a long and rambling tale about getting stuck in the mud crawfishing with his daddy. When everyone had gathered around the table, Adi handed them each a double stacked Dixie plate.

"Time to eat. If you're waiting on me, you're backing up."

Adi served a heaping plate of crawfish, potato, and corn and handed it to Bertie. She sat and waited for everyone else to get their fill. The food and company was perfect, and they spent far longer at the table than Griffith had expected. They went from tale to tale, laughing and joking. She expected everyone was getting loose because of the beer, but she realized no one had had more than one or two. This was just how this community of friends spent their shared time.

The entire thing was so at odds with the superficial times she'd spent with friends in LA. There everyone was watching to see who was coming in the door, making sure they were noticed in a good way. No one connected like this. And not one cell phone had come out all evening. That was unheard of at home. She and her friends had made a pact that the first one to pull a phone paid the tab. That wasn't even a consideration here. It was delightful and she felt lucky to experience it. When they were finally winding down, she saw Bertie nod at Adi.

"Okay, y'all. Rolling time."

Everyone stood, and Griffith followed suit. They began at the table's edge just in front and rolled toward the center. She did her best to keep up. When she reached a particularly large pile of shell or corncob, Adi helped get the roll over the bump. Soon the whole shebang was pushed down into the lined trash can. *Such a smart way to do this. We wouldn't think of using a trash can this way at home.*

"Well, that was easy."

"Sure enough. We like it easy. Come on. Let's go sit on the porch."

Now Griffith understood the abundance of rockers and the large swing. The evening continued in the comfort of the porch. *I could get used to this life. It's so laid back.* Adi sat beside her on the swing, her long legs stretched out in front of her. T'Claude pulled out a cigar case and offered them around. Bertie took one, as did Jose. Rosa and Adi declined.

"Okay now, California, check out this fine tobacco. I know you ain't got nothing like this where you come from."

"That sounds like a challenge. I'm sure it's fine tobacco, but I don't know if it can top what we have in LA. I'll try one." She took a long, slender cigar from the case and ran it under her nose. The light scent of whiskey and vanilla was appealing. T'Claude held out his torch lighter to each of them, and they were soon surrounded by the fragrant smoke. He was right. This was finer tobacco than any she'd ever smoked. But then, maybe it was just the company. *I can't remember a nicer evening.*

"This has been so wonderful. I hate the thought of the evening ending, but I'm really tired. Is there anything I can do before I head home?"

"No, ma'am. You did plenty today. If you hadn't helped Adi with the fishing, there wouldn't have been any eating. You just go on home and rest up. Adi, take this girl on home."

"Yes, ma'am."

They walked out to the truck. Adi took a few minutes and unhitched the trailer. After they had buckled in, Adi reached over and held Griffith's hand in her injured one. They drove to the hotel in comfortable silence.

The lights of the hotel seemed harsh after the pleasant evening, and Griffith felt the loss. Adi turned off the truck and faced her. Her face was a study of light and shadow, so serious.

"What is it?"

"Nothing. I just wanted to look at you. Can I have a good night kiss?"

"You can."

Adi leaned over and kissed her deeply. Griffith wanted the kiss to last forever. *The perfect ending to a perfect day.* When they parted, she smiled. "I'm going to miss spending the day with you tomorrow."

"Me too. We're going to be busy at the Pot, but you can, I mean, if you want, you can come over and hang out."

"I'm sure I'd just be in the way. Don't worry. I have work to do. I've got a deadline on your story, remember?"

"Oh, that's right. I almost forgot what brought you here."

"Me too."

"So, are you ready to write it now? Do you have everything you need?"

"Pretty much, but I'd still like to know what you ran away from when you were a child."

Adi looked down, avoiding the issue. "I don't want you to leave. I want you to stay, at least until Monday. I want one more day with you."

"I'll stay. I want one too." She kissed Adi then, a kiss that said she trusted her. That said she would wait and hear her story. That she valued the time they spent together. At least, she hoped that's what Adi got out of it.

Adi's gaze as they moved apart was piercing. "That means so much to me, Griffith. Thank you."

"You're different from anyone I've known. I like being with you. Thank you for the crawfishing lesson. Next time I get to drive the four-wheeler," Griffith said.

"Next time, huh? Think you'll be here long enough for a next time?"

"You never know. I know being with you is an adventure. I like adventures."

"It would be nice to have more of those with you," Adi said.

"Yes, it would. I guess I should go in, unless you'd like to join me?" Griffith watched as the overhead light illuminated Adi's blush. *Damn, she's gorgeous. She doesn't have a clue how sexy she is.*

"I...uh...I don't think I'm ready for that. I better get back home."

"You sure? I promise you won't be disappointed." Griffith gave her best come-hither look, but she could tell Adi was just too shy to jump.

"Thanks, but I wouldn't even know...I mean, I'm not sure... heck, I don't know what I mean."

Griffith let her off the hook. "It's okay. If you decide you're ready before I leave, you'll let me know, right?"

"Yes, I will. I promise."

Griffith climbed down and closed the truck door. She watched as Adi pulled away. *What am I doing? I'm so drawn to her. Is it just because she's different, that this whole world is different? Is there more here than simple novelty?* If not, she really needed to pull back. Hurting Adi to slake her own lust and curiosity wasn't cool. Adi wore her heart on her sleeve. Messing with her meant messing with her heart. *Is that something I want to live with? Am I that shallow?* Maybe in the past, but not now. Not anymore. She was going to do her best to leave Adi undamaged, no matter what her libido dictated or her journalist's instinct demanded.

CHAPTER ELEVEN

Adi watched Griffith in her rearview mirror as she pulled out of the parking lot. *What's wrong with me? She just invited me into her room. Am I crazy?* There was something about Griffith and the way they were together that Adi didn't want to spoil by rushing things. She briefly wondered if she should worry about being so open. Lots of people could have seen them kissing and carrying on, and in this town, that news would spread like wildfire. But was she willing to keep that part of her quiet anymore?

She thought about the way it felt, the way her stomach flipped over and she felt like jumping out of her skin with happiness, and she knew she was done worrying about what other folks thought. Sure, maybe she'd never get the chance to sleep with Griff, but if not, that was okay. She wanted to really know her before she took that step. Griffith was like a shiny new penny. Something you wanted real bad, but when you had it a while, it ended up as tarnished as all the others. *I don't want that. I want Griffith to keep her shine. What if sleeping with her changed everything? What if it made it weird to be together?* Adi hadn't had many friends, really just the gang at the Pot, and way back, Rachel.

When the thing with Ransom happened and J.B. made her more a part of his business, she'd lost the connection she had with Rachel. He'd kept her so busy, and when she was free, being with Rachel made her feel dirty. Like the things she'd had to do were marks on her skin that Rachel could see. And there were so many secrets, things she couldn't say…their friendship had been poisoned by the life he made her live. Adi had just stopped hanging out with her. She convinced herself it was to protect Rachel, but she knew that wasn't totally true. It was what she had to do to survive.

She thought about her conversations with Bertie and felt the truth of them deep in her soul. *I'm tired of being afraid. I don't want to hide any more. How can I tell the truth without putting all of us in danger?* What if she laid it all out for Griffith and asked her for her help? Would she be able to do anything? Would she know how to safeguard Bertie and T? *Can I trust her enough to ask?* She was starting to think she could. That maybe Griffith would treat her story with the kind of care it needed.

She wanted to believe it could be that simple. That with Griffith's help she could get out from under the threat of J.B. and maybe live a normal life. *But what about the things I did? What about Ransom? Am I going to end up behind bars? That's probably where I belong. I killed him and helped hide the others.* She needed to think about it, long and hard, before doing anything stupid. When she drove into the driveway, she was no less conflicted than she was before. Bertie and T were still on the porch. She dropped into the swing and sighed in frustration.

"What's up, puppy? Why you moping around?" T asked.

"No reason. I'm tired, I guess."

"You didn't hurt your hand out in the mud, huh?" Bertie said.

"No, the hand's fine," Adi said.

"Well, just tell us what it is that's got you in a funk," Bertie said.

"I don't know what it is. I'm just all mixed up inside."

"You know what I do when I'm not sure which way to go? I just plain stop. I sit and open myself up to all the choices I've got, then I just wait. Eventually, my heart leads me one way or the other. It's never failed me. You should try it," T said.

"Maybe," Adi said.

"Want to talk about it? It usually helps," Bertie said.

Adi looked at Bertie and T. The two people who meant the most to her in her life. She'd already told Bertie about J.B. and the things she'd done, but not T. He knew nothing about her past.

"Maybe later."

"I think it's about time for me to go. Y'all sure put on a good feast tonight. Thanks for the party," T said.

"You don't have to go, T," Adi said.

"I know that, but I think it's a good time. I'll see you in the morning."

"Good night, T'sugar," Bertie said.

"Night, Mama Sass. Night, Adi."

"Night, T." Adi felt like she'd chased him off by being moody, but was grateful she'd have time to talk with Bertie.

She waited while T loaded his cooler in the car and drove off.

"I'm all mixed up, Bertie. I don't know if I should tell Griffith everything or hide out until she leaves town. She's got me so confused."

"Hm, confused how?"

"I don't know. I mean, when I'm with her, all I can think about is holding her. My heart says trust her, but my head says stay away. Then she kisses me, or I kiss her, and I forget to be careful. It's all going to slip out if I keep spending time with her."

"And that's a bad thing? You don't trust her enough yet?"

"How can I? There's so much at risk, and her job is to tell stories. If she prints my story before I've figured out what to do, we'll be in all kinds of danger. I can run again. I know I can keep him from finding me, but the Pot and you and T, y'all can't disappear so easily. I can't let her write about my past at all."

"I understand your fear, baby, but I also know you got to make a stand at some point. You can't just live your life ready to disappear. What you going to have when I'm gone? How're you going to build a life when you so scared you can't connect to anyone? You seem a bit partial to that reporter. Seems like maybe she's somebody you might want to build something with. You going to deny yourself that? With her or with anyone? To keep a secret for an evil man?"

"I'm not keeping it for him, Bertie. I'm trying to keep all of us safe. If he comes after us, he won't stop till we have nothing left. And I don't want to go to jail, either."

"But don't you get it? In keeping us safe, you're freeing him to do more harm. Plus, you're keeping yourself trapped. You're closing yourself off from life because of that secret. That means every day you let him walk free is a day less you have for living? How many days are you willing to give up for that man? You're already in a kind of jail, child."

"I don't know. I'm scared and I hate him. I don't want him to ever touch my life. Not mine or yours or anyone's, but I can't keep him out once he knows where I am. He's like a hurricane, Bertie. He's relentless. I can't do it. I can't unleash that hate on all of us. I just can't."

"Thing is, all of that hate is already loose. You won't be unleashing a thing, just giving it a different direction. Maybe we can direct it right into prison, if we can get some help. I want you to see if Griffith can help us put that man away. Then your life can truly begin."

"Could that work? Do you really think so?" *Can I trust her enough to find out?*

"You'll never know unless you ask. It's going to take trust. I don't know if you're ready for that or not. I get a sense that you are either going to take that step and let it out, or you're going to leave me. I fear you running off. You mean the world to me, Adi. You're my own child as far as I'm concerned, and I can't take losing you."

Adi shook as the truth of Bertie's words sunk in. She'd made herself believe that running would be the only way to keep Bertie safe, but it would hurt. Not only her, but Bertie and T as well. They mattered to her; their pain mattered.

She grasped her head in her hands, trying to quell the pounding that erupted behind her eyes. *Why did this have to happen? Why couldn't I just stay hidden and safe?*

"I don't know what I'm going to do, Bertie. All I'm sure of is that I have to keep everyone safe."

"There's no telling what's ahead, Dink. Truth be told, even if you keep quiet, we aren't none of us safer than if you don't. He's out there, and if he wants to find you bad enough, he will."

"If I go away, at least you and T will be safe."

"No, child, there's no guarantee of that. Plus we'll be worried about you. Running ain't a solution. It's just stretching the problem out more and more. You know what happens when you stretch something too far. It snaps back and bites you. Don't be stretching this secret more than you have. It's past time for you to deal with it. The best place to do that is right here where you have family that loves you and can support you."

"You don't know what he'd do if he found me, Bertie. There's nothing that could keep me safe."

"I don't believe that. There has to be a way to keep us all safe, if we work together. I won't be losing you, Dink. I won't let that happen, hear?"

"I hear ya. Let me think on it some. I promise I won't do anything without talking it out with you," Adi said.

"Well, that's gotta be good enough, huh? All right then, I'm going to put my tired bones to bed. Be sure you lock up when you come in," Bertie said.

"I will."

Adi sat back in the swing and willed her mind to stop racing. The rapid-fire sequence of things that could happen just wouldn't stop. What if J.B. came after her? How would she possibly be able to stand up to him? Would he even show himself? He could send someone to take her out without even getting his hands dirty. Maybe he was dead? What if one of his international partners took him out of the delivery chain? She didn't even know at this point. She needed information so she could think of a way out of this.

Griffith was her best possible resource when it came to finding out about J.B. If she talked to her openly and asked for her help she had to believe Griffith would help. *Why do I believe that?*

She called the number she had for Griffith and paced while she waited for an answer.

"Hello?" Griffith sounded like she'd been sleeping.

"Hi, it's me. I need to ask you something," Adi said.

"Okay, I'm all ears."

"If...I mean what would you do if I told you something that could hurt me, could hurt all of us?"

"I guess that depends on what it is and what kind of hurt we're talking about," she said.

"Serious hurt, the kind you don't walk away from."

"I'm not sure. I mean, I won't know how I'll react without the facts. I can say I would do my best to keep anyone from getting hurt. Is this about your past?"

Adi swallowed. *Once I say it, I can't take it back. It will be out there and whatever happens will happen.*

"Yes." It wasn't more than a whisper, and its passage through her lips left her feeling gutted. Raw and vulnerable.

"And you're afraid whatever it is can hurt you or those you love?" Griffith said. Her tone was very gentle.

I hope that's a good sign. "Yes."

"How can I help?"

The flood of relief that rushed through her made Adi feel weaker than a newborn foal. She leaned back against the wall and let the cool wood hold her up.

"I'm not exactly sure; it's all so complicated. There's things I've done. Things I'll always have to live with, but I want to tell you. I just have to know I can trust you to handle this carefully."

"You can trust me, Adi. I promise. Tell me."

"Not tonight, not on the phone," Adi said.

"When, then? Do you want me to come back to Bertie's?"

"No, not tonight. Can we sit down and talk it out on Monday? I'm going to be slammed at the restaurant through the weekend. That always happens when we've been closed," Adi said.

The silence on Griffith's end of the line was deafening. *Did I blow this? Is she still with me?*

"Okay, sure. Monday it is. I'm going to write the article for Dawn tonight. Your past doesn't really play a part in your cooking. Is there anything in what you're going to tell me that I need to know before I send that to her?"

Was there? Did her childhood have anything to do with now? Would it reflect badly on the Pot?

"I don't think so. It's all from so long ago," she said.

"Fine then. I'll write my piece, and on Monday we can sort out your past. I'll do everything in my power to help, Adi. I promise."

"Okay," Adi said.

"And, Adi? Thank you," she said.

Adi disconnected the call. *It's done now. There's no going back. I hope to hell I haven't made a mistake. Don't you let me down, Griffith.*

CHAPTER TWELVE

G riffith tossed her phone onto the side table. She was finally going to hear Adi's story. From what she'd said it could be a doozy. She didn't seem like the type to exaggerate, and if she was this frightened, it must be big. *I have to know as much as possible before I write Dawn's piece. If whatever she's hiding is so terrible,* Epicuriosity *could be caught in the backlash.* She needed facts; that was how she operated. If she didn't have all the facts, the ones she wrote lost their credibility. *I need Adi to understand that.* She flashed back to all the bitter encounters after the Moore affair, and the fair accusations that she'd failed to check her facts. That she hadn't done her job.

Adi's going to tell me on Monday. If I spend the weekend doing a bit of research, I'll feel better about the whole thing. Why do I feel like I lied to her? When has it ever bothered me to hash out a story? Her gut was screaming at her to dig, to get to the bottom of things. *Why am I even hesitating? Tomorrow, I start looking for young Adi.*

She rose early the next morning, knowing she had a bit of a drive to get to Dulac. She had checked her maps app and figured it would take about two hours to make the trip. She also checked where to find the Parish records office and the local policing agency, located in Houma.

She still felt uneasy about it, but she couldn't set it aside. She had to give due diligence to the story. *It's just groundwork. Adi will flesh out the story personally on Monday. I'm doing the right thing.*

No matter what she told herself, it felt like a rotten thing to do, invasive and underhanded. Why hadn't she just told Adi her intentions? Something had held her back last night, knowing that Adi wouldn't like her plans. *My mother always said if you can't tell someone you're doing something, you shouldn't be doing it. I should have told her.* She sighed and kept getting ready. Sometimes real journalism meant taking a road less desirable to get the story. If she did her own research, she'd know for certain Adi hadn't held anything back.

She loaded up her tablet and a couple of bottles of water for the drive. She would be in Houma before lunch and could grab a bite to eat there. She'd go to the Parish office and scan some records before the final drive down to the coast.

The drive was uneventful, mostly farmland broken by the occasional patch of swamp. When she reached Houma, she had little trouble finding the courthouse. It was a massive limestone building in Greek revival style, with a distinctly 1950s feel. *I hope this beast is air-conditioned.* She climbed the narrow steps to the massive doors and walked in to start her explorations. The man at the information desk sported a checked vest and a bowtie.

"Hey, there. How can I help you?" he said.

"Hello. I'm doing research for an article I'm writing. Where would I find population and demographic records for Dulac, Louisiana?" she said.

"Dulac?" He frowned. "I don't know that place, but hold on."

He scrolled through pages on his computer screen, his frown deepening. Finally, he stopped and smiled.

"Got it. That's one of the tiny communities on the estuary. Not much of record in the database, but there are some basic things listed. Want me to print out what I've got?"

"Thank you, that'd be great."

The printout he handed her was thin, records for Dulac sparse. The population had always been small, and after the hurricanes of the last decade, it had dropped by over forty percent. The median income was well below the state median, and it seemed to have a high percentage of Native American residents.

After an hour of searching records, she gave in. *This isn't telling me anything. I need more.* Something that would point her in the right direction. She would eat and then give the police department a try.

The Houma Police Department covered the area of Dulac as well as other small cities near the coast. Hopefully, they would have some information that would help.

She found a small café near the courthouse for brunch. The food was good, but not close to Adi's. She missed the company and banter she'd been enjoying with her New Iberia friends. That's what they'd become, her friends. If you'd asked her a week ago if she made friends easily, she'd have said no, but Adi and the others made it effortless. *It's like everyone is their friend until they aren't. I hope this trip doesn't change how they feel about me. Especially Adi.* She knew she had to pursue the root of the story, but she needed to do so in a way that kept everyone at the Pot safe. She couldn't draw attention to what she was doing. If anything she did led to her friends being harmed, she'd never forgive herself. *I won't let that happen.*

After settling her bill, she headed to the police department, still conflicted about what she was doing. When she arrived, the place was bustling with activity. She went to the information officer and asked where she should go to read old missing persons reports. He was none too happy when she pulled out her press credentials and he had to take her to the records room. Freedom of the press had its benefits.

"Look, lady. I don't really care who you are. These records aren't to leave this room. You ask for a specific date and John will bring you the records. That's how it works. Oh. You need to check your phone in at the desk. No photographs are allowed. When you finish with one set of records, you can request another. We close this office at four, so you are done at three forty-five. Understand?"

"Yes. Thank you."

She had been around her share of grumpy, uncooperative officials, and she knew the best way to handle them was to be small and efficient. Operate within their guidelines and perhaps, if she needed something extra, they would oblige because she hadn't been difficult. She could throw her power around if she needed to, but found it better to work within the system.

She requested reports from June of 2007. John, the records clerk, who was decidedly more cheerful than Mr. Information, was happy to bring her the entire month's reports. He was curious about her search and asked lots of questions.

"So you're looking for a runaway from Dulac? Heck, I'd guess about half the kids born there run away. You ever been to Dulac? It's not a place people generally want to stay, if you know what I mean."

"Yes, I'm looking for someone who ran away from there. A young girl, maybe fourteen?"

"You got your work cut out for you, that's for sure. I'll bring you the next month's report. Don't worry about Phil. He's just a pain. If you want, I'll even run some parameters through my computer. You know? Narrow things down a bit? It might help."

"Oh, would you? That would be great. Thank you."

"Sure. Write down the particulars and I'll see what I come up with."

Griffith jotted down Adi's age, ethnicity, and estimated disappearance date. John took the slip and went back to his office while she pored over the reports. So many young people had been reported missing it was staggering. There were twice as many boys as girls, though, which helped. Her eyes were beginning to blur with the effort when she finally closed the last file. This wasn't going to get easier. She needed a break. She took the files back to the window and handed them to John.

"I'm going to stretch my legs. Can I bring you anything?"

"Well, that's awfully nice, ma'am. I would love a Coke if you go by the vending machines."

"Which way would I find those?"

"Just go left out the door to the elevator and go to the basement. The cafeteria and vending area is down there."

"Will it be a problem for me to go down there?"

"Oh no. That's all in the public area."

"Great. I'll be back shortly."

She walked slowly down the corridor, enjoying the stretch in her stiff legs. She hoped the computer search would turn up something useful. She wondered how Adi's day was going. Would she have trouble cooking with her knife wound? She managed just fine yesterday.

She mentally ran through the list of possibles for Adi she had written in her tablet. There were really only five likely candidates so far. Two of them were strong possibilities, disappearing without a known companion. One of the others was suspected to have gone to meet an Internet acquaintance. That could be Adi, although the fact that she didn't have any Internet presence now made Griffith doubt it.

She reached the vending area and began feeding dollar bills into the drink machine. She got a cola for John and a lemonade for herself. Drinks in hand, she headed back to the records room. She walked to the window to hand John his soda and he in turn handed her two files.

"These two are the most likely records to match your mystery girl according to my computer. You were off on the date for one of them though. She disappeared in March. Good luck, and thanks for the drink."

"Thanks, John. I appreciate your help."

She took the files to her table and opened the first one. The picture of the girl was blurry, but she could be Adi. Same facial structure, right age. Tall.

She read through the file. This girl, Kendrick Baptiste, had left her home on the night of June twelfth. She had been in and out of trouble, apparently, and didn't care for her parents' brand of punishment. The report stated that police had been called to the home on two prior occasions. Once for truancy and once after a teacher reported suspected abuse. The father had been arrested in the second instance but released when no charges were filed.

Griffith recorded the pertinent information on her tablet. She would check out the Baptiste family. Maybe discover something to solidify whether this might be Adi.

The next file was from March of 2007. A fourteen-year-old girl named Merley Nerbass had disappeared without explanation. Her parents had reported her missing and were reported as being distraught over her disappearance. Foul play was suspected, and the parents had been interviewed extensively, but there had been no leads on her disappearance.

Griffith flipped to the last page of the report and there was a picture. It could also be Adi. She was younger, softer. If it was her, she had changed a good deal in eight years. She wondered why Merley had run. Nothing in the file led her to believe there was abuse at home. No records of police visits. No arrests. Yet, the police had suspected something anyway. The last known address of the parents was listed, and Griffith noted it.

She closed the files and returned them to the window. "Thanks again. You made this a lot easier."

"No problem."

Griffith pushed through the door and out into the corridor. She contemplated which family she should check out first. The Baptiste family held more promise, the daughter having trouble at home and not wanting to be there. The other family, the Nerbasses, sounded more like a child abduction or something of that nature. Showing up on these people's doorsteps to ask about their missing kids was problematic, though. She had to come up with some way of getting the information without directly asking about the girls. That way, if she found Adi's family and the perceived danger originated there, she wouldn't lead them back to Adi. She'd promised Adi she'd be careful, and although Adi didn't know about this part of what she was doing, it didn't make that promise any less relevant.

She would use the extremely high rate of runaways as a starting point for a cover. When she approached the families, it would be to hear how losing their child affected them emotionally and economically. She could explore the possibility that the recessed economy was a contributing factor to the runaway issue, and the effect such an event had on the most vulnerable families.

She headed south on state Highway Fifty-seven. The rural highway was sparsely traveled. Most of the buildings she encountered were metal frame buildings housing oil and gas enterprises. She did pass a couple of restaurants, but none that encouraged her to stop.

She noticed suddenly that water was now on both sides of the highway. She slowed to a stop. That wasn't right. Dulac was just before the waters of Lake Quittman and Bayou Dulac converged. She looked at her GPS and realized she had driven right through the small town. She turned her car around and slowly backtracked.

Apparently, Dulac was really more of a postal code than a town. Her GPS assured her she had reached her destination, but there wasn't really any way of knowing you were there. She pulled to the side of the highway and reached for her tablet. She punched the address of the Baptiste family into her maps app and the computerized voice directed her to the small house on piers.

The cedar-sided house was elevated about ten feet off the ground. She pulled into the driveway and parked. She looked up at the house, wondering if she was making a mistake appearing unannounced. She opened her door and started up the wide staircase.

"That's far enough, lady. What you want here?"

Griffith couldn't see where the voice was coming from. She smiled and called, "Hello. I'm here researching a story. My name is Griffith McNaulty. I'm a freelance journalist."

"A reporter, huh? What story are you here about?"

"I'm writing a story about the high number of runaways in this area. May I come up?"

"Well, sure, come on."

Griffith climbed the remaining steps to a wide wooden deck. She could feel the salt in the air that blew steadily from the Gulf. The woman who had spoken to her was waiting at the door of the house. She appeared to be in her fifties, dressed in a light cotton housecoat and slippers. She had her hair wrapped in curlers and an unlit cigarette hanging from her overly rouged lips.

"Hi, Mrs.?"

"I'm Mabel. Mabel Baptiste. Come in out of the sun."

Griffith entered the darkened house. She was hit with the smell of stale cigarette smoke and musty furniture. She waited while her eyes adjusted to the light.

"Mrs. Baptiste, thanks for being willing to talk to me."

"It's Mabel. Here, let's sit." She pointed to the scruffy sofa.

Griffith walked to the hard wooden dining set and pulled out a chair. "Is this okay? I have a bad back, and I have to sit on hard chairs."

"Heck, I know just what you mean, dear. Want something to drink?"

"I'm fine, thank you."

"So you say you're writing about runaways? What's that got to do with me?"

"I'm exploring how families cope with the long-term effects of losing a child. I understand you have a daughter who ran away in her teens."

"Kendrick? Oh Lord, you're digging up really old news there."

"I'm sorry if I'm opening old wounds, but when she ran away, and you reported her missing, what did you feel? How did you manage the anguish of not knowing where she was?"

"Anguish? Nah, you got that wrong. I wasn't worried. I mean, sure, she ran away, but I knew where she'd gone. Ran right to the scumbag she's with now. She wasn't even gone from home more than three weeks. I turned her in to the cops so they'd scare her into staying home. I knew she'd turn up, just like a bad penny."

"I guess I was given the wrong information. I understood she was still missing."

"No, no way. She was freeloading here till last March."

"Oh, I see. So she wouldn't really fit into my story."

"What? Aw, come on now, I'm sure I can think up something that would be a good story. Lemme just think a minute."

"Oh no, really, that's okay. I need to talk with parents who haven't recovered their children."

"Well, couldn't you use Kendra as, like, I don't know...the happy ending, kind of?"

"I don't know about that..."

"Really, I mean, sometimes kids run away and come on back home. I think that's important to show, you know? Come on, please?"

"I guess it wouldn't hurt to hear your story. So tell me about when Kendra ran away."

Mabel's eyes lit up and she railed about her wayward daughter and the fights they'd had.

"Really, I mean, what was I supposed to do? Her daddy sure wasn't interested in helping keep a handle on her. So I grounded her. No way did I think she should be running off to see a twenty-year-old man when she was just coming up to fourteen. That just wasn't right. Didn't do me no good, though. She waited till I had to work a double down at the diner, and she packed up and left. I was madder than a nest of hornets when I found her gone. I called up the sheriff right away to hunt her down. She never let me forget that."

"I'm sure it must have been a trying time. Did the sheriff locate her or did she just return home?"

"Ha. That sheriff was just about as useful as a case of ringworm. No, he didn't help at all. I finally got tired of her running wild and went after her. She came home, but the sour grapes. Ugh. Anyway, that's all I can say about it."

"Well, thank you for your time, Mabel. And thanks for sharing your story with me."

"You going to send me a copy of your story when you get it published?"

"It will probably be in an online journal. I can send you a link."

"Well, shoot. That isn't going to work. I don't have a computer." She looked thoughtful. "Are you going to talk to any other folks around here? Some of them has computers and might let me take a peek."

"Yes, actually. I was going to talk to the Nerbass family next."

Mabel's entire body stiffened and she squinted suspiciously at Griffith.

"Nerbass? You mean J.B. Nerbass?"

"Yes, John Bertram and Eloise. I understand their daughter ran away."

The tension amped up in the room. Mabel grabbed Griffith by the elbow and propelled her to the door.

"I never did talk to you, you hear me, lady? You were never here. I swear on the Bible, I never laid eyes upon you. Now you get on out of here."

"What is it? What did I do?"

"You just get on out of here. And don't you be talking to no one else, if you know what's good for you. Just get back in your shiny car and get."

Griffith was stunned by the vehemence in Mabel's voice and puzzled as to what she had said. She complied with the request and drove out of sight before pulling over to assess the situation. Something she had said had turned an attention seeking woman into a closemouthed, hostile person. Who exactly was John Bertram Nerbass, and why did his name inspire fear?

She considered her next move carefully. Her plan had been to do much the same as she had done with Mabel. Enter the Nerbass address into her maps app and show up at their door. Now she wasn't sure that was a good idea. She drove up the highway a little farther and found a small diner. She would call them first, get an idea of how she would be received. She could always come back on another day.

She ordered a shrimp po'boy and an iced tea. Armed with her search engine, she looked for a contact number for the Nerbasses. The number of pages that came up with the J.B. Nerbass search surprised her. She'd expected it to be hard to find anything about the family, but clearly, the name J.B. Nerbass held some clout. She randomly clicked a link. It opened to a picture of Mr. Nerbass with a state senator at a black-tie function. She read the text.

"Senator Landry shakes hands with businessman J.B. Nerbass at annual gala."

She looked at other articles. John Bertram Nerbass was a self-made millionaire. He owned a multistate sports fishing tour company and a helicopter ferry service that transported workers offshore to oil rigs in the Gulf. It appeared he had amassed his wealth in the past ten years, starting with a small bait shop in Dulac. His JB Dulac Transport now had helipads up and down the Gulf Coast. His fishing charter companies set out from Morgan City, Louisiana, as well as Galveston, Rockport, and South Padre Island in Texas, and Gulfport, Mississippi. He had been fortunate to contract with BP prior to the spill and was responsible for all transport to and from the spill sight. He also had contracts with several other large multinationals.

Was that what caused the animosity with Mabel? The fact that this man had started in Dulac and had become overwhelmingly successful? It had seemed deeper than simple jealousy; she'd looked terrified. If Adi was his daughter, surely he would've exhausted every lead searching for her. *That is, if he wanted her found.* Men with money were so often dangerous, it was almost cliché. But was that the case now?

She would have to tread cautiously. He was probably unapproachable without an appointment. Her oil spill cover wouldn't work with him, but she figured selling the interview as a rags to riches feature piece might. The one thing she couldn't do was mention Adi in any way. After Mabel's reaction, she wouldn't dare bring attention to her. She called the number listed as his headquarters in Morgan City. The person who answered dutifully took her information down. She was unable to speak with him, but was assured that her query would be given to Mr. Nerbass directly.

Griffith didn't hold out hope that he would get in touch anytime soon. She paid for her meal and decided to head back to New Iberia. She would mosey down to Morgan City in the morning and see if she could find out anything else about Mr. Nerbass.

She was unlocking her car when her phone rang. She smiled at the number displayed. Adi.

"Hi there, tall one."

"Hey, yourself. What are you up to?"

"Just about to get in my car and drive back to the hotel. I've been doing research today."

"Cool. You want to come by here and spend half an hour with me?"

"Sure I would. It'll be a couple of hours before I can get there, though."

"A couple of hours? Where are you?"

Griffith hesitated. She knew Adi would be upset if she knew where she was, so being vague was better than an outright lie.

"I'm just out and about in the countryside."

Adi was quiet, and Griffith worried she could tell she was prevaricating.

"Okay. I'll keep working until you get here."

CHAPTER THIRTEEN

Griffith pulled into the parking lot of the Boiling Pot two hours later. Adi was waiting on the porch.

"Hey," Adi said.

"Hey, yourself. So what are we going to do for your thirty-minute break?"

"Let's go for a walk."

"Okay."

Adi held out her hand and Griffith took it. They walked to the back edge of the parking lot where there was a trail beside a small waterway.

"Is this a creek?" Griffith said.

"No, this is a coulee."

"A what?"

"A coulee. That's what we call them anyway. I suppose you'd just call it a ditch anywhere else. It's for drainage."

"Why do you call it a coulee?"

"Just Cajun for ditch."

"Hmm. Okay. Are there any fish in the coulee?"

"Just crawfish," Adi said.

"Well, it's pretty anyway."

"I think so. This is one of my favorite walks. Even though we're pretty much in the middle of town, it feels like we're out in the country because of all the trees."

"Yeah, I get that."

"I missed you today."

"I missed you too."

"I think we need to get to know more about each other. Let's play a game," Adi said.

"Okay."

"Let's play the question game. I ask you a question, then you ask me one. You have to answer or the other person gets to give you a task."

"So, like truth or dare?"

"Yeah, but not as treacherous." Adi shrugged, almost embarrassed to suggest it. But she'd realized during the day she hardly knew anything about Griff, and she wanted to know more.

"Okay. Ask."

"Who was your first kiss?"

"Easy, Eleanor Grimes. I was twelve. My turn. If you only had one day to live, what would you do?"

"Hmmm. I guess I'd spend it out on the bayou in the canoe. Just being with nature. What's the most embarrassing thing you ever did?"

Griffith winced. "I got a story wrong. I defended someone who was guilty, and she ripped my heart out and nearly destroyed my career. All because I didn't check my facts thoroughly enough."

Adi stopped walking abruptly, suddenly understanding Griff's obsession a little bit more. "Wow, I'm so sorry. That had to be horrible."

"It wasn't a walk in the park, that's for sure."

"That's awful. You want to tell me about it?"

Griffith sighed and closed her eyes. "Yeah, I would. Can we sit somewhere?"

"Over there, by the oak tree, there's a bench."

Adi led Griffith to the bench that encircled the wide oak. They sat side by side, leaning on the tree.

"It happened two years ago. I was doing an in-depth story on the players in a big fraud scheme at an energy trading corporation. There were a lot of innocent people who lost everything they had saved because of these crooks. I was interviewing Tabitha Moore, the financial planning and analysis manager, and she convinced me she had been completely duped by the chief financial officer.

Unfortunately, I let myself become infatuated with her and missed the red flags that would've given me the truth. She was a liar.

"She wouldn't tell me much about her past. I went to her hometown and talked to people who knew her, or tried to, anyway. Every door was closed, though. No one wanted to talk about her. I just blew it off as jealousy and accepted what she was telling me. In the end, she was indicted, and she would've gone to jail, but she fled the country. She had me completely fooled."

"That's horrible." Adi's stomach turned at the thought of Griff being infatuated with anyone else. *Don't be stupid. She's got history. So what?*

"The worst part was that other journalists had no trouble seeing her for who she was. They were able to get the background story because they hadn't written pieces defending her. I was scooped and betrayed. Not to mention heartbroken. I'm still working on regaining my credibility."

Adi processed what she said and asked, "What were you researching today?"

"I drove down to Houma and looked at old records."

"What records? What were you looking for?" Adi felt like she was going to be sick. She knew the answer, but needed to hear it anyway.

"You. I was looking for you. I have to know your truth, Adi. I don't have a choice. I can't print an unsubstantiated story again. That could mean I don't work anymore."

"But I'm not her. It's not at all the same. I haven't stolen anyone's money. I'm no liar."

"It's about my journalistic integrity, Adi. Telling the whole truth."

"You can't tell my whole truth, Griffith. You can't. You said you wouldn't. People I care about could get hurt. Don't you get it?" She wanted to scream, to shake Griffith by the shoulders until she could see.

"How can I get it? You haven't told me a thing. Only that I can't know. That's not okay with me. I can't ever let that be okay with me again."

"You're mixing up two very different situations. You had a liar, a crook, who convinced you not to look into her past. I'm not a liar or a crook, and I want to tell you my past. I just don't want you to write about it. You're supposed to write about the restaurant, about me as a cook. What's that got to do with my past?"

"But where is my integrity in that? Huh, Adi? If I promise you I won't write about your past, and then your past turns and bites my ass where does that leave me? I can promise that I'll be careful, and if it doesn't matter, genuinely, to the story or to the magazine, I won't say anything about it, but I can't promise not to check the facts. I just can't. It's what I do. It might not matter a lot to the article, but it matters to me."

"You're not being fair. I told you I would tell you. I said I would. But you can't promise to keep my past secret, even if it means the people I love will be hurt or worse? I can't trust you. Just get away from me." Adi jumped up from the bench and turned away from her. *I knew better. Trust is for weak people.*

"What?"

"You heard me. Get away from me, Griffith. You have to leave me alone. You lied to me, and I'm not about to put people I care about in danger because of some article in a magazine. Find someone else's life to blow to hell."

❖

The empty feeling grew and threatened to overwhelm her as Adi rushed back the way they had come. What had just happened? Griffith leaned against the tree, its solid mass grounding her, helping to keep her from drifting away. What could she do to repair the situation? She watched the ground blur and realized she was crying, tears obscuring her field of vision. *Damn. Why did I get so obstinate? I've already decided not to write about her childhood. Why couldn't I just say that? Because I'm a stubborn oaf.* It felt like her soul was being stripped away as she watched Adi leave. She needed to get a grip. *Pull it together.* She rubbed furiously at her eyes. *Damn tears.* She went after Adi, but she was fast, and already out of sight.

When she got back to the restaurant, she hurried to the kitchen. Adi was nowhere to be seen.

"What's got you all messed up?" Bertie asked

"Adi. We had a fight. I think I really upset her."

"Aw, don't you fret over that one. She runs hot and cold. You just got a taste of hot. She'll cool down and come on back. She's probably running the coulee. Just sit here a bit and settle yourself. I'll get you a Coke."

Bertie handed her an icy cold bottle of Dr Pepper. The cool plastic felt good. She held it against her cheek and let herself calm down. Adi would be okay. They would work through this. Bertie would help. She opened the bottle and took a long swallow.

"What did y'all fight about?"

"Her past. I was stupid and pushed her."

"What'd you mean you pushed her?"

"I wouldn't promise not to write about her past, but that was stupid, because I've already decided I wouldn't. It was just my defensive reaction to being told not to. Now she's gone. I didn't mean it, Bertie. I'd never hurt her."

"I believe you. But you sure have stuck your hand in a hornet's nest. She don't hold that part of herself back because it's all sunshine. No, she has some serious trouble she's lived through. You have to let her do the telling. Make sure when she comes back that you're clear about what you will and won't write about. And make sure you know what, and why, you're doing it yourself, girl. Get that right in your head before you talk to her again."

"I will. You're right, Bertie. She'll be back. Would you mind telling her I came back here to apologize?"

"Why don't you just wait here and tell her yourself?"

"I think she's probably going to want more time before she sees me again. I'll be at the hotel. If she wants to talk, she has my number."

"Well, all right then."

Griffith walked out to her car. She still felt hollow inside. That would be with her until Adi filled it again. She would go back and soak in a hot tub and watch a movie. Tomorrow she would go to Morgan City. She had a job to do, and Adi had asked for her help. Okay, maybe she shouldn't have pushed, and maybe Adi was right to be afraid. But Griff had never let fear run her life, and she wasn't about to start now. If she was going to help Adi, and keep her career on the right path, she had to do it her way and hope Adi would understand. *Back on track.*

❖

Adi ran. She ran until the sound of her own breathing and the beating of her heart drowned out the fear chasing her. She moved into the groove she hit when her running was optimal. There, nothing outside could touch her. Nothing mattered but the beat of her heart and the sound of her shoes on the trail. She ran with the skill of one who knew her surroundings, adjusting easily to the ruts and bumps in her path.

She stayed in her safe zone as long as the wind was with her, never wondering how far she'd gone, just letting her body tell her when to stop. She listened when her legs said enough and slowed. Jogging, she thought about the fight. Griffith was telling her about something that was very painful and took a long time to heal. The fact she'd been checking up on Adi was born of that stuff. Stuff from her past. *Guess we've all got skeletons with baggage.*

She wanted to trust Griffith. She was her best chance to finally be free of J.B., and Adi cared about her. She believed Griffith cared about her too. But her past didn't have anything to do with her cooking or the Boiling Pot. Just like her being a lesbian had nothing to do with cooking or the Pot. Griffith had been surprised when Adi asked her if she was going to put that in her story. If the truth about her and her past with J.B. turned out to be something Griffith couldn't help her with, she'd have to figure out something else. She owed Griffith the truth, had planned to lay it all out for her on Monday. Why couldn't she just wait until then? Why'd she have to go poking around now? Did that mean she couldn't trust her, or that Adi needed to understand why Griff couldn't just accept things? *I need to ask her.* She wanted to be free, but she needed to trust Griffith to do the right thing, and not put them in danger. Maybe, if she understood that it had nothing to do with the Pot, things would be okay. She tried to understand the credibility thing Griff had talked about, but she just couldn't see how her messed up childhood would matter to some high-flying magazine. It wasn't like anyone would ever associate the adult Addison with the child Merley. Especially not folks just wanting to read about food. But then, maybe it was the world Griff lived in, one Adi couldn't well understand.

Resolved to try to get Griffith to understand her situation and what was at stake, Adi felt her whole being lighten. Her jog became even more effortless as the tension fell away. She rounded a corner and headed back down the trail toward the Pot. She hoped Griffith was still there. She needed to fix this, so they could move forward, but Griffith had to want it fixed, and she needed to meet Adi somewhere in the middle.

When she reached the back of the restaurant, she paced to cool down. Bertie had hung her customary damp towel outside the door so Adi could wipe down. She had often told T'Claude she was going to put in an outdoor shower. This would've been a great day to have it.

After cooling down and wiping off, Adi went into the kitchen and down the short hall to the office and the shower there. She had an extra uniform in the closet for days like this. She washed quickly and dressed.

When she walked back into the kitchen, Bertie was standing at the range with her hands on her hips.

"Hey, Bertie. Thanks for the towel."

"Umm-hmm."

"You mad at me?"

"What I got to be mad at you for? You want to be a fool, go on ahead and be one."

"What do you mean?"

"What do I mean? I mean asking Griffith for help but having a fight with her instead and making a right mess of things. How're you supposed to get her to help you when you go getting all mad and up in her face? You got more sense than that. I know you're scared, and rightly so, but this ain't the way to go about it, Dink. I know she's been looking around for clues to your past. That's why you got to step up and let her know what she will find. You got to be the one tells her, hear? She needs to know where that fear comes from. And since she's sniffing around, better sooner than later."

"You're right, Bertie. I was a fool. I'm sorry."

"You bet I'm right. I know I'm right. You don't need to be telling me I'm right. Look here. You better get on out of here and go find that girl. You need to make peace with her. She's the best chance you've got."

"I can't leave now, you know that. It's almost dinner time. I'll go as soon as the rush ends."

"That ain't going to work. You can't leave that mess festering. You got to deal with it now. The longer you wait, the harder it's going to get. That Griffith McNaulty is just about the nicest woman I ever met, and for some durn fool reason, she happens to like you. You got to hold on to that. You hear me?"

"I hear you. And I know you are right. I'll deal with it, Bertie. I promise. Before I lay my head down to sleep tonight, I'll call her or go over there and clear this up. I promise. Just let's get through the rush. We've been closed two days, and figuring how busy we were at lunch, we're going to be slammed tonight."

"Well, I don't like it, but I guess I'll have to accept it. I got the pork roasting. You better start prepping the fish. You making Oysters Ernie?"

"Yeah. And Snapper Pontchartrain. I know, get busy." Adi turned to her prep counter. Bertie hadn't spoken so strongly to her since she was a teenager. She would call Griffith and set things right as soon as things slowed down.

She loved the fevered pace of the kitchen when things really started rocking. That was when Adi knew who she was. The plate was her canvas, and she filled it with the bounty of her heart and her kitchen. This was her element. Bertie was getting over being mad too. Adi could tell. She had kicked the music on and was swaying as she prepped salads for the next order.

Life was back to normal. Everything would work out just the way it was meant. She would apologize to Griffith. She just had to get through tonight's dinner service, and that was going well.

They plated seventy-seven dinners in an hour and a half before things began to slow. Adi pulled off her toque and grabbed a water bottle as she stepped onto the back porch. She slid her cell phone out of her pocket and dialed Griffith's number.

The phone rang and rang without answer. She had hoped to talk to Griffith, but it seemed that wasn't going to happen tonight. The phone went to voice mail, and for a minute, Adi considered hanging up. *Be a grownup.*

"Hi, Griffith. It's Adi. I'm just calling to apologize for reacting the way I did. I know it wasn't easy for you to share that story about Tabitha. But this isn't the same thing. I want to trust you. I need you to understand the danger of my situation before you dig anymore. This is life or death. Please wait until you know who and what you're dealing with. Call me back as soon as you get this." She hung up, then and took a long pull on her water bottle. What if Griffith didn't call back?

"Adi, there's a fool out there wants to send back your boudin. He says it has too much rice in it," Bertie said from the doorway.

"No way. Take it in the back, reheat it, and send it back out. Bet he says it's fine now."

"Right on. Did you call that girl?"

"I tried, but only got her voice mail."

"Did you leave a message?"

"I did. Come on, let's finish this night."

They worked until closing time with not much of a letup. People had missed the Pot the last two days. It felt good to be appreciated, but better to be closing. Jose was busy at the pot sink and Adi was wiping down the prep surfaces. Bertie was putting things into the cooler for the next day's service. The weekend help, Ellen, was closing out the register. Another successful night.

There was a loud crash from the cooler.

"Bertie? You drop something?" Her question was met with silence. Adi rushed to check on her, worry quickly welling inside her.

Bertie was on the floor, bleeding from a small gash in her head, and she didn't seem to be conscious. "Bertie?" Adi felt for a pulse, trying to ignore her own as it raced with panic, and finally, she felt the small pulsing under her finger. Bertie's breathing was labored, though. "Jose! Call 911. Bertie needs an ambulance."

Adi knew the best thing was not to move her. She didn't know what Bertie had hit, or how hard. She stripped off her coat and laid it on top of her. *Keep her warm. Monitor her breathing. Stop the bleeding.* The mantra from her first aid class kicked in hard. She pulled a clean cloth from the hanger and pressed it against the gash to stem the flow of blood.

"You're going to be fine, Bertie. Help is on the way. Just hang in there. You're going to kill me when you realize we called an ambulance. Don't worry. All the customers are gone. Just hang in there."

Adi's heart was beating so hard it felt like it would come right out of her chest. *She has to be okay. Bertie is all I have.* She kept talking to stay calm. She started telling her about watching Griffith crawfish. How cute she looked in those hip waders. She kept talking until the paramedics arrived. They ushered her out of the cooler so they could have enough room to work. They went straight to it, putting on a pulse oximeter and starting an IV line.

While those two worked on Bertie, another two paramedics entered with a transport gurney. One of them threw questions out to the room in general.

"What alerted you to something happening?"

"She fell. I heard her fall."

"Was she conscious when you got to her?"

"No."

"Has she regained consciousness at all?"

"No."

"Any medications she takes that you know of?"

"She takes Lisinopril for blood pressure."

"No heart medications? Is she diabetic?"

"No and no."

"Okay. Good. We're going to load her up and take her to Iberia Medical Center. Can you contact next of kin?"

"I'm her next of kin."

The man stopped and looked at her. "You're her next of kin?"

"Yes. She's my mamma. You have a problem with that?"

"No, not at all. You can ride with her in the bus. We're going to need you to fill out paperwork when we get there."

"Jose, call T'Claude and get him to meet us down at the hospital. He has all the information on Bertie's insurance, and I need to be with her."

Fear flooded her now that she didn't have to be the one in control. Her whole body began shaking. Her knees were like Jell-O, and she felt like she was about to fall. The paramedic grabbed her arm.

"Are you okay, ma'am?"

"I'm okay. Just shaky."

"Well, sit down here. Once we have your mom on the truck, I'll come and get you."

Adi slid down the outside wall of the cooler, far enough out of the way not to impede the paramedics. She was cold and sweaty at the same time, plus it felt like she was going to lose her lunch.

"Here, Adi. Drink this. You'll feel better. It's just the shock."

Jose pressed a can of juice into her hand and wrapped his own coat around her shoulders. She gave him a grateful smile. "Thank you."

"She's going to be okay. She's too tough to go out like that. Don't you worry. Everything is going to be okay. Mr. T'Claude is on his way to the hospital now. I'll lock up here and find you down there."

Adi nodded and watched as the team of responders wheeled Bertie carefully out of the kitchen area and to the parking lot. Soon she felt an arm grip her above the elbow.

"Okay, time to go. Let's take care of you too. Sam is going to be in the back with you and your mom. I'll be driving. We're doing everything possible for your mom. Come on. Time to go."

He gently tugged, and Adi stood and walked out to the waiting ambulance. An EMS truck was pulling out as she climbed into the back of the ambulance.

"Thank you for getting here so quick. I appreciate it."

"No problem. It's what we do." He closed the doors and soon they were on the way to the hospital.

Adi struggled to come to grips with what was happening to Bertie. She looked so small and frail strapped to the gurney.

"Is she going to be okay?" Adi said.

"She's a little shocky right now, but we're getting her stabilized. She'll be evaluated as soon as we get to the ER. Listen, Adi, is it?"

"Yes."

"Adi, your mom has probably had a major event. When we get to the hospital, things are going to happen really fast, okay?"

Adi nodded. *A major event? What's that mean?* She couldn't get the words out.

"Good. We're focused on your mom. You'll be able to follow us into the emergency doors, but the hospital staff will keep you from following us any further. Don't freak out. That's so the patient can remain our priority. They'll take you to a seating area to wait for news from the medical staff. Try to stay calm and let everyone do their job. That's the best thing you can do if you want the best for your mom."

"Okay."

"Good. We're pulling in now. If I see you on my way out, I'll give you any update I have."

"Okay."

The doors flew open, and in seconds, Bertie was whisked into the emergency bay. Adi hurried to follow and wasn't surprised when she was stopped by the staff. She watched the doors swing closed behind Bertie. Her nausea was receding, but the shaky feeling was still there.

"Ma'am, let's get you settled in the waiting area." The nurse had kind eyes, and Adi followed without resistance. She sat in the hard plastic chair as directed. There was a large clock on the wall opposite her, and she noted the time. Eleven fifty. She wondered how long it would be before they could tell her what was wrong with Bertie.

"Adi?" T'Claude entered from a different door. He was holding a folder. "How're you doing?"

"Oh, T. She didn't wake up. She didn't even seem to hear me."

"I'm sorry, kid. She's in a good place, though. They'll fix her up." He wrapped a burly arm around Adi. She leaned into him, grateful for his comfort.

"We have to call Jacques and tell him about Bertie. He's her brother; he should know."

"I'm her kin."

"Well, sure, Adi. I meant besides you. He lives in Tupelo, right?"

"That's right. I have his number in my phone. Shouldn't we wait until we can tell him what's wrong? He's an old man, T. We can't just give him a shock without information."

"They might need to talk to him, you know, so they can do what they need to do."

"Listen. I am Bertie's next of kin. I have her medical power of attorney. We did that for each other long ago. She can make decisions for me; I can make decisions for her. We made sure of it."

"Oh, good. That's a relief. I was worried. How about a Coke? Something to keep us awake until we hear what's up."

"Okay."

He got each of them a Coke from the vending machine and they sat quietly, waiting to hear something. For a moment, Adi considered calling Griff. But this was family business, and although she wanted to get closer to her, this wasn't where she belonged. Even if Adi really wanted to be in her arms. She leaned against T and waited.

CHAPTER FOURTEEN

G riffith stood in the Boiling Pot parking lot wondering where everyone was. She had decided to come here first, before heading to Morgan City. Adi's voice mail from the night before made this stop her priority.

She wanted to clear things up with her, make sure Adi knew her intentions, and get as much information as possible before making contact with J.B. Nerbass. She'd left her hotel determined to get Adi to understand why she had to do this and to acknowledge Adi's request about not doing anything before they talked again. Now she was here, and the place was deserted. By this time on most mornings, there would be a steady stream of breakfast diners. Other people came and went, seemingly as puzzled as Griffith. But the restaurant remained locked. None of the staff vehicles were in the parking lot.

She glanced at her watch. Nine twenty. She needed to get on the road. She had managed to get an appointment with Nerbass's assistant at ten forty-five, and the drive would take nearly an hour. She would have to catch up with Adi later, since she hadn't returned her call from earlier, and now it went straight to voice mail.

She made it to the offices of JB Dulac Transport by ten thirty. The place was really state-of-the-art. The building felt organic to the space it occupied. The design was modern but had the feel of belonging to its environment. She wasn't surprised to see it was designated a green building by the USGBC. The natural lighting and wood used in the construction made the place feel warm and welcoming.

"Hello, my name is Jacob. May I help you?" A young man entered through a half door and greeted her.

"Yes, hello. I'm Griffith McNaulty. I have an appointment with Randy Pecot at a quarter to eleven."

"Ah, yes, ma'am. You're welcome to wait here. Can I get you anything?"

"No, thank you."

"Great. I'll be right in my office if you change your mind. Feel free to look around. The fishing boats are docked out back, if you'd like to see them."

"Thanks. I might do that."

He nodded and went back to his work. She wandered around the pleasant lobby, looking at various displays and photographs. There was a model of the pier for the JBN Sports Fishing boats. Apparently, they were also touted for their green design and energy efficiency. The boat engines were designed to use less fuel, and that fuel was much cleaner than industry standards. She wondered if his helicopters ran on biodiesel. She made her way out the back door onto the dock. It was impressive. The entire structure was lined with reused materials. The covered boardwalk used photovoltaic cells cleverly camouflaged as ceiling structures. She had to admit that Nerbass truly seemed dedicated to environmental responsibility. That was a fresh point of view on the Gulf Coast.

"Ms. McNaulty?"

Griffith turned to see Jacob at the door.

"Ms. Pecot is ready to see you now. If you will follow me, please."

Ms. Pecot? Griffith had fallen for the old gender trap and assumed Randy Pecot would be a he. That was a mistake she rarely made. She followed Jacob down a hall walled in silver metallic cork strips, with a bamboo floor. The office was fronted with glass and with a smaller glass wall facing the Gulf. The woman seated at the desk smiled warmly and stood as they approached.

"Ms. McNaulty, what a pleasure. I'm Randy Pecot."

"Hello, Ms. Pecot."

"We aren't that formal here. Feel free to call me Randy."

"Okay, Randy, I'm Griffith."

"Nice to meet you. Go ahead and have a seat. How can I help you?"

Griffith sat on the comfortable overstuffed couch Randy indicated.

"I'm not sure if you can help me. I'm actually hoping to get an appointment with your boss."

"So I understand. You have to know, Griffith, J.B. is a very busy man."

"Clearly."

"He's also not quick to give interviews to reporters. He has been vilified in the press often enough to want to shield himself."

"Oh, I understand that. Believe me. I'm writing a story on how losing a child affects people. I'm trying to pinpoint why people react so differently by interviewing a wide range of people, from those in difficult economic circumstances to those in more fortunate circles. Mr. Nerbass is an excellent example of overcoming grief and honoring his child with his success."

"So, you know about Merley?"

"Yes. I came across that sad fact in my research."

"That's a very touchy subject, Ms. McNaulty. J.B. never recovered from the loss of his daughter. It devastated him. He actually began his green building and sustainable energy plans in her honor."

"So he considers the loss of his daughter a reason to build in a sustainable way? That's admirable. When did he give up on finding her? I think that would be the hardest thing, not knowing."

"She's been missing eight years. He searched everywhere for Merley after she disappeared. He finally resigned himself to the fact that she was gone. If she had been alive, I am certain he would've found her."

"So you worked for him even back then?"

"Well, no. I've been with the company for five years. Back then, JB Co. didn't really exist. He started with a small bait shop in Dulac. After he lost Merley, he started the helipad transport business. That took off like crazy, and he expanded again and again. The sports fishing branch developed once he was headquartered here. So I've been in this office about four years."

"You mean he's built this entire empire in the past eight years? That's pretty remarkable. He must have had some strong investors."

"He's completely self-made. He purchased the first helicopter secondhand with a loan from a good friend. I have a pamphlet here somewhere with his whole story. Hold on a second."

She rummaged around in her drawer, finally handing Griffith a slick brochure with the J.B. Nerbass story inside, but something about it felt shady. It was possible for a person to build a business from the ground up in eight years, but it was unheard of for someone to reach the heights that Nerbass had so quickly, especially from a small dock with no capital to invest. She had already checked his net worth. He was listed as just under $70,000,000 in assets. Unheard of growth, even by LA standards.

She had assumed there had been substantial investment in the company by others to help create such a balance sheet. To hear it was done with virtually no help in such a short time period had all her alarm bells going off. Nerbass wasn't a part of her story, unless he did have something to do with Adi, but she might make him the center of her next piece.

"Thank you. I really would like to sit down with him and talk about how losing his child changed him." Griff hoped like hell she wasn't drawing attention to Adi, just the way Adi'd been afraid she would. It was too late now, though. If this was the person responsible for Adi living in fear, she'd damn well find out why and help put a stop to it.

"I wouldn't hold your breath, but I'll check his schedule and find a time for you to meet."

"Thank you, I really appreciate that. Would you know approximately when the meeting might be? I need to arrange my schedule as well."

"He won't be in town this week. He's at a conference in Mexico City. He should have some time next week, before his trip to China."

"He's going to China?"

"Yes, he has some new ventures in development with the Chinese."

"But you think I'll be able to have a moment of his time, don't you?"

"I'll do my best to find time for you."

"I appreciate your help with this, Randy. I'm covering quite a few families who have lost children, and I think his story would be an inspiring addition."

"I'll be in touch as soon as I have something confirmed."

"Thank you."

"I'll walk you out."

She led Griffith to the door and politely excused herself. This new information about J.B. Nerbass had Griffith excited about doing a piece on him. She could always use this time in Louisiana to develop a storyline for Nerbass. She could multitask and maybe do a new piece off the back of the cooking article, one she could use for her next step back up the ladder. If it didn't have anything to do with Adi, of course.

The swift rise of his company was really tweaking the investigative journalist inside her. *Time to get to work.* She needed to know more about Nerbass. If he had anything to do with Adi's fear, she could expose him, help Adi, and get her story. It could be a major win, as long as she didn't screw anything up.

She left the waterfront and drove directly to the local library to use their Internet access. She logged on to the public library system and pulled up Hoover's Online. She searched JB Co and found the preliminary information she needed. J.B. Nerbass was the principal partner and president. His wife was listed as a board member and CFO. There were a total of five board members, including the Nerbasses. The other three names were interesting: Senator Ruben Landry, of the news article photograph; Ramon Zuniga, owner of a Mexican oil and gas exploration company; and Gao Feng, president of Lumera New Materials, a Chinese chemical company.

The company had been established as a limited liability corporation five years ago. Prior to that, J.B. Nerbass was the Sole Proprietor of JB Dulac Transport. Something big had happened when the switch to LLC had been made. Nerbass had been gaining steadily with his transport company and fledgling sport fishing charter company, but things grew exponentially when he added Zuniga and Gao to his board.

She noted the dates of each incorporation, then dug further back, to the purchase of the first helicopter for JB Dulac. The sale was registered from a group called Controller. It appeared to be a cash sale of a used Sikorsky S-76C. The listed sale price was just over two million dollars. Where had Nerbass acquired that amount of cash?

He had been a bait shop owner, running shrimp and mullet out of a fair-sized store on a private pier in Dulac. He still held ownership of the pier and the shop. How could such a small enterprise give him access to that size of an investment?

Randy Pecot had mentioned a loan from a friend, but what kind of friends had the ability to loan two million dollars? She thought about the board members. Had one of these men lent the cash for the purchase of the Sikorsky? She brought up a page on Senator Landry.

He was born in a suburb of New Orleans, son of a restauranteur. Landry had begun his political life while still in school at LSU. He had campaigned on and off campus for then Democrat Trent Foster. He was an active and vocal campaigner, and when Foster won his seat on the state senate, he brought Landry along as a political aide. Landry followed his mentor into the Republican Party in the early nineties. He won his first elected office as comptroller of accounts for the city of New Orleans in 2002. His political rise was marked by questions of ethics and concern over misuse of funds, but he weathered the storm and came out of the 2006 elections as state senator.

Griffith checked her time line. The purchase of the Sikorsky was dated June of 2009. Two years after Adi arrived at the Boiling Pot. She had no proof that Landry was the source of Nerbass's loan, but she had a suspicion. Loaning someone money wasn't illegal, in and of itself. But their motives and what they used the money for certainly could be.

Next she looked up Ramon Zuniga. He was born into wealth, the son of Emilio Suarez Zuniga, the president of the state-owned oil company. He was educated in the U.S. in petroleum engineering, graduating the same year as Landry from LSU. He had begun his own state-sanctioned exploration company only a year after graduation. His company was responsible for most of the recent discoveries of oil, including the Macondo reservoir. He had made the state and himself extremely wealthy with his discoveries and his powerful gift of persuasion.

From the outside, Zuniga was spotless. No whisper of corruption or back room dealing touched him. If he had a connection to Nerbass before his appointment to the board in 2010, she couldn't find it.

The last in the cast of characters was Gao Feng. He had assumed the role of director of Lumera New Materials when his father, Gao Jin, retired. There wasn't a great deal of information about Mr.

Gao online, but there was plenty about Lumera. The corporation fabricated metals and precision oil drilling parts as well as chemical processing and supply. It was the single largest exporter of Chinese chemicals. There had been six major stories involving Lumera in the past three years: A leak of toxic gas at their plant in Guangxi Province; a huge story about misappropriation of funds, resulting in half of the upper management of the company being replaced; a massive fire and explosion at a plant in Fujian Province; a clash with protestors near Beijing over the planned building of a new plant that made news worldwide; and two other unfavorable stories about the basic management of the corporation.

Griffith wasn't sure when Mr. Gao entered the radar of Mr. Nerbass, but somewhere the two had connected and since 2010, Gao had made regular trips to the Louisiana Gulf Coast. It still didn't explain how Nerbass had created his empire so quickly before the other people got involved, though. And why was he tied to these three powerful men? Where did they connect before 2010? She had to get out there and talk to people who held some knowledge of Nerbass prior to 2010. She knew right where to start, with Mabel Baptiste in Dulac.

❖

The drive to Dulac was interrupted only by a stop at Façon's bakery for éclairs. *Might as well have a peace offering.* Griffith could tell that Mabel was home as she neared the house. The porch door stood open to the wide deck. She cautiously made her way up the staircase.

"Mrs. Baptiste? I'm sorry to bother you, but I have a few questions."

"Shhhh! Quiet. Come on up off the stairs and be sure nobody sees you."

"Okaaay?" Griffith climbed the remaining stairs, happy she wasn't being ordered off the property.

Mabel was standing at the door waving her inside. "Hurry up, and duck down."

Griffith obliged and bent down to hurry through the door. The blinds inside the house were all closed, making the small room even less inviting. The stale cigarette smell had increased since yesterday.

Mabel followed her in and quickly closed the door behind her. She pulled aside the blind on the door, as if expecting someone to be outside.

"I promise you, it's just me, Mabel. I didn't bring a team of assassins with me."

"Well, aren't you the funny one, Miss High and Mighty. It wouldn't be the first time someone crept up my steps to cause trouble. Why the hell are you back here, anyway? I told you to get yesterday."

"I know you did. I had to come back, though. I need some information I think you can help me with."

"What information?"

"About J.B. Nerbass. I want to know about him, before he became what he is now."

Mabel paled and sat heavily on the recliner. "I don't have anything to say about that man."

"But your body language says you do, Mabel. Look, I don't want to cause you any trouble. In fact, I brought you a treat. Here." She handed over the éclairs.

"You can't buy me, lady. I'm not for sale."

"I'm not interested in buying you. I just want to ask you a couple of questions."

"I mind my own business. I don't have anything to say."

"Let me tell you a story, then? Would that be okay?"

"Go on." She flipped open the bakery box and pulled out one of the pastries.

"There was a young girl, from a really small town. Her father was a really nice guy, a shrimper, but he died, and the girl was left with her mother. The mother wasn't a very nice person and didn't treat the girl very well. Then the mother met someone, a man. And one day, when she was about fourteen, the girl disappeared. No one knew what happened to her. Does this sound familiar?"

"Familiar? Hell, girl, that story happens all the time. In my case, though, the girl was a delinquent and she ran off to her boyfriend's house. It's a story that plays out down here about a hundred times a year. What makes your story different?"

"My story is about the girl who disappeared. She's a woman now, and still hiding from what she left behind. I want to help her."

Griffith watched Mabel's eyes narrow. *She knows exactly who I'm talking about.*

"Maybe you should just keep your yap shut. Maybe that girl ran for a reason."

"Maybe. She's kind of shut down, you know, not living her life completely. I think if she can face what she ran from, she can let it go." *Please don't be someone I shouldn't have trusted.*

"And I say maybe what she left behind should be left alone. Maybe she knows it could hurt her."

"But I have to find out, don't you see? I have to know so I can support her, either way." Griffith heard herself say the words and her breath caught as their meaning registered. *I want to be there for Adi. I don't want to be anywhere else. I really, really want her to be safe and happy. Screw the article.*

"What's this girl to you? Aren't you just a reporter?"

She could be everything to me. I have to find out what I am to her. "I am. But she's also my friend and I care about her. I want to see her free of the weight of her past."

"You're stirring up a hornet's nest, messing with this. The people you want to talk about are serious people. Dangerous people."

Griffith had guessed as much. Why else would Adi be so afraid of him? It was good to know Mabel felt that way too. She wouldn't be running to Nerbass to tell him about Griff's questions. And if she was right about who it was, dangerous probably wasn't the right word. But in her line of work, she'd come up against plenty of vile people who deserved to be taken down. That in itself wasn't going to get her to back down.

"So, why would you think this girl would be in danger if she came back home?"

"Seems to me, if you run away you probably have a reason. If you run away when you're fourteen, it's probably a *good* reason."

"Okay, but a reason that could hurt her now that she's an adult?"

"Look. You said J.B. Nerbass. I know all about his daughter and her disappearance. I always figured her body was out in the marsh somewhere. Never thought she might still be alive. Now you come around here with this story, and you make me wonder. I'll tell you right now, if your friend is Merley Nerbass, she's lucky she got away.

Everybody in Dulac knows J.B. would've made sure she didn't live to see fifteen if she'd stayed around."

"Why? What reason would he have to harm his daughter?"

"That man has two faces. He could get you to believe he's a saint, but that ain't the real man. She lived under his roof. She'd know."

"Who is he, then?"

"I can't say. All I know is that when she disappeared, J.B. gave the papers and the police every kind of anxious face they wanted, but when he come around asking after her with her friends, he let us all know she was in for big trouble."

"He came here? Were Kendrick and Merley close?"

"They knew each other from school, of course, but they had a good friend in common back then. Rachel Comeaux. If anyone knows about Merley running away, it would be her."

"Does she still live here?"

"Oh sure. Rachel's family owns the grocery store. Conq's. She still works there."

"Thanks, Mabel. I won't trouble you any further. I appreciate your help."

"Listen. You steer clear of J.B. Nerbass. We have a name for him down here."

"What's that?"

"*La mort cachée*. The hidden death."

Griffith saw that Mabel was being completely serious. Her fear was tangible. She nodded her thanks to Mabel and left. *I'm coming for you, Nerbass.*

CHAPTER FIFTEEN

Adi felt someone shaking her. She was disoriented when she opened her eyes, unsure where she was.

"Get up, Adi. The doctor is here."

It was T'Claude. The hospital. She sat up and looked at her watch. They had been at the hospital since eleven forty-five the night before. It was well after ten in the morning now.

"Ms. Bergeron? I'm Dr. Klein."

"How's Bertie?"

"Let's go sit in the conference room, okay?" He pointed to a nearby door. T'Claude and Adi followed him and stepped into the small room when he motioned them ahead. There was a small couch and two stuffed chairs in the room, as well as a table and a phone.

"Sit down. Please."

They sat side by side on the couch.

"Ms. Durall suffered a severe stroke. We've done all we can for her, but her prognosis isn't good."

Adi felt like she had been punched in the gut. Her ears erupted in white noise, and she struggled to make sense as the doctor continued to talk. She held out a hand.

"Wait, wait. Give me a minute." She put her head down and took deep breaths to gain control. She needed to hear everything he had to say.

"Could you say that again, please?"

"Yes, of course. I was saying, we've done all we can. She hasn't woken and is unlikely to regain consciousness. Her stroke was hemorrhagic, bleeding into her brain. We have stabilized her, but as I said, it doesn't look good."

"So what does that mean? You've stabilized her? If she's stable, why won't she wake up?"

"Ms. Bergeron, in a stroke like this one the tissues of the brain get flooded with blood and die. The location of Ms. Durall's bleed is causing her to remain unconscious. When I say we have stabilized her, I mean we've inserted a breathing tube and have done our best to stop the bleeding. She remains unresponsive, but we're keeping her alive with the ventilator. Her chances of waking up from this are very slim, and even then, she'll be very different than she has been."

"So you're telling me she's only alive because you're breathing for her? And if you took the tube out…"

"Yes, that's basically it."

Adi didn't know what to say or ask at that point. She was numb with the shock and frightened at what it all meant.

T'Claude's arm tightened around her. "I'm here, Adi. We're going to get through this together."

"I'll let you all have a moment. I'll be right back." Dr. Klein rose and left the room.

Adi turned into T'Claude and let him hold her. She couldn't hold back her tears any longer. She felt the dam burst and the warm, hot trails racing down her cheeks. "What are we going to do, T?"

"First, we're just going to feel. Then we'll listen and decide what we do next. For sure, we aren't going to decide anything right now."

Adi heard his grief in his voice and knew he was right. Whatever Bertie's prognosis, they would wait until they had a handle on all possible outcomes before they made any decisions about next steps.

"Listen, I'm going to go call Jacques. Bertie's brother needs to know what's going on. I'll call Jose too. Will you be okay on your own for a few minutes?"

"Yes. I'll be fine."

"Okay then. I'll be back." T'Claude pushed through the door and Adi was alone. *Brain hemorrhage.* That wasn't good at all. She wished she had Bertie sitting here beside her. She relied on her to help her with the hard stuff. She never expected Bertie to *be* the hard stuff. When they had filled out the medical powers of attorney, she felt that was a precaution in case her past ever found her. She never imagined she would be the one using it. She pulled out her phone and started searching for articles about hemorrhagic strokes.

Twenty minutes later, Dr. Klein returned and Adi felt more able to process the conversation.

"How are we doing?"

"Better."

"Good. I'm here to answer any questions you might have."

"Is Bertie going to survive this? I mean, what part of her brain is involved?"

"The bleeding was in the lower brain, specifically, the brain stem. This is the part of the brain that controls breathing, heartbeat, and blood pressure, as well as speech, swallowing, hearing, and eye movement. I want you to understand that it is possible, but rare, to have a good recovery from a brain stem bleed."

"Then why did you tell me her prognosis isn't good? If it's possible to recover, Bertie will."

"Ms. Bergeron, the bleeding has been controlled now, but there was quite a bit of damage done before we could stop it. We really won't know the level of her impairment until she wakes, but I can tell you, there will be impairment. I can't tell you if she *will* wake up. Best-case scenario, she wakes and can respond when spoken to. She will need months of therapy, physical and occupational, possibly speech. But she could recover."

"What's the worst-case scenario?"

"Providing she wakes up?"

"Yes."

"She could be trapped in what we call 'locked-in syndrome.' That would mean her entire body, with the exception of her eyes, would be paralyzed. She could learn to communicate through eye movements, such as blinking. She would essentially be on a ventilator, a catheter, and a feeding tube for the remainder of her life. That's providing she wakes up. I have to say, though, given the severity of the bleeding she experienced, the chances she will regain consciousness are really quite slim."

"So what do we do now?"

"This is hard, Ms. Bergeron. I know how hard, but you have to decide whether or not you want to take a gamble and see how she does. I understand from Mr. Michaud that you hold her medical power of attorney."

"Yes, I do."

"And you can produce it if requested?"

"Yes. There is a copy in that folder. But the certified copy is in the safe deposit box at the bank."

"Okay. Well, it falls to you to decide whether or not to continue care."

"What? What does that mean?"

"You have to decide if Ms. Durall would want to risk any of the outcomes we have discussed. If you decide she would want to take a chance, we will continue life support and place her in a medically induced coma. That way we can slowly bring her out as the healing process works. If you decide she wouldn't like to risk these possible outcomes, then we discontinue care. Basically, we would turn off the ventilator and allow her to pass peacefully."

"What? You mean... I have to decide whether or not Bertie lives or dies? I can't do that. That's not for me to decide. What if I want her body to decide?"

"That's what this is about, Ms. Bergeron. If it were me, I would let nature take its course and not go to extreme measures to skew the outcome. I would allow her to be slowly removed from mechanical care and see what happens. The problem is that the most likely scenario would be death. It's a truly difficult decision. It's hard not to think of yourself and how the loss would affect you. You have to decide, though, and try to think about what she would want, and if she could live with the possibility of being paralyzed, fed by tubes, unable to communicate. I'm going to leave now, but I'll be back in after my rounds for your decision."

Adi felt like her heart was being ripped out of her chest. Bertie was everything to her. *It's not fair.* No one should have to decide something like this. She rubbed at her arms, trying to warm them. Why were hospitals always so darn cold? And where was T'Claude? She got up from the couch and walked into the waiting area. Suddenly, she needed to get out of there, be somewhere without cold walls and squeaky floors. She headed toward the exit door.

"Hey, where you running off too, Adi?" T'Claude called.

She stopped and let him catch up with her. "I have to get out of here for a minute, T. I can't breathe."

"Okay. Let's go get some coffee."

He drove them to a coffee shop nearby and ordered coffee and Danishes. "So what upset you enough to get you to leave the hospital?"

"I have to decide whether or not to keep Bertie's ventilator on. I have to choose if she lives or dies."

"Now wait, you don't have anything to do with her living or dying, kiddo. That's out of your hands. See, when Bertie had the stroke, the decision went into the hands of someone higher up. She lived through the night. She's alive now. So you aren't in charge of that decision at all."

"But, T, they want me to tell them to either unplug the breathing machine or keep her body alive, whether or not she ever wakes up. Doc said she could very well be alive and conscious but paralyzed except for her eyes. How could I choose that for Bertie? How could I decide she should live but never taste again? I can't do that. She wouldn't want that."

"I think you just answered your own questions. And again, it's not in your hands or the doctors. It's up to Bertie and whoever looks out for her up there." He looked up at the ceiling and put his hands together in prayer. "Those machines they have breathing for her? Those aren't Bertie. If she wants to live, then she will. Let her decide."

"So tell them to stop breathing for her?"

"It's not like she had an accident she can recover from. She had a stroke. A big one. Seems to me we're robbing her of choice by keeping her on those machines. Let her decide. She'll stay if she has a mind to. If not, well, then she was probably already gone to the good Lord, and it's just her body here anyway."

"But what am I going to do without her? If she doesn't wake up? Bertie is all I have, T."

"I know you feel that way, but you have me, and Jose. I know how hard this is, but believe me, we did all of that mechanical breathing and therapy stuff with my mamma. She was never the same. It was hard to watch her live but not live."

"What if you're wrong, T? What if she wants me to let her keep breathing?"

"If she wants to keep breathing, don't you think she will?"

Adi didn't know how she felt about that answer, but most of what T'Claude said made sense. She knew Bertie would fight to live if she wanted to. She also knew Bertie was a spiritual person on good terms with God. Bertie had never feared death. She had often talked about when her time came and was content that she had lived a good life.

She thought about what Bertie might do if Adi was the one on life support. Would she choose to let Adi fight without help? Or would she extend her life artificially? She was pretty sure Bertie would believe that she would fight if she were meant to go on. How would Adi feel if she were lying there waiting for Bertie to decide? Heck, she probably wouldn't even know she was in that bed. If it were her, she wouldn't know to fight until life started slipping away.

She had to let go and let Bertie fight or let Bertie die. It couldn't be right to keep her pinned to earth if it was her time to go. That's what Bertie would choose, she was certain.

"I think I know what to do. It's going to be so hard, though."

"Life ain't easy, kid. We both know that. I'll miss that ornery old woman like she was my own too. She practically raised me. But life is life, right?"

"I guess we need to go let Dr. Klein know our decision."

"Yeah, let's finish up and go."

❖

Adi watched the ventilator as it slowly stopped, and looked to the monitors. Bertie had been placed on a drip of what the nurse called "comfort medication." Morphine for any pain and Ativan. Adi wasn't sure how to feel about that, but Dr. Klein said it would guarantee that Bertie didn't feel as if she were suffocating. T gripped her hand tightly as they stood watch. Bertie seemed to be sleeping. Her heart rate was still strong. The alarms from her machinery were all set to silent. The doctor and the nurses left them but monitored Bertie from the desk area.

Adi moved away from T and took one of Bertie's hands. T took the other.

Their vigil lasted well into the evening, and just before eight p.m., Bertie's breathing stilled and her heart rhythm dropped to nothing. The staff entered and unhooked the monitors and were quietly respectful of their grief. They did nothing to hurry them out. Tears ran down Adi's face, but she didn't wipe them away. She leaned down and kissed Bertie's cheek one last time.

"Good-bye, Bertie."

T'Claude started really crying, then. Sobbing like his heart was broken. Adi couldn't take it. She walked out into the corridor, then kept walking until she felt the night air hit her.

Run. Just run. She started slowly, heading off with no idea of direction. She hit a sidewalk and turned to follow it, her pace increasing. The cement gave way to dirt, and still she ran. She ran to keep from feeling. Her heartbeat was the only thing holding her focus. She ran until her lungs were burning and her legs felt like they were on fire. She ran until finally, the pain of her grief overwhelmed her.

And then she screamed. She screamed out her anger at being helpless. Her regret at not keeping Bertie here, because she needed her. She screamed at the pain of losing her family, and the fear of being alone. When her voice gave out and her screams were silenced, she dropped to her knees and pounded her fists against the damp earth in futility.

Finally, she collapsed onto the gritty path and rolled to the grass beside it. She lay on her back, staring at the vast, empty sky, as empty as her heart.

CHAPTER SIXTEEN

Griffith found Conq's Grocery about two miles up the highway. It looked as if it had been there for quite some time. The door was plain wood fronted by a full screen door. There was a little bell tied above the door to announce visitors.

"I'll be right there," called a voice from the back room.

Griffith felt nostalgic looking at the mid-high wooden display shelves packed with assorted dry goods. They had probably been built when they built the building. The register was at the front with a door to the back open to the left. It wasn't long before a young woman came out carrying a baby on her hip.

"How can I help you?"

"Hi, my name is Griffith McNaulty. I'm a reporter working on a story about runaways and the way those left behind cope. I understand the daughter of the owners had a friend who ran away."

"You're kidding, right? You trying to trick me into something? What's your scam?"

"No scam. The girl may have been a friend of Rachel's?"

"What? That can't be. I'm Rachel, and I didn't have any friends who ran away."

"No? I could have it wrong, but I was led to believe you knew Merley Nerbass."

The woman froze, visibly paling. "Merley didn't run away. No matter what they say. I know what happened to her."

"I don't mean to upset you. I'm just following a lead. She was reported as a runaway, but if that's wrong, I apologize for my mistake."

"She never ran away. Her father. He killed her and dumped her somewhere in the marsh."

Griffith was shocked at the strength of her belief. *How did she come to that conclusion?* "And how do you know this?"

"Because. He told me he did."

"What? He told you he killed his daughter? If that's the case, why isn't he in jail?"

"He's too rich to go to jail. He has the law in his pocket."

"What made him tell you he killed Merley?" If it were true, that Merley was dead, this lead wasn't going to be anything to do with Adi, and she could follow it to the article she wanted to write. If it wasn't true...

"I was angry. I knew he had something to do with her being gone. She wouldn't have run away without telling me. I went right down to that bait shop when I heard and asked him to his face what he had done with Merley. He tried to laugh me off, but I wouldn't shut up. I got louder and practically screamed at him. He grabbed me by the arm and shook me so hard. He said, 'Listen. Merley is feeding the gators and you'll be feeding them too, if you don't shut up.'"

"Didn't you go to the police?"

"Of course I did. I told my mamma and we went down to the police station. Back then they had a little office on the highway. I told the policeman what Mr. Nerbass had said. He acted like it was old news. He didn't even try to act like he was going to do something. No. He just looked up from his paperwork at my mamma. Then he told her that she should take me home if she knew what was good for me. He told me if I ever told any more lies about Mr. Nerbass he'd throw me in jail. *Me.* For reporting my friend's murder."

"Why do you think the police officer reacted like that?"

"He was on Nerbass's payroll. That's what I think. Mamma said he just thought I was making up tales. She told me we should wait and see if Merley came home, but she never did. I never saw her again."

Or maybe he'd had experience with distraught teenagers and knew enough not to overreact. "And you really believe her father would've killed her?"

"Listen here, lady, my best friend disappeared and her squirrely stepfather tells me she's feeding the gators. What would you think?

You think he admitted to killing her just for fun? I do believe he killed her, because if she were alive, she would've found a way to let me know."

"Losing a friend is hard, especially hard when you're young. I'm sorry you had to go through that. Do you think it affects your life now? The loss? Do you think of Merley often, or have you mostly moved on from that time?"

"What do you think? Of course it affects me. She was my best friend. She...I mean, we were very close. Really close. It hurt so bad when she was taken from me. And that asshole just got clean away with it. Got to throw up his big helicopter company and get rich. He never loved Merley. Never missed her. It was like she was an obstacle he had to overcome. And man, when he gets those big ole gator tears and cries about losing her as he dedicates this and that to her. Jerk. I hate that man."

"Her stepfather has spent several thousand dollars searching for her. Did you know that? He has a standing offer of twenty-five thousand dollars to anyone who can help locate his daughter. Why would he do that if he knew she was dead? Why not just let the memory of her fade away?"

"Ha. That's easy. He knows he'll never have to pay that money, that's why. And looking for her makes him look innocent. Plus, it makes people feel sorry for his ass."

"The second part of the story I'm working on is about how adults who ran away reconcile their past. How disconnecting from their roots affects the way they develop and build relationships as adults. I've tracked down several former runaways and talked with them at length about why they did what they did. For the most part, they've been happy with their decisions, but some of them can't let go of the regrets and fears of their youth. It hampers them, you know? Keeps them from living fully. How would you feel if you found out that your friend really *had* run away? What if she'd built a new life?"

Rachel sat on the bench behind the register and gently placed her baby in the nearby playpen. "Why?"

"Hmm?"

"Why would they run away and never let folks know where they were?"

"That's a question only they can answer. I will say, some of them are frightened about things beyond their control in their early lives. Something made them run. They need to be able to let go of their fear and live life free and happy. Sometimes that means confronting their past and making amends. Sometimes it just means forgetting and forgiving. Each case is different. There's no single answer."

"I don't know how I can help you."

"I don't want to put you in any danger. If Nerbass is a killer, I don't want him looking your way for anything so I'm just going to ask some questions, and then you should forget I was here. What can you tell me about Merley's life here? Where did she live? What about her mother? Anything you can tell me might help me put the pieces together and find out the root of her fear."

The baby started crying then, and not a subtle fussing, but a full-on rage. Rachel picked her up and tried to soothe her, but she wouldn't be calmed.

"I'm sorry, but my Merley, this one, is hungry and won't be put off. Could you leave me your contact information and I'll call you later?"

"Sure. I appreciate any insights you can give me. This article is going to be about more than one singular runaway, but they all matter. I'm really sorry I upset you. Thank you for your time."

Rachel nodded, tears still running down her cheeks, as she moved into the back with the crying baby Merley.

Griffith walked back to her car and thought about Rachel's reaction to Merley's disappearance. What if her Adi Bergeron was, in fact, Merley Nerbass, stepdaughter of J.B. Nerbass, millionaire? Why had he told Rachel that Merley was dead? Was he trying to scare Rachel? Make her stay away from him because she reminded him of his lost child? Or was there something more sinister to it? Every question she posed led to more questions. *I need to try to call Adi again. This is all so convoluted, and if she is Nerbass's daughter, no wonder she's afraid.* The call went to voice mail again. *What's going on? Why can't I reach you?* She wanted to get in her car and drive right back to the Pot. But if Adi'd had second thoughts about her phone call the night before, maybe she was just avoiding her phone calls. *Besides, if I did reach her she wouldn't be happy to hear where I am. I don't want to lie to her. I'll just wait until the morning.*

Griff checked the time. It was just after six and most businesses in the area would probably be closing. Maybe she could find a restaurant or a bar, grab a bite to eat, and see if any of the patrons cared to shoot the breeze about Dulac's favored son.

She made a slow circuit of the tiny township and had no luck finding any sort of dining or drinking establishment. She had just about made up her mind to go back to Houma when she thought of the shrimpers and the pier area. There would be someplace there to eat. She drove the last mile to the waterfront and found a place to park.

There were any number of rusty old cars and trucks parked along the embankment. There were five or six shrimp boats tied to cleats along the cement bulkhead, and random piers jutting out into the bay every few hundred yards. One of the piers had a small building lit up in neon called Shanghai Redd's. She wasn't sure if it was an eatery or a bar, but there were bound to be people inside.

She pushed open the wooden door and was greeted by loud Zydeco music and the smell of week old spilled beer. There was a long bar on the right and a scattering of scarred tables, mostly empty. The pool tables were busy, with most patrons gathered around watching a game. TVs above the bar had sports talk shows on. Three of the twelve bar stools were occupied by a couple and a single woman. She felt herself relax a bit with the knowledge that she wasn't the only woman in the place. She sat on an empty stool and waited until the barkeep looked her way.

"Yeah, what can I get you?"

"I'll have whatever you have on tap. Dark, if there's an option."

"Got it. Coming up."

She watched the animated people at the pool table. *It must be a money game.* There was a tall blond fellow who seemed to be struggling. His opponent was a wiry brunette, not much bigger that Griffith. She seemed too young to be in a bar legally, but that wasn't unusual for a small town.

The bartender set a tall glass of deep mahogany colored ale in front of Griffith. "There you go, pretty lady. A nice ale for a beautiful face."

"Thanks. What is it?"

"That's an Abita Turbodog. I hope you like it."

She noted that the glass wasn't overly chilled, always a good sign. She took a long pull and savored the rich chocolaty-nuttiness of the ale.

"Oh yeah, that's a nice ale."

"I'm glad you like it."

"Tell me what's going on at the table over there."

"What, that? That's just Sherry, showing off again. She comes in once a week to take the money off these poor gullible fishermen."

"Ah, a shark, huh?"

"Nah, just gifted. She never takes all their money and is mostly just having fun. Makes for a bit of excitement. What brings you in? I know you aren't from around here. "

"I'm just looking for information. I'm a writer and I'm trying to get a feel for the area."

"Oh, like a novelist? That's cool. We got lots of color down here. This is a good place to set a book. You know, like a mystery or something? Easy to get rid of unwanted characters, if you get my drift."

"Oh? How so?"

"Well, you got the Gulf right there in front of us. Want to get rid of something or someone, just take them a mile or so out and dump them. Won't be much ever found. Or the marsh. Just get a jon boat and run it up into one of the bayous. Dump your trouble and cruise away. Gators will eat anything. Nothing ever coming back out of the marsh that's been put there to stay."

"It's that easy, huh? Just dump your victim and they're gone for good? Are you sure about that? Seems too simple to me."

"I'm telling you, it's been done. Been done around here. More than once."

"How could you possibly know that?"

"People talk. You know, after a drink or two, they forget what they should say and what they shouldn't."

"Are you telling me people have confessed to dumping bodies to you? Right here in this little bar?" Griffith grinned at him to let him know she wasn't judging, just interested.

"No, now, hold on. No bodies, but stuff they wanted to get rid of, you know. Like stolen goods and stuff. But I'm sure there have been people who were taken into the marsh and never came back. No doubt about that."

"If you could think of anyone in this town who would've taken a body into the marsh, who would it be? Who should I model my villain on?" *C'mon, take the bait.* If she brought up Nerbass, she'd probably get the same reaction she'd gotten from Mabel. But if he did it himself...

"Could be any of these guys. Maybe they get tired of giving Sherry their money. Maybe they decide to take it all back, and she fights them. Maybe she ends up falling and, you know, accidentally gets killed. Then here's this poor scumbag, killed a girl while trying to rob her, so what's he gonna do? Call the cops? No way. Dump her. That'd be a good story."

"I don't know. I mean there's not a lot of motivation there, and how does an accident carry a whole novel? It needs to be something more sinister, something that will hook readers and make them want to stay until the end. We have to have a really despicable villain. Someone people just naturally want to hate. Is there anyone around here like that?"

"So you mean someone with power? Someone who could hurt people and it wouldn't even faze him?"

"Exactly. That's more like it. Maybe a law officer gone bad? Or a businessman? The guy who owns the shrimp boats?"

His eyes lit up, and he glanced around before he leaned toward her. "Oh, I got just the guy! You need to use Nerbass. He's just the ticket. Only, you have to be real careful, like. You know? That guy is serious bad. He won't want to have anything to do with any mystery writer. But heck, he probably has a bunch of convenient bayou trips he could tell you about."

"Nerbass? Tell me about him. Why does he make a compelling villain?"

"Shoot. He's pure evil, that's why. And I'm not lying, neither. He could kill you with a look, I swear."

"What's his story? Is he the guy that owns the boats?"

"Nah, that ain't him. Nerbass is serious big. He runs the crews out to the oil platforms on his helicopters. Not him personally, but his pilots. Has a high-end fishing outfit too. I remember when he first came to Dulac, him and me, we used to hang out sometimes. But he got way too big for us little people."

"So success changed him?"

"Damn straight it did. J.B. used to be the nicest guy. Happy-go-lucky and all that. Then he started his bait shop. The first couple of years, he was still just himself. I guess it was about the time Ike ripped through here that he started to change."

"Hurricane Ike?"

"Yeah. He got some kind of connection hooked up with his old college buddy, Raymond something or other. Then he started being squirrely. Lots of money started rolling his way. Suddenly, we wasn't good enough for him. Started hobnobbing with the New Orleans and Houston clowns who come down here to fish. It was like he became a completely different guy."

"You don't say. Where do you think the money came from?"

"Well, from that Raymond guy. I'm sure of that. Loaned him the money to buy his first helicopter."

"That's quite a big loan. Those aren't cheap. How do you think he paid Raymond back?"

"Well, if anybody asks, you didn't hear this from me, but I think he has some shady business on the side."

"Like what?"

"Heck, I don't know. Maybe sometimes his choppers come in loaded with more than oil roughnecks."

"Smuggling? Like human trafficking?"

"Could be. Who'd notice down here? Might be more than that too."

"Are you just speculating or do you have some proof?"

"What?"

"I mean, if he's involved in illegal activities, I'm not sure I want him to know I'm writing a book modeling a character on him. I kind of enjoy breathing."

"Ha! I know what you mean. For a minute there you made me think you might be a cop or something. I'm no snitch. I'll tell you about J.B. for fiction, but if you was to ask me proper, I'd have to say he's an upstanding businessman."

"No worries. I appreciate your help. So if I want to find out more about Mr. Nerbass, for my research, who would I talk to?"

He shook his head and wiped the bar down in slow circles. "I told you, you have to be careful. You really don't want to be on his bad side."

"But what is he like? I mean does he have a family? Is it obvious that he's shady? If I met him would I get a sense that he was dirty? I like to know my characters inside and out."

"He has a family, but no, you'd never know he was anything but a gentleman if you met him. In fact, you would believe it to your core until the moment he took you out."

"What is his family like? Trophy wife and requisite kids?"

"Now, sure, but once, he had a real family. He fell hard for a local gal with a young daughter. Married her and they seemed really happy. Then one day the daughter up and disappears. No one ever heard from her again. The cops figured she ran away, but nobody could figure out why. She and her mamma had a hard time before J.B., but once he was in the picture, that kid was all smiles all the time. For a while, anyway."

"What do you think happened to the daughter?"

"I can't say. I suppose she could've run off, but I don't know. To me, it seems strange she would leave when she was so happy. She couldn't have been much more than thirteen or so. Too young for it to be about a boy. It sure imploded the rest of the family. J.B. was crazy with grief. He searched everywhere for the girl. The mother, Eloise, she didn't seem too upset. It was like she was relieved or something. She and J.B. were split by the year's end."

"Is the mother still around?"

"Oh yeah, she still lives in the house they shared back then. Down at the end of Old Bridge road. She lived there before J.B. entered the picture. I wonder sometimes how she feels now that he's a big deal. Making money hand over fist, living in that big old mansion in Morgan City, and her, still in that tiny little worn out cabin, her daughter gone too. I bet she's sorry she let him get away."

"You think she'd talk to me about him?"

He inhaled with a hiss. "I don't know, lady. You'd be getting awfully close to being on J.B.'s radar. I wouldn't risk it if I were you, especially for a made-up story, but it's your call."

"I appreciate your candor in talking to me. I can't wait to start writing. What do I owe you for the drink?"

"Ah, that's on the house, but the next one you can pay for. You're going to come back and keep me in the loop on your book, right?"

"Once it's written, you'll be the first to know."

"Most excellent. Take care now, and stay out of trouble."

"Thanks."

Griffith made her way back to her car, thinking about Eloise Nerbass. Would she be likely to answer the door if she just showed up? *Good probability.* She looked at her maps app and found Old Bridge Road. Her instincts were on overdrive, the scent of a real story driving her on the way it used to. *We're going to get him, Adi. Somehow, we're going to turn things around for you.* As soon as she had something more, she'd call Adi to clear things up between them. Until then, she needed to keep doing what she was good at.

CHAPTER SEVENTEEN

W e need to plan her service, kid. It's what we have to do. She ever say anything about what she'd like?" T'Claude said.

"I can't, T. I'm not ready."

"Adi, you don't have a choice. Bertie deserves to be celebrated, and it's our job to arrange things. Now where do you think we should look for her will and stuff? Maybe she has a plan written there."

Adi tried to pull herself out of the deep depression that had fallen on her after Bertie's death. She really couldn't. It hurt too much to think about, and being in the house without her made it so much worse. She needed to get T to understand.

"I need you to just go home, T'Claude. I really can't do this right now."

"I know you're hurting, but we have to plan now. Folks are going to start getting upset if they don't hear something soon. It's been two days."

Two days. Was it only two days? Time seemed to fracture without Bertie. Every bit and piece of the last two days was a part of a kaleidoscope of numbness bordered by pain. Adi felt like a grain of sand being whirled in that cylinder, landing in one space and then another. Why did Bertie have to go? How was she going to find a way to anchor herself and move on?

"Come on, Addison. You need to get a grip. Bertie gave you everything, a home, a life, a family. Are you telling me you can't find it in yourself to give her the send-off she deserves? I never thought of you as selfish."

The words stung, but Adi knew he was right. She needed to be strong and give Bertie her best. That was what Bertie had taught her to do.

"You're right. I know you're right. It's just so hard. Let me think a minute." She considered where Bertie might have put directions regarding her funeral. *Maybe in her room somewhere.* Adi hadn't had the willpower to go in there yet. *Or maybe with the papers in the safe deposit box at the bank?*

"There might be something in her room, and we should check the bank box too."

"Good, let's go check her room."

They went into the small bedroom near the back of the house. The scent of Bertie was everywhere, but somehow Adi found it comforting. She walked to the tall chifforobe in the corner where Bertie had her most precious things. The top was adorned with pictures of Bertie and Adi, Bertie and her brother, and Jacques and Adi individually. The top drawer held Bertie's nightclothes, mostly full-length silk gowns. The second drawer had as assortment of knickknacks, a St. Anthony medal, several rosaries, some memorial cards from the funerals of family and friends. A small box with mostly costume jewelry. The third drawer finally revealed Bertie's bible. Adi knew she kept some papers folded within its pages.

She carefully lifted the book from the drawer and sat on the edge of the bed with it. T'Claude dropped down beside her. They looked at the gilded cover for a while, both lost in their thoughts.

"Bertie loved the Lord, that's for sure," T'Claude said.

"Yes, she did. This book meant an awful lot to her." Adi opened the cover and found the family genealogy page covered with names dating back into the early 1800s.

"Wow, a true family bible. That's so rare to see these days. This book was held by Bertie's ancestors. See here, that's her mamma's name there. And here, at the end, that's you."

Adi looked at her own name carefully inscribed in Bertie's family bible. *She claimed me as her own.* She felt her chest tighten as the depth of Bertie's love became clear. Adi had always felt like Bertie was her mother of choice, but now she knew Bertie had shared that feeling. She wasn't just being kind to Adi; she truly loved her.

Adi flipped the page, not wanting to confront the grief that this realization brought. Several papers fluttered to the floor with the quick motion. T'Claude bent to retrieve them. He opened the first and read.

"This is her will. She left her house and her share of the Pot to you, as should be. We need to give this to her lawyer for probate. And here, this is a life insurance policy."

Adi nodded. She couldn't talk about it. She carefully continued to turn pages in the book. Near the end of Genesis, she found a sealed envelope marked "In the event of my death." She handed it to T'Claude without opening it. That would surely have Bertie's directives for her service.

"I'm going to go call the lawyer. I'll be right back."

"Okay."

Adi kept flipping through the well-worn book. She turned to the New Testament and found several faded newspaper clippings folded into the binding.

"*Father searches for lost daughter,*" the headline read. June 20, 2007. About three months after she had arrived in New Iberia. The article was about her. Had Bertie known all along who Adi had been running from? Why hadn't she turned her over to the authorities? Adi truly owed her life to Bertie now. The other clippings were dated later, the last in February of 2010. Adi was the subject of all of them. J.B. hadn't given up looking for her. He still owned the bait shop, but wasn't married to her mom anymore and lived in Morgan City.

She would burn those clippings. She didn't want anything to tie her to Nerbass. That life was a lie. Her truth was right here in New Iberia, with Bertie and T'Claude.

"You should have that bible. Bertie would want you to have it. That's why she wrote your name in it. I'm so sorry, Adi. I know what a loss this is to you, to both of us. I've been there and it's not easy, but it does get better," T said as he walked back into the room.

"Better? I don't know, T. I haven't ever hurt like this before. I just want to wake up and have it all be a nightmare."

"I know, kid. Let's go outside and get some fresh air. We can open the envelope out there."

"Okay."

They went to the wide front porch and sat in the rockers. Adi looked out at the azaleas blooming in the yard and the vegetable garden with its freshly turned soil. She would put in the summer garden, just like she'd promised Bertie. She would go on living, even if it hurt. She would do it because Bertie would want her to.

"You want to open this? Or should I?" T'Claude said.

"Go ahead and do it, T."

He ripped the seam of the envelope and pulled out a few sheets of paper. He read them aloud.

"At this time, I know you are all being silly fools, crying and all of that, but don't be sad for me. I'm going home, and it's about time. I'm not in that empty shell you got there. I'm up here dancing and singing with my mamma and other folks I love. Don't waste your time being sad for me. You all have things to do in that world. That's why you're there. Be sure and do them. Don't be stuck. Let life take a hold of you and fly free.

Now, when y'all start thinking about how to send me off, here's what I want. I want my pastor to get all fired up about the joys awaiting in the afterlife. There needs to be singing and dancing, lots of dancing. Don't be burying my leftovers, now. Just fire me into nice clean ashes and send me off. You know where, Adi. Smile for me, laugh for me, and be happy. I know I am."

Adi had to smile as she listened to T read. She could hear Bertie, and nothing in the note surprised her. She knew just the place Bertie wanted her ashes scattered. The Atchafalaya Basin, where she liked to canoe. She had shown Bertie the pictures she took there and knew it had been Bertie's wish to be able to share that with Adi, but she'd sworn she wouldn't get in some creaky little boat. This way, whenever Adi went to the Basin, Bertie would be waiting for her. She took to heart the message of Bertie's note. To live free, not to be stuck. That was meant for her. It wouldn't be easy, but she would do her best.

"That's just like Bertie. Make us feel silly for missing her. She would do that. Are you going to be okay with a happy celebration? I mean, if you need it to be more solemn, I'm sure Bertie wouldn't mind."

"No. It has to be just the way she wanted. It's better that way. It will help me break out of this funk. She always did know exactly what was good for me."

"Okay then. I'll call Reverend Peters and set up a memorial for her. Can you take the will and stuff to the lawyer? He said he'd wait at the office for one of us."

"Yeah. I can do that. Thanks."

"Good. I better go on down to the Pot and see if Jose has things under control. I hired a cook off Greg Landry, over at Iberia Kitchen. He should be ready to start today. Just someone to help keep things going."

"That's good. I'm glad you did that. I don't know when I'll be able to go back to work. I'm afraid I'll hear her falling every time I'm in the kitchen."

"That's understandable. You take whatever time you need. We'll be okay until you're up to it again. What ever happened with that reporter?"

Adi hadn't thought about Griffith since they'd turned off the machines. What had happened to her? She'd mentioned something in her voice mail about where she was going, but Adi couldn't remember where it was.

"She's still around somewhere, I think. I'm sure we'll hear from her soon." The thought of being held by her caused an ache in Adi's soul. If she was still around, maybe they could fix things.

"Good, then. We're going to need all the good publicity we can get with a new cook and no Bertie."

"I think I have her phone number inside. I'll call her when I get back from the lawyer and see what's up."

"I'd appreciate that. And hey, it matters to you too. You're a partner in the business now. Regardless of when you come back to work, you profit if the Pot profits."

"Thanks. I'll let you know what I find out."

After T'Claude left, Adi hit the shower and drove down to deliver the will and insurance to Bertie's lawyer. She still felt numb and had flashes of grief, but she reminded herself of Bertie's parting message in the letter, and it helped. Healing would come with time.

She thought about the last time she had seen Griffith. The walk on the coulee the evening of Bertie's stroke. How she'd reacted and how she'd told Griffith to get away from her. Had Griffith even heard her voice message apologizing? What if she hadn't? What if she had no plans to return to New Iberia and had already gone back to California to write her article? Adi couldn't blame her if she'd chosen to leave town. And that also meant she didn't have to explain her past.

Fresh pain tore at her as she thought of never seeing Griffith again. Never stealing kisses from her on a moonlit night. She shook it off. *No sense worrying about something you can't control.* She pulled out her phone and called her.

After six rings, the voice mail answered and she had to leave yet another message. Maybe something was wrong. Maybe Griffith was avoiding her calls. She could spend all day worrying, but it wouldn't help a darn thing. Griffith would call her back, or she wouldn't. Adi had done all she could. Time to move on.

CHAPTER EIGHTEEN

Griffith hadn't had any luck at Eloise Nerbass's house. Apparently, the woman wasn't in town. Just when she had paid her motel bill and was pulling out of the parking lot to head back to New Iberia, Randy Pecot called, letting her know that J.B. Nerbass had been delayed in Mexico and wouldn't return until after his China trip.

"He wants to help with your story, though, and he'd be happy to fly you down to Mexico City to interview him. He'll fit you in between business meetings. Shall I book you a flight?"

"Mexico City? I'm not sure if I can do that. Can I get back to you in an hour?"

"Of course. I know it's last minute, but that's how J.B. is. When he decides he wants to do something, he makes it happen. If you'll just confirm with me by four this afternoon, I can get you on a flight this evening," Randy said.

"Okay, I'll let you know as soon as possible." She was both anxious and excited. She knew there was a story here, one that would see her star rising again in print journalism. The worry was over how Adi would react. *I don't want to hurt her, and this is going to hurt, if I'm on the right track. She's not going to accept that I went to meet with him and didn't mention it to her. I have to talk to her before I go through with this.* The fact that she was willing to discuss it with Adi told her more about how she felt than she'd realized. She never asked permission from anyone, ever. But Adi's feelings, and safety, mattered more than her career ever would. She drove back up the coast to New Iberia. Hopefully, she'd be able to talk to Adi before she grabbed her bags from the hotel. When she arrived at the Pot it was still deserted. Why had they closed down? She drove to Bertie's, dread building. The house was empty as well. *Where is everyone?* She called Adi's cell again, but there was no answer and the message box was full. She called T'Claude and had the same result. *This isn't good. What could possibly have happened?* She glanced at her watch. Three fifty. She had to decide what to do.

If something had happened to Adi, she was sure Bertie or T would have called. Maybe they were avoiding her because of her article, or because of her fight with Adi. But that didn't make sense, as it wouldn't be a reason to shut down the Boiling Pot. She didn't know if she should stay and figure this out or take Nerbass up on his offer. She sighed and considered the options. Whatever was going on here, she wasn't a part of it. But she was a part of the story, Adi's story, which included Nerbass. She needed to follow her instincts and get to the root of Nerbass's business dealings. This could help Adi in the end. There wouldn't be another chance like this one.

She would be back in a few days and she could find out what had happened then. *I wish I could see her before I go. I don't want to lose her.* She called Randy and confirmed her trip details, then packed her bags and headed to New Orleans. Then she called a friend in LA and let her know she was meeting a contact in Mexico. If she suddenly disappeared, she wanted someone to know where to start looking.

She arrived in Mexico City, more anxious than she had been in New Iberia. Something was wrong. Something big. She could feel it. She tried calling all the numbers again as soon as she was off the plane but had no luck. There was a driver holding a sign with her name on it as she exited customs. He whisked her away to five-star hotel and spa. A hotel representative greeted her personally and showed her to her room. The whole time, she wondered if Adi was okay and what was going on in New Iberia.

"Mr. Nerbass has instructed us that anything you desire is to be added to his bill. Please feel free to enjoy all we have to offer. If you need anything at all, here is my personal number. Don't hesitate to call me. Enjoy your stay," she said. She handed Griff an embossed card and left her to unwind.

She'd been told Nerbass would call her when he was ready for their meeting. She tried to relax and gather her thoughts, but her head and her heart hadn't made the trip. They were back in Louisiana. *Why can't I get in touch with anyone? Does Adi even know I've tried to reach her?*

She was playing the waiting game with Nerbass, and she didn't like it. She had to pull it together so when she finally did get an opportunity to talk with him she wouldn't give anything away. He couldn't connect her to Adi. She'd made sure of it, and she'd rehearsed her story to sound as plausible as possible. By the second day of waiting, her nerves were beginning to fray. Her concern over Adi and the others was growing exponentially, and the urge to leave was strong. But this was important. She needed to find out who he was, behind the flashy veneer. She was certain he was the source of Adi's fear, and she couldn't free her without the facts. *I have to stick it out. He's scheduled to leave for Beijing in the morning. Whether he calls today or not, tonight I'm on a plane back to New Orleans.*

She felt bad about the way she'd left things with Adi. She had every intention of talking out their disagreement, but her sense that meeting with Nerbass would give her a big break was overwhelming, and she didn't want to miss her chance. And knowing she could help Adi, even if nothing more ever happened between them, made her determined to figure it all out. The past two days had given her ample time to evaluate Adi's reaction and her own defensive stance on editorial control. Realistically, the situation with Adi was nothing like the one with Tabitha. No one was at risk except Adi and those she loved. There weren't life savings involved, nor was she a criminal. At least, she didn't think she was. In fact, her deceptiveness over her past was most likely purely protective. The locals she had talked with certainly made it sound as though J.B. Nerbass was a dangerous man.

Adi made her feel things. Things that went deeper than ever before. The way Adi's smile made her tense inside and flush with warmth. The tingle that rippled down her body when they touched. Feelings she'd turned off after Tabitha. It was more than just a passing attraction, and Adi was worth the risk of being in a dangerous situation in a foreign country. It was theoretically possible Nerbass wasn't the connection to Adi after all. *Can I live with it, if I never really know where she comes from?* The truth surprised her. She could. And she could write her piece for Dawn completely confident that nothing could arise from it that would harm her or the magazine. She trusted Adi fully. The question of whether or not Adi would trust her, knowing that she'd invaded her past even though she'd asked her not to, was another question. One she'd deal with as soon as she got back.

She looked down at her phone to check the time. Ten forty. She needed to book a flight back to New Orleans. She would be back in New Iberia before another day passed.

As she was gathering her things to pack, her phone rang and she was asked to meet Nerbass in one of the hotel conference rooms in an hour. She was glad the trip wouldn't prove fruitless, but was nervous about the meeting. She let ideas flow as she showered and dressed. She wore her Armani suit, knowing that looking as sharp as possible with the corporate set paid dividends. The conference room door was guarded by a tall hulking fellow in an equally fashionable suit.

"Ms. McNaulty?"

She nodded.

"He's waiting for you inside." He held the door for her.

Nerbass looked slightly older but no less impressive than the photos she had seen in the Morgan City headquarters. His dark hair, silver at the temples, was slicked back. He rose gracefully from a couch and held out a hand in greeting. His smile was warm, but his dark eyes were cold. He was shorter than she'd imagined, but trim and athletic. His hand was smooth and well manicured. He exuded confidence, but Griff found something about him repugnant. *That's because you have a broader view of him. Keep it cool. Be yourself.*

"Ms. McNaulty. Thank you for taking me up on my offer of travel. I find it so very difficult to squeeze in time at home these days. Come, won't you sit down?"

"Mr. Nerbass. Thank you, I will."

"Would you care for anything to drink? Cocktail? Bottled water? No?"

"Thank you, I'm fine."

"Wonderful." He sat across from her, his hands folded in his lap, his head tilted slightly. "Randy tells me you're writing about how losing a child affects a parent. Is that an apt description?"

"Yes, that's correct. I find we focus so much on the devastating reality of loss that we overlook how it can change a person in a positive way. I've come across a number of stories where parents have made positive changes to the world because of that loss. Your story particularly intrigues me, especially as your business success came about after your daughter disappeared, and how you've made certain decisions in her honor."

"And why does my story resonate with you? What is the goal of your article going to be? Am I going to be a beacon for other parents experiencing loss?"

Griff couldn't tell if he was being sarcastic or not, but she continued with a smile. "That's a part of it, but there's more. How would it affect you if your daughter returned after all these years? What would change? Would you accept her and welcome her back into your life? I know you've never given up on finding her. I know about the reward. Some of the families I've spoken to said they wouldn't know what to do, or if it would change the things they were doing. What would you do if you found out she was still alive?"

Griffith didn't know why she was taking this route, but it felt right, like her intuition was shoving her down an unavoidable path. She watched Nerbass as he processed what she had said. His face went pale, registering shock, then red with anger.

"Why on earth would you propose such a thing? I'm not amused." He motioned toward his bodyguard, signaling that the meeting was nearing its conclusion.

"I certainly mean no disrespect, Mr. Nerbass. I just wanted your perspective on a reunion with a lost child. This is completely hypothetical. I've asked all my interview subjects the same question. Some people were taken aback, but the majority were overcome with the what-ifs and had really great constructive ideas of what they would do if their child returned. Do you find more comfort in the idea that your daughter is gone from your life forever?"

"That is a completely outrageous thing to suggest. How dare you even contemplate such a thing."

He was becoming visibly enraged the longer she stood there. *Why? If he loves his child and wants her back, why would the possibility enrage him?*

"Let's take a step back from this, Mr. Nerbass. I can see this was the wrong question to ask you. How about you tell me how the loss of your daughter affected you? What did you change about yourself, your goals and dreams, when you lost her?"

"You want me to forget you asked the question? You want me to continue as if you hadn't just ripped open an old wound? What kind of person are you? How did I change? I was gutted. Literally destroyed by the loss of my daughter. She was the world to me. Did I throw myself into my work? Yes. Did I benefit financially from that? Absolutely. Is that wrong? Does it make my pain any less? Not in any way. You want to know what I would do if my daughter walked into this room right now? I would fall to my knees and thank the Lord. I loved my child. I love her still. Write that in your little article. Now, if you'll excuse me, I have a busy day ahead. Jones will see you out."

The anger in his voice and the acrimony in his body language gave Griffith a taste of what Mabel and the barkeep saw in Nerbass. He came off as smooth as melted chocolate, but rub him the wrong way and his spines came out. She knew if she analyzed the puzzle of his rise to wealth and power, she could uncover a big story, but that didn't interest her at the moment. Right now all she could think about was how that anger would've felt when directed at a fourteen-year-old. *Poor Adi. Growing up with that kind of hidden monster.*

What had taken place in that little house in Dulac? Why would it still cause him to lose his temper, eight years later? She thanked him for his time and tried to appear calm as she left his office, though she could feel the animosity of his glare on her back. She hurried to her room and gathered her belongings. The rest of the answer wasn't here in Mexico. It was back in Louisiana.

❖

On her way out to the waiting cab, Griffith noticed Nerbass walking toward a black sedan. The back door swung open and he slid inside. She thought about it for a minute and then asked her driver to follow the sedan at a safe distance. She wanted to see where he was going.

The driver didn't blink at her request, just pulled out after Nerbass. *Must be plenty of subterfuge in Mexico.* They drove along Paseo de la Reforma heading toward Alameda Central. The sedan slowed as it neared the Palace of Fine Arts. When Nerbass stepped out onto the plaza, Griffith had the cab pull in, closer to the park. She watched him walk up to the winged statue and stop.

Soon a second figure walked up to the statue. A man who looked familiar to Griffith, though she couldn't place him. He was older than Nerbass, dressed in jeans and a work shirt. They remained at the statue for several minutes. The man and Nerbass shook hands before they headed in opposite directions.

The man, flanked by two younger men with the posture of bodyguards, walked toward Griffith's cab, passing almost directly in front of her. She snapped a discreet picture with her phone. She knew that face but not where she had seen it, and her instincts told her it was important she find out.

"You ready to move on, miss?" the cabbie said.

"Yes. The airport, please."

What was Nerbass up to? Who was the man in the jeans, and why did he look familiar? She wondered if her old contact, Martin Beltran, still worked at *El Sol de Mexico*, the local paper. Maybe he could identify Mr. Jeans. She pulled up the masthead for the paper and was happy to see her friend still listed. She shot him a quick email asking for his help just as the cab pulled up to the departure entrance.

"Gracias, señor." She paid the cabby, adding an extra tip for his efforts.

Security and Customs were the typical time consuming annoyances she had always known, and after an hour or so of lines and searches, she was comfortably seated at her gate. She slid her phone out of her pocket and checked her emails. Martin had responded and was more than willing to lend a hand. She sent him the photograph without much explanation. She didn't really know what she had witnessed or how to relate it to her current story, so she avoided the question.

He responded quickly, but his message was perplexing. He didn't identify the man outright, but asked her why she wanted information on him. Not sure how to answer, she asked him for a number so she could call him. It would be easier to explain over the phone than in email. His response was downright baffling.

"I will call you from a safe line. Where can I reach you? It won't be until late this evening."

She sent back her number and let him know she would be in transit and not available until after six. *A safe line?*

The flight was unremarkable in every way, leaving her plenty of time to think about what she'd found out, and to daydream about Adi's beautiful smile and strong arms. As she left the plane, she tried calling Adi again. Why wasn't she answering? What had happened? T didn't answer either. She wanted to drive straight to the Pot when she finally left the airport, but she was tired and needed a few hours' sleep before she tried to get behind the wheel. She booked a room at the Hilton and arranged a rental car for the morning. After a quick shower and a bite to eat, she fell into bed. Although she couldn't wait to see Adi, she needed to get her feet under her before she could face her with what she knew. She didn't want to risk another fight, especially if it could mean she'd lose Adi altogether. She hadn't heard from Martin yet, but he might have gotten called away. *If I'm asleep when he calls, the phone will wake me.*

She was asleep minutes after her head hit the pillow. When she woke the next morning, there was still no message. She sent him an email, but worded it vaguely. If there was something about Mr. Jeans that would cause Martin problems, she didn't want to exacerbate them. It bothered her that she hadn't heard a word from him, especially given his need for security. She called Adi's cell phone, but had no luck. She was on the road to New Iberia before nine.

Something felt off at the Boiling Pot. There were only a few cars in the parking lot, but this time, Griffith could see a handwritten sign in the window. When she read the sign, she understood the disquieting feeling she had, and why no one was answering their phones. *Bertie's gone.* How could that have happened in just the few days she'd been away? *She seemed so full of life. How can she just be gone? And what about Adi? This had to devastate her.* She entered the restaurant on the off chance Adi would be there. It didn't smell like Adi's cooking, and the conversation at the few occupied tables was subdued. The feeling of loss was palpable. She headed for the kitchen.

"Hello, Ms. Griffith."

"Hi, Jose. Is Adi around?"

"Ah, no, ma'am. She's taking some time off."

"That makes sense. I guess I'll check her house. I really need to talk to her."

"She should be there. The service is tomorrow, so I'm sure she'll be around. Mr. Michaud has been in and out today, but I haven't seen Adi."

"Thanks. If she does drop by, would you tell her I'm looking for her?"

"Sure thing."

"Thanks."

Griffith drove to the house, hoping to see Adi. The driveway was empty, but she knocked on the door anyway. When there was no response, she tried to think of where else to look for her. There was too much to say, too many questions. *Maybe I should park myself in a porch rocker and wait for her to come home.* She eyed the comfy rockers. *Yep, that'll do.*

Her phone rang as she settled into the chair. It was an unidentified caller.

"Griffith McNaulty."

"Griff? It's Martin. What are you getting yourself tangled in?"

"Hey, Martin. I'm trying to stay clear of tangles these days, but I'm following a lead on a story I hadn't expected. Why do you ask?"

"What in God's name would possess you to not only take a picture of El Mayo, but to email it on an unprotected number? You're going to end up dead, and quick, if you keep that up."

"El Mayo? The drug lord?"

"Exactly. You took a really good picture of him too."

"Damn. Refresh my memory, which cartel is he with?"

"Umberto Ismael Garcia, El Mayo, runs a faction of the Sinaloa Cartel. He's the shit, man. You don't want to mess with that."

"Are you kidding me? The guy in jeans is el jefe for Sinaloa? He looked like an average guy."

"Yeah, he lives real. He was a farmer before the cartel, knows all there is to know about botany and agriculture. He is also muy paranoid. He would kill you if he knew you took his picture. This guy is very dangerous. Why are you looking at him?"

"Funny thing, that. I'm not looking at him for anything. He just happened to meet with the guy I'm checking out. J.B. Nerbass?"

"The businessman? Seriously? What has he got to do with the Sinaloa?"

"That's a very good question. And exactly what I'm trying to find out."

"Word of advice? Keep your shit far from Garcia. You don't want him thinking you were breathing in his direction. I'm talking serious, graphic death. Not what you want to experience. Trust me. And listen, you never heard any of this from me. I have to live in this city. I'm also somewhat fond of my head and want to keep it where it is."

"Got it. Thanks, buddy. I owe you one."

"Damn straight. Hit me up next time you're here. We'll talk about things that won't get us killed."

"That's a promise. Take care."

"Bye."

So why was Nerbass meeting El Mayo? Is drug cartel money funding his little empire? She considered various possibilities, allowing her experience to guide her as she examined one possibility after another. A drug cartel would certainly make Adi wary of divulging information from her old life. She wasn't sure it was the best way to broach the subject of Nerbass and El Mayo, but her time was limited and her options few. She sent the photo she had taken to a friend in the DEA. She might lose the story, but she didn't care at this point. She'd do anything to help Adi.

Griffith nearly gave up waiting after an hour. It was getting dark and she really had no idea where Adi might be. She called her again, but only got a message that the voice mailbox was full. *Where are you?* The need to connect with Adi was becoming overwhelming. *She's got to be hurting so bad. I need to find her. I have to let her know she's not alone, that I'm here for her.* She tossed her phone on the chair beside her. *I'll sit here until you get back, no matter how long it takes. I'm not going anywhere.* More than anything, she wanted to wrap Adi in her arms and let her know how she felt, what it meant to be with her. She wanted take her pain away and hold her. Just hold her.

Headlights suddenly illuminated the yard. She stood, hoping it would be Adi at last. When the truck was fully in the driveway, she realized it was T'Claude. He'd know where Adi was.

"Hey. I'm really sorry to hear about Bertie," she called as he exited the truck.

"Oh, hey there. I didn't see you. Thanks. It was sure unexpected, but at least she didn't have much pain. Is Adi here?"

"No. I was hoping you knew where she might be," she said.

"Nope. I called her about six times, but she hasn't called me back. I figured maybe she was sleeping or something so I decided to drive by."

"Well, she's not here."

"That's strange. I know she planned to be here tonight. We were supposed to go over some stuff for the service tomorrow," he said.

"Do you think we should be worried?"

"No, not yet. She's taking all of this real hard, but she's tougher than you think. She'll be okay. It just takes time. But she sure could use a friend right now. I kinda hoped you would show up at the hospital. We figured you'd gone back to LA."

"I would have gone to the hospital, if I'd known what was going on," Griffith said.

"I don't get how you didn't know. Seems like you'd have called or gone by the restaurant."

"I did call. So many times. You and Adi both have full mailboxes and weren't answering. But that's beside the point. I'm here now and I need to talk to Adi."

He nodded and gave her a small smile. "I stopped checking my phone, sorry. Too many well-wishers, making it even harder. I imagine Adi has done the same. I need to talk to her too."

"Where could she be?" Griffith didn't want to worry, but it was hard not knowing what was going through Adi's mind. She wouldn't be able to relax until she knew she was okay. T looked just as concerned.

"She probably went out on the bayou. She had to go to the lawyer's today. I'm sure she needed to clear her mind. Tomorrow's going to be hard on all of us, especially Adi. I guess I'll go check on the Pot. You're going to stick around, right? You'll be there tomorrow?"

"Yes, without question. If you talk to Adi, please tell here I was here."

"Will do."

Griffith left him on the porch, disappointed that she had missed seeing Adi. She headed to the hotel, hoping to hear something soon. The Boiling Pot wasn't going to be the same without Bertie. She needed to fill Dawn in on what had happened. She called from her room and they spoke at length about the evolving situation. Griff told her there might be more to the story, something particularly interesting, but wasn't free to talk about it just yet. Dawn decided to put a hold on the article for the time being. Griffith knew Adi would be relieved, and now that she knew who Nerbass was connected to, she was relieved as well. It would give her time to reconnect with Adi and talk to her about what she'd discovered. *If he's her stepfather no wonder she's terrified he might find her. That's one scary man.* For Adi to not only survive him, but to make something of herself as well, was amazing and made Griffith admire her that much more. Whatever it took, she would help Adi be free of him for good. Then, maybe they could find their way back to each other.

She might not have any future with Adi, but she had to give it her best shot. She would regret it if she didn't. As she slid into the soft sheets of her bed, the memory of velvet kisses wrapped around her, and she knew she would never change a second of the time they had spent together. If these fleeting memories were all she had in the end, at least she would understand the value of what they'd shared. The last thing she remembered as she fell asleep was Adi's smile.

❖

Adi loaded the kayak into the back of her truck. She had driven down to the Basin after dropping the papers at the attorney's office. She needed time and quiet to deal with her feelings. She didn't know why this had been Bertie's time to go, but it had. She couldn't change that. She needed to come to grips with the fact that life was going to move on. She'd have to make some serious decisions in the next week or so.

I don't want to go back to the Pot. I don't know what I want. Damn, Bertie. What am I supposed to do now?

No matter how many times she asked, no answer came. She was utterly alone, and all the choices were hers now. *What do I want? I used to want a bigger place, a larger crowd to lose myself in. Is that what comes next? Do I cast off the old and start fresh? Maybe I should. Maybe it's time to grow up, see the world a little.*

That sounded good inside her head, but she wasn't sure about the reality. Could she make it in New Orleans or Houston? Would anyone hire her? She felt the knots of dread building in her gut. Why was it so hard? People did it every day. Kids left home, went to school, built a life of their own. Why did it seem so insurmountable?

She ratcheted down the tie on the boat and it hit her. *Bertie knew this would happen. She knew you'd have questions, doubts. She already answered you, "Don't be stuck. Let life take a hold of you and fly."*

Adi jerked as the meaning of Bertie's words became clear. She knew Adi better than anyone. She'd know how losing her would lock Adi up like a bike left out in the yard. Chain rusted, stuck fast. But she also knew a little grease and a few good knocks would get that chain moving again. She'd given her the grease, a stake in the business and a house, and with her parting words, the first good knock. It was all there for her. She just had to let herself fly.

She'd talk to T'Claude about selling her share of the Boiling Pot to him and put the house on the market. If she had a big enough nest egg, she'd build a life somewhere else. She'd have the funds to settle in and a bit of time to wait for the right job opportunity. It was time.

She felt her chest constrict as anxiety about starting over kicked in. *This is what you need to do. It's time to grow up and take charge of your life. I'm not going to even think of looking back. Bertie, I'm going to fly.*

Her fear gave way to excitement. She'd leave as soon as possible. She was sure T'Claude would help her with the details.

She'd found just the place for Bertie's ashes. A cypress tree with the face of a woman in its weathered surface. She'd call the tree

"Bertie's rest." She had circled it several times, taking pictures from all angles so she would know exactly where it was. A printed copy of the place would be the cover to Bertie's memorial program. Her phone had been dead since four due to all the pictures, and she couldn't deal with the amount of voice mails from people calling about Bertie, so she'd ignored them, and was somewhat relieved when the phone died and stopped ringing all the time. She grabbed her car charger and plugged it in. T'Claude had probably been trying to get a hold of her, but it couldn't be helped. She'd call him when she got home.

I'm sure he's pissed, but I needed this. Now I'm ready to say good-bye. He'll get over it. I needed to find the right place for her.

When she finished off loading the kayak and getting her gear inside, she called him.

"Where have you been, kiddo?"

"Out on the Basin. I found the spot for her, T. It's perfect."

"Good. Listen, how about I grab some wings and head over there? We need to get things settled for tomorrow."

"Okay. I might be in the shower when you get here, but come on in," she said.

"Right. Oh, hey, McNaulty was at your place this evening."

Adi's pulse sped up. *She didn't just leave. She's still here.* "She was? Did you talk to her?"

"Yeah. She was hoping to see you. Would you mind giving her a call? That story is going to mean a lot. We need to do whatever we can to make the Pot stand out."

"Sure. I'll call her now," she said.

"Thanks," he said.

As much as she wanted to hear her voice, she dreaded talking to Griffith. She didn't know what to say. The last time they'd spoken was in a different world. She couldn't even remember what she'd said. She knew she'd been rude, and they'd fought. So much had happened, though. How could she talk to her without going through the whole ordeal? The whole business seemed so trivial in comparison to the past few days.

But Adi had decided her life was about to change, and with Griffith going back to LA at some point, there wasn't any point in keeping what they'd started going. *I need to treat this like we're just a reporter and her subject. It's way too personal and deep. I made a mistake letting her into my life. I'll just make it a professional call.* The thought of pushing Griffith away, when she really wanted to pull her close, made her ache inside.

She steeled herself to any reaction Griffith might have and called.

"Adi, thank goodness. Are you okay? I'm so sorry about Bertie."

"Ms. McNaulty. I understand you were looking for me tonight?"

"What? Okay...so we're going back to formality?"

"Did you need something?"

"I need to know that you're okay. I want to be here for you. I don't even remember what we argued about, and it doesn't even matter. I care about you. Are you okay?"

"I'm doing well. Did you need something for your story?"

"My story? Why does that matter? What's going on, Adi?"

"There's nothing going on. Thank you for your condolences. If I can't be of further help, I have things to take care of." Adi hated the sadness in Griffith's voice, but she couldn't back down. She had a road to take, and someone like Griffith, with all her worldliness, wasn't on that road.

"You're seriously just going to say good-bye? Did you hear me at all? I care about you. Damn it, let me in."

"If that's all, I'll say good night."

"Don't. Talk to me, please."

"Good night."

"Merley..." Griffith whispered.

Adi felt her blood run cold as goose bumps prickled her skin. She dropped onto the couch, breathing rapidly.

"Did you hear me? Merley? Are you there?"

She felt severed, disembodied as the name she'd cast off rung in her head. Merley was dead. She was never coming back. The acrid smell of gun smoke ghosted through her nasal passage as the memory of her past crashed down on her. She could see the rain of red mist wash through the room just as it had that night so long ago. The sound of her phone hitting the floor barely registered. She jumped up and ran to her room. She stuffed random items of clothing into a bag she grabbed from the closet. *Run. He's found you. If she knows who you are, he knows. Run and don't look back. Run, run, run...*

She was out of the room moments later and racing for the porch. She reached her truck in seconds and fired the engine. When the squeal of her tires on the asphalt echoed through the night, she was gone. She wouldn't stop until she was in New Orleans. She would start again, but not as she'd hoped. She'd have to scratch out a life all over, since she couldn't go back to do the legal stuff, but she wouldn't face that place again. She wouldn't be there when he found out where she was living. She'd forget this life too, in time. Hopefully, no one would look too hard for her. *Bertie, I wish you were here. I never should have talked to that reporter. I knew it.* She let the tears fall as she said good-bye to her home, to Bertie, and T, in her rearview mirror.

Chapter Nineteen

W *hat did I do? Why'd I open my mouth? Surely she won't miss Bertie's service?* Griffith looked around at the gathering of friends and family who had arrived to send Bertie on. It was a large group, showing how well loved she was. That Adi wasn't there was noticeable, and she could see the questions circulating among the gathered. *I'm so stupid. Where is she?* The fact that she could have caused Adi enough panic that she'd miss Bertie's service brought bile into the back of her throat and tears gathered in her eyes. She couldn't breathe properly.

"Where is she? She was going to call you, last I heard. When I got to her house, the front door was wide open and her phone was lying on the floor. What happened?" T'Claude said, his arms crossed over his chest, his eyes narrowed accusingly.

"I...I said something stupid. I don't know where she is. We were talking, and then she was gone. I don't know what else to tell you."

"What did you say that made her run?"

"I can't tell you. It's not something she wants anyone to know about. You're going to have to wait until she surfaces and ask her."

"You're kidding me. You waltz in here, get all cozy, then scare the shit out of her and walk away scot-free? I don't think so. You're going to sure as hell help me find her. You hear what I'm saying? You're going to turn that investigative journalist thing to our advantage and help Adi. You made a mess. You clean it up. Not like last time you made a mess."

Griffith was stunned with the acid in his words.

"Yeah, I know who you are, lady. Don't look so surprised. I can research too. You have some serious skills in hunting information, and we're going to need that if we're going to find her."

"I'm happy to help. I want to find her too. I'm not backing away from this at all. I'm just not sure where to start. I've got to talk to her. I can't tell you what I said, but I can tell you it was a mistake. I want her back just as much as you." Griffith realized it was true. No matter what, she had to make things right.

"Like hell. But you're going to help, no matter what. Let me get through this mess, then you and I are going to get to work."

The service was lovely in spite of Adi being missing. Everyone danced and sang and sent Bertie off in a big way. Griffith pasted on a smile and was polite, but all she could think about was Adi, and where she might have gone. When they finished the fantastic buffet Jose and the new cook had prepared, people began to say their good-byes, and T'Claude found Griffith sitting at a back table.

"I know you're angry with me, and you've every right to be. But believe me, the last thing I wanted was to cause Adi pain or make her run. I just wanted to get through to her. She wouldn't talk to me. She'd shut me out. I had to say what I said so we could have a chance," she said.

"What chance? What did you expect? You know her well enough by now to know that girl isn't but barely held together on the outside. She's deep. Real deep, on the inside, but she doesn't handle stress at all. She's like a chocolate dipped ice cream when you first take a bite. That shell just cracks and falls away. How could you do that to her? I thought you cared."

"I do care. I care a great deal. When she wouldn't let me in I panicked. I had to get her to react. To acknowledge that I existed in her life. I was scared, damn it."

"Well, hallelujah. You were scared, so you destroyed her. Great plan, there. How's that working out for ya?" He crossed his arms and glared at her.

"Not so good. Damn it, T'Claude. Let's stop this crap and find her. Can we do that, please? Can we not focus on what an ass I've been and instead focus on where she would go?"

He was a solid slab of anger, and Griffith wondered if he would budge. She knew his love for Adi would win in the end. He needed her as much as she needed him.

"Fine. For now. I'm not letting this go, though. Selfishness like that? It's not caring about someone. But we'll get back to that later."

"Good. Where do you think she's most likely to go? She didn't take much with her."

"No, she didn't. Her phone, for one thing. She used to talk about New Orleans a lot when she was a teenager. I don't think Bertie ever managed to get her over there, but she might have headed that way."

"New Orleans. Good. I have some contacts there. They owe me some favors down at city hall. I'll email one of them, and he can run her plates through the system and see if she shows up anywhere. Her truck will be pretty hard to miss too. Maybe he could run a check on her credit cards," she said.

"That's a good plan. I can call my buddies down there and get them to look out for that truck. Plus, if she's looking to put her skills to use as a chef, I can pull some strings so we'll hear about it."

"You don't think she'll just come back? You know, after a few days?"

"No. She didn't come back for the service, so there's no way she's planning to come back at all."

"I'm so sorry to be the cause of this, T."

He sighed. "I know you are. Mind me now, I'm not forgiving you, but I know you didn't mean to chase her off. Let's get going on this stuff so we can hear something soon."

"Okay. You have my cell number. Please call me if you hear anything."

"You do the same. We should head down to New Orleans ourselves. She isn't going to just up and call us," he said.

"You're right. Let's do it."

"Good. I'll tie up some loose strings here and we can head out later today. Let's say, by six?"

"I'll be ready."

Griffith headed back to her room and called her New Orleans contact. She had covered a story on fiscal misconduct he had been involved in. She had found proof he had no part in the misappropriations and had basically saved his butt, so he was more than happy to help.

"Sure, no problem. If I find anything, it should be in the next few hours. I'll send you a text."

"Thanks. I appreciate it," she said.

That complete, she packed an overnight bag and waited to hear from T'Claude. Sitting around was making her crazy. She felt trapped and helpless. The longer she waited, the higher the tension rose in her until she felt like she could scream. Why? Why did she open her stupid mouth? She knew the subject of Dulac made Adi jumpy. What had possessed her to throw out the name she had run from? T was right. It had been her selfish need to show Adi she knew who she really was to get her to let her in. *Talk about backfiring.*

Just when she thought she'd burst if nothing happened, her phone rang. She didn't recognize the number, and with blind hope, she answered.

"Adi?"

"Excuse me? Is this Griffith McNaulty?"

Not Adi. The voice was familiar, but she couldn't place it.

"Yes," she said.

"This is J.B. Nerbass. I did some follow-up after our visit, Ms. McNaulty. I now understand you have quite a reputation as an investigative journalist. I had my people look into your recent movements and I see you've been all over South Louisiana."

"How is this a concern of yours, Mr. Nerbass? I told you I was doing a story. It includes various people in various places."

"It's very much my concern. Just what kind of game are you playing?" he said.

"I'm not playing any kind of game. I don't have time for this right now, so if you'll excuse me?"

"I will not. You have a lot to answer for. My attorneys will be doing the talking for me if you're too busy to hear me."

"Mr. Nerbass, I assure you, I'm not playing any game. Right now I'm in the midst of a personal crisis. Please understand."

"I understand one thing. You came to me about a very personal matter. You have caused me unbelievable pain, and I'm not the kind of man you want to make angry."

"Is that right? And what kind of pain have you caused? I'm done with this conversation. Good-bye." She disconnected the call and resisted the urge to throw her phone across the room. If ever there were a shit storm with her name on it, this was it. He knew where she'd been, and quite likely, who she'd been talking to.

Where was T? What was taking so long? She had to get to New Orleans and find Adi, before anyone else did.

❖

The sound of the street drummers calmed Adi as she wandered through the French Quarter. It was so crowded with people she felt anonymity surround her like a cloak. *This is good.* No one would ever notice her here, much less be able to find her. The room she had taken at the Super 8 was clean, but not something that would work long-term. She needed to find a place to disappear.

There had been a guy at the place where she had breakfast who mentioned a job at Tujague's. It wasn't much, just a line cook position, but if she got the job, it would be a secure source of income with the potential for promotion. He had given her directions and the name of the person to speak with. Hopefully, this would pan out. She wouldn't have any references to offer, so she couldn't be sure. Pain knifed through her as she flashed on Bertie and T joking around in the kitchen at the Pot. *So much loss. When will it stop hurting?* She blocked it out, numbed herself to the memory. She would forget.

The man at Tujague's was happy she had some experience as a cook. He accepted that she had drifted around New Iberia as a short order cook.

"Here, fill out this paperwork, and when you're done, tap on my office door. I'll walk you through our system and get you a T-shirt and cap. You can wear any pants for now. If you move up, you'll have to get the full uniform," he said.

"Yes, sir."

"Just call me Jake. No sir-ing around here."

"Okay, Jake," she said.

He nodded as he slipped into his office. Adi filled in the forms, putting in the names of several restaurants near New Iberia. They might call, but she chose places that she knew had high turnover rates, or that had closed. When she tapped on the door, Jake tossed her a black T-shirt and cap.

"Be here tonight at six. You'll start on a trial basis. If things work out, great. You have the Super 8 listed as your residence. Is that right?" he asked.

"For now. I just got into town and don't have a permanent place yet."

"I have a buddy who owns a building in Bayou St. John. The bottom floor is an ice cream joint, but he rents out the apartment above. It's pretty nice. I think it's available. Let me get you his number," he said, searching his desk. "Here you go. His name is Steven. Tell him I gave you his number."

"Thanks."

"Forget it. See you tonight."

Adi was a little shook up at how easy it was. She had a job and now a connection to an apartment. She was going to be okay. She grabbed a bite to eat at a café on Decatur. Everything was just so alive here. She liked the feeling the city gave her. It was so much more than New Iberia had been. More movement, more laughter and music, it just breathed life. She concentrated on that, and people watching, rather than think about Griffith's betrayal and how she'd lost everything because of her.

I can be this place. This is who I am now.

She called about the apartment and got an appointment to see it that afternoon. The place was small, but had some great features. It was small enough to feel safe but big enough not to feel claustrophobic. She loved that it had a good-sized deck too. The neighborhood seemed safe, with a number of little shops with apartments above them. The rent wasn't cheap, but she thought she'd be able to swing it. She might have to get a second job, but that would be good. Less time to think about what she'd left behind. She signed lease papers, month to month, and paid two months' rent in advance. The lady who showed her the apartment ran the shop downstairs. She said Adi could move her things in between nine p.m. and ten a.m. *Things.* She'd have to get some of those. It wouldn't do to move into an apartment with only a backpack. Briefly, she thought about Griffith and wondered what her place in LA looked like. The thought was quickly followed by the feeling of being wrapped in her arms. But then... The whispered name that sent her running, made her heart ache. *Dangerous. Too damn dangerous.*

When she returned to her room, she set her alarm for four thirty. That would give her plenty of time to shower and get back to the restaurant. She was desperate for a nap, and it wasn't long before she was asleep.

J.B.'s arm wrapped around her waist. The smell of his aftershave was strong in her nose. He forced her hand around the grip of his pistol. The blue-black gun filled her vision, its cold surface cutting into her skin. What's happening? She watched as his finger tightened around hers, causing the gun to explode with heat and smoke. Her ears felt like they were bleeding, but she couldn't hear a sound. She looked up the length of the gun and saw the carnage the bullet had created. The body collapsing, red mist hanging in the air, and then the face, obscured by dark hair. Who was that? It should be Ransom, but it wasn't. She watched as the body continued its fall in exaggerated slow motion. The head hit the floorboard and bounced up, hair slipping off the face. Her own face. Suddenly, she was looking out of dead eyes at herself, holding a smoking gun.

Adi sat up, covered in cold sweat. *It wasn't real. You didn't kill yourself. It was Ransom. It was J.B. making you shoot Ransom. You're safe.* Sound slowly returned, the smell of blood and gun smoke finally fading. Her skin was cool and her head ached. She made her way to the bathroom and climbed into the shower in her undershirt and briefs. The water helped, but the dream lingered. She felt the tears building up before they fell. She gave in to her grief as she slid down the shower wall into a crumpled heap.

When the water turned tepid, she made herself get up and get dressed. It was almost time to head to the restaurant, and she didn't want to be late.

The place was already full of diners when she arrived. The staff entrance was in the alleyway behind the restaurant, but she had to negotiate the crowd on the sidewalk to get to it. One thing about this town, everybody was happy. The other kitchen staff gave her a lukewarm welcome, showed her where to toss her bag, and gave her space at the counter to help prep the dinner service. She chopped so many onions and celery she wondered what the special was, but noticed others preparing like amounts of all sorts of ingredients. The head chef was cantankerous, and she made sure to stay out of his way.

The first time she got near the cooktop was to reduce a beef stock. She happily took on the task, even though it caused some of the other workers to grumble. Apparently, there was a hierarchy she needed to learn. During her first break of the evening, one of the friendlier guys joined her in the alley.

"Hey, new girl," he said.

"Hey, yourself. I'm Sonny."

"Chris. So how's it going so far?"

"I'm not sure. You tell me," she said.

"Not bad. You could work a little slower, though."

"Really?"

"Yeah, you're making the rest of us look like lazy bums."

"I didn't mean to do that," she said.

"Of course you didn't. Just trying to impress the big guy. Look, Chef won't like you, no matter what you do. You work so hard trying to get his attention, and when you do, it's only so he can shoot you down. Trust me. Been there, done that."

"I'm not trying to get any attention. I'm just doing my job."

"Okay, if you say so. You chop faster than anyone I've ever seen," he said.

"I'm used to having to do it all pretty much on my own. I never had a kitchen full of folks to help," she said.

"Where'd you work before?"

Adi stopped. She couldn't just tell him about the Pot. "Just around."

"Yeah? Not around here, then. Take my advice and slow it down. Some of those guys will kick your butt for trying to brownnose," he said.

"Thanks. I will."

"Later." He walked off down the alley. She watched him go, wondering how many other things she needed to adjust in her cooking style to fit in. She'd get the hang of it before long. Adapting was something that she could handle. The rest of the night was uneventful.

She made a point of slowing down a bit, while still doing her best. The glares coming her way lessened, and she felt good about her first service. When she left for the day, Jake gave her a second T-shirt, this one white, and told her to arrive at eleven the following morning. She barely remembered showering again before her head hit the pillow.

Griffith was standing in front of her, a light sheen of sweat from the humid air coating her arms and face. Suddenly, she was wrapped in her arms and Griffith was stretching up to kiss her. The electric feeling racing through her as the kiss deepened, God. She'd never felt anything like this before. Don't stop. Please don't stop. She opened her lips slightly and felt Griffith's lip slide between hers, the soft swell of her tongue as Adi opened her mouth. The tightness as her nipples reacted to their connection. Wetness between her legs and tension in her abdomen. Don't stop.

Adi woke, aroused and confused. The kiss in the bamboo. She had felt that way, hadn't she? She hadn't wanted Griffith to stop kissing her. If only she had kept on kissing her and hadn't been asking questions Adi couldn't answer. If only she had stopped looking for the past and stayed with her in the present. Maybe, then, they could have been more.

CHAPTER TWENTY

G riffith watched the headlights illuminate the white strip along the highway. The miles were rolling by, but she still felt like they weren't moving fast enough. She felt caught in some kind of limbo between the darkness and the roadway. New Orleans was so close, but so far from where she wanted to be. If she could go back and change things, she would. She should have been there when Bertie died. She should have listened when Adi shut down about her past. If she knew then what was coming, she would have found a different path to the truth.

It mattered that Adi face her truth. It was keeping her from truly living, but Griffith hadn't looked for her truth to help her. At least, not at first. *And who the hell am I to force Adi to face that truth?* Griffith had forced her way into Adi's past to gain security for herself. Her reputation was her motivation, not her concern for Adi. What an ass she had been, and she was still far from the answer. She still had no real reason for her running away, although she had a far better idea of the possible terror that Adi had grown up with.

Her phone buzzed in her pocket, pulling her out of her head. When she looked at the screen, an email from the DEA popped up. She looked at T'Claude, but he seemed as lost in his thoughts as she had been a moment ago. She looked at the reply.

From: MHague@usdoj.gov
Re: Photo

Need more 411. Call secure (202) 370-1087
M

She should call him, but didn't want to do that in the car. She sent a reply that she would call as soon as possible. As soon as she hit send, her phone rang.

"McNaulty."

There was no sound on the line, and she wondered for a minute if maybe it hadn't rung after all. She looked at the screen and it showed an open connection.

Maybe it's Adi?

"Adi? Is that you?"

Nothing but silence. She disconnected.

"Was it her?" T'Claude asked.

"No. The call must have been disrupted. There wasn't anyone on the line." She tried to shake off the feeling something was seriously wrong.

"Weird. We should be there in about ten minutes. I'm going to head straight to the quarter. That's most likely where she'd have gone. We can find a couple of rooms once we're there."

"Okay."

They exited I-10 and drove into the French Quarter. The crowds of pedestrians and the narrow roads made going slow. *So many people.* It would be a challenge to find her here, if this was even where she headed. Griffith hated not having some proof that this was where she'd be, but it was the best option. T navigated through the streets until they hit Canal. He drove toward the river and the hotel zone.

"Look, I'm thinking the Hilton is a good option. They have parking and it's close to the trolley line. We can cover a lot of the area from there."

"That's fine with me."

Once they figured out the valet parking, they were able to get rooms without much trouble.

"Let's get freshened up, then meet at Spirits downstairs. We'll come up with a plan. Say in a half hour?" T'Claude said.

"Okay. I need to call a source, but that should be plenty of time."

"Yeah, I'll call my guys here and see if Adi turned up at any of their places."

Griffith opened her door and tossed her bag onto the bed. She kicked off her shoes and called Mike Hague at the number he'd given.

"Hey, Mike. It's Griffith McNaulty."

"What was the purpose of the picture, Griff? What's your angle?"

"No angle. I ran across J.B. Nerbass while I was doing a story about a runaway. He made all my little hairs stand up, so after our meeting, I followed him. That photo is the man he met."

"Seriously? You just 'happened' to meet with him? Come on, who do you think you're talking to? This is big and all kinds of ugly. You don't want to be standing anywhere near this guy when it all blows up."

"I'm not going to be anywhere near him. Like I said, our meeting was incidental. I just thought you'd want to know who he's talking to across the border."

"We know. We've been on this guy for the past eight months hoping he would slip up. We don't have anything concrete to pin him with. This meeting you observed was surveilled by the Mexican DEA and our operatives there. You want to stay out of the crossfire on this one."

"He has my number in connection with my story. I can't help it if he contacts me. What should I do to protect myself?"

"Damn. Can we put a tap on your line? That way we can filter his communication with you and see if it helps us trip him up."

"I don't know, Mike, that seems a little much. What are my safeguards?"

"You'll be kept strictly out of it. You're just a door, an opening to him on a different playing field. Come on, Griff. This is huge."

"And how will it work to my advantage to do this?"

"Okay, look. I'll talk to the coordinator and see what we can work out. It's possible I might be able to get you an exclusive on the takedown story. Would that work for you?"

"You get me that in writing and we'll talk."

Griffith heard him sigh into the phone. "You'll be hearing from me shortly," he said and hung up.

So the DEA knows Nerbass is dirty. That changed so much of the story. They would have evidence of his movements from the time he became a suspect. She would be able to give Adi that when she saw her, and maybe that would give her some piece of mind, knowing he was being watched. If his drug activity had anything to do with her running away, she could let go of that fear. Provided Griffith and T'Claude had any luck finding her.

She quickly washed her face and ran a brush through her hair. Not feeling very refreshed, she headed to the bar. Hopefully, T's connections had some good news for them.

He wasn't there yet, so she ordered a drink and waited. An email came in with a signed letter from the coordinator of Mike's team. She had her guarantee, if it was worth anything. She replied that she was willing to be snooped on and promised to call in later. Mike would take care of the details.

Will I even notice they're listening? Will there be some kind of tell? She doubted it. More than likely Mike had started monitoring her phone as soon as she sent him the picture. They didn't need her permission, not since nine-eleven. It was a farce for him to pretend they did, but she was happy to go along with it. At least it felt like she had some control.

"Sorry about that. It took longer than I thought." T'Claude looked as if he'd taken a shower. Griffith wished she'd taken the time.

"That's okay. Did you find out anything?"

"Some. My friend over at Tujague's said they have a new hire and Antoine's has three newbies. We just have to go check them out. We have to plan what we're going to do, though. If she spots us, you know she'll bolt again. Especially if she sees you. How're we going to play this?"

"Can you text a picture of her to your buddies? Then we'll know for sure if she's there?"

"That's a good idea. I'll do that."

He sent the photo and they waited for a response.

"It's her at Tujague's," he said when there was an almost immediate response.

Griffith felt a rush of relief knowing Adi was there. She would have a chance to talk to her if they did this the right way.

"So, we should probably find a place where we can watch for her. I think it's best if she doesn't know we're here until we know where she's staying. That way if we lose her, we know where to go."

"That feels shady to me. I've known her since she was a kid. I don't feel right spying on her."

"You said yourself that she'll bolt if she sees us. How can we keep that from happening? If we know where she's staying, we know where she might run," she said.

"But it's just wrong. I don't like it. I think we should just show up there after her shift and talk to her."

"It's risky," Griffith said.

"You stay back and spy on her then. If she runs from me, you can follow her," T'Claude said.

"I'd like it better if we knew ahead of time where she would go."

"Well, tough. That ain't happening. I won't do it."

"Okay, okay. We'll do it your way. Just don't blame me if we lose her."

"The hell I won't. I blame you for her not being at home where she belongs."

He's right. If not for me, Adi would be at home, but the potential of her past popping up wouldn't have gone away. But then, maybe her past wouldn't have ever caught up with her, if I hadn't come around at all. If I can help the DEA take him down, she'll be safe. What then? Will she even want to see me? The possibility of losing Adi altogether after this made her ache inside. Their worlds were different, their geography problematic, but she still wanted to know if there was a chance they could build something.

"Fine. Lead the way."

They walked from the hotel to the restaurant. It was less than a mile. The area was crowded with tourists. It would be a challenge to keep T'Claude in sight, much less watch for Adi. *We'll never be able to follow Adi in this crowd.* She was on foot and didn't know the city. Hopefully, Adi wouldn't run, but if she did, they were out of luck.

"I'm going to go in and talk to my buddy. You hang out by the right side of the building. The alley runs one way out to there. She'll have to come past you if she runs."

"I hope you know what you're doing," she said.

"Trust me."

He disappeared into the crowded dining room. Griffith walked to the right side of the place and leaned against the old brick wall. She could see the back area of the restaurant pretty clearly. She watched the door swing open and a guy in jeans and a T-shirt came out for a smoke.

How long do I watch? What if she comes out the front? She moved across the alley so she could watch both doors. Her view was obstructed from this angle, but it couldn't be helped.

After twenty minutes, Griffith stretched her back and wondered what to do next. Either they were wrong about Adi being there, or she had decided to talk to T'Claude. She'd just started to relax when the back door of the restaurant opened with a bang. Adi flew out the door and directly into her path. She braced herself for impact as she neared, but it never came. Adi skidded to a stop in front of her.

"What are you doing here? Why can't you just leave me alone? Isn't it enough that you destroyed my life? Go away."

"I can't. How could I know your life was so fragile that one word would send it over the edge? What's that about? I don't know everything, but I do know where you started. I know the man who pushed you to run, but I'm not him."

"You don't know anything. You just have to keep digging for your damn story. You don't care who you bury."

Griffith watched T'Claude approach from behind. He stopped and waited for their confrontation to end.

"You're wrong. So wrong. I stopped looking at your past for my story and started looking just so I could help you. I kept digging because I care, because living scared is no way to live, and I have the means to help. Okay, the man is damn dangerous. Why face that alone? Why let it continue when you have people who can make it stop? I want to know what has you so on edge that you run from everything you love. You sacrifice yourself out of fear. That's not living, that's surviving. You deserve to live."

"What do you know about surviving? You want to be the rescuer, the hero. You're nothing to me. You hear that? Nothing."

The words were like needles piercing her heart, but she wouldn't give up. "That's all I, or anyone else, can be to you. You can't have anything you value when you live your life in fear. That's what I know about surviving. And it's one thing if you count me as nothing, but obviously everyone you love is counted as nothing when you drop them and run like you did."

"Stop. You're wrong. Just stop."

"Why? Is the truth so painful you can't even hear it? Oh, wait, that's right, you run from the truth."

"Damn you, Griffith. Stop."

"Adi, the truth is you ran from something in your life when you were just a kid. You left behind everything and everyone you ever knew, and probably for damn good reasons. Now you want to do it again, but this time it's different. This time those you leave behind won't be left, and you're an adult, not a kid. We can keep trying to find you, and we're not heartless and indifferent to your pain. This is your new truth. Get used to it. We care. We love you. T'Claude loves you. Bertie loved you. I love you. Can you get that through your head? Break through those walls and let it sit in your heart? We love you. You're not alone, and we can help."

Griffith watched as the words affected Adi. She seemed to pull herself in and started to slip down the alley wall. Griffith reached out and caught her, pulling her into her embrace. T'Claude came from behind and wrapped his arms around them both.

"She's right, Adi. We aren't going to let you run away from our lives. If you want to leave us, you're going to have to tell us to our faces. I, for one, won't settle for a kiss-off. You are going to have me in your life for as long as forever. The distance between us might be big, but we're always going to be family," he said.

Adi didn't respond with words, but she held them both as though to keep from drowning, and Griffith took that as a good sign. It didn't matter anyway; she wasn't going anywhere until this was truly over, and then, only if Adi said there was truly nothing between them.

"Come on. Let's get out of here," T'Claude said. He led them out of the narrow alley and into the mass of moving bodies that was the French Quarter. They walked down Dumaine, with Adi sandwiched between them. When they reached Bourbon Street, they turned and walked to Lafitte's Blacksmith Shop.

It was dark, only candles lighting the place. They sat at a table away from the piano so they could talk without interruption. Griffith ordered a bottle of wine, figuring they could all use some. Adi was quiet, and the look of fear was gone, but she seemed deflated.

"Adi, you know I love you, kid. You have to tell us once and for all what it is in your past that has you so messed up. We can't help you if you don't share with us," T'Claude said.

Adi looked from one to the other of them, her lips quivering and her eyes bright with unshed tears. Still, she remained silent.

"We aren't going to let this go. You have to tell us," Griffith said.

The waitress arrived with the wine and poured for the table. Adi grabbed her glass and drained it in one gulp.

"That's no way to treat a good wine," T said, "You didn't even taste it. Slow down."

Griffith poured her a second glass. *Maybe she needs the courage this will give her. Anything that helps.* "Please tell us, Adi," she said.

Finally she spoke, her voice a child's whisper. "I...it's hard."

"Okay, take it as slow as you need to, but just talk to us," Griffith said.

"I was eleven when it all started. He...J.B., he made me do it. I didn't know what he was doing. I didn't mean it."

"What? What did he make you do?" Griffith asked.

"Kill Ransom. I didn't mean to, T. I didn't, I swear."

"Kill Ransom? You mean he made you kill someone?" T'Claude said.

"He put the gun in my hand. He squeezed it, his finger over mine..."

"That's not your fault. He forced you, Adi. You aren't to blame," said Griffith.

"I'll force him, that bastard. How could he do that to you? You were just a kid," he said. "How do you know he was even dead? This Ransom guy?"

"He had to be. There was so much blood."

"Blood don't mean much. We got a ton of blood in us, kid. How do you know he was dead? Did this J.B. call an ambulance? Did someone tell you he was gone?" he said.

"No, I mean, I don't know. There was no ambulance. J.B. took him off in his skiff, said he was going to dump him in the marsh. I don't know where he took him. He just gave me bleach and told me to clean the place up."

"So there's no proof this Ransom was dead. It's possible he took him somewhere for help. But why? Why did he make you shoot this man?" Griffith said.

"The business. That's why. He told me Ransom was trying to cheat him. He said he was proud of me for taking him out. It made me sick."

"What business, kid?" T'Claude asked.

"Drugs. Drug trafficking, I think, but I don't know for sure. He showed me a baggie of this crystal stuff and told me all we had to do was get it from the shrimpers and pass it on through the shop. I never wanted to know more. It was evil."

"You said you were eleven when this happened, but you didn't leave until you were fourteen Why?" Griffith said.

"I couldn't. I didn't know how. From the minute that gun went off, all I could think about was running away. I tried to run that night, but the sheriff found me and brought me home after a couple of hours. J.B. watched me all the time after that. And then...then he made me go out with him all the time. To the marshes, to dump bodies. And I had to wash down the room every time he put a beating on someone. Life became...hell. The deepest, darkest hell. And I knew it wouldn't be long before he took me out to the marshes and left me there too. It took years to be sure I could get away and he wouldn't find me."

"None of this is your fault. You don't have anything to be afraid of, Adi," Griffith said.

"You can't know that. You don't know him. He won't stop if he finds out where I am. That's why I had to run. He will destroy everything I love, to make sure I don't tell what I know. And I was an accessory, wasn't I? That means jail time, right?"

"We won't let him get to you," T'Claude said.

"No, we won't," Griffith said.

Adi looked at T'Claude, then at her. She finally let go of the tears she had been holding back. Griffith wasn't sure if they were from fear, relief, or just anxiety, but she was glad to see Adi let them go.

She moved closer and put an arm around her. T did the same from the opposite side. Griffith did all she could to send comfort to Adi, hoping the strength of her feelings were coming through the gentle hug. *You mean so much to me. Feel me; know that I'm here for you. Let me prove you can trust me. Please.*

Adi wiped the tears from her face, and for the first time in such a long time, Griffith saw her beautiful smile. It was like the sun coming from behind a cloud and it warmed every inch of her.

"Let's get out of here. I bet you haven't had a good night's sleep since Bertie," she said.

Adi nodded. They headed back to the Hilton, and T'Claude walked them to Griffith's door.

"Okay now, you get some sleep. I'm just across the hall if this one won't stop nagging ya," he said.

"Okay, T," Adi said.

"Seriously, don't even think about leaving. I mean it."

"I won't," she said.

Griffith opened the door and they went into the darkened room. Adi was at her side, and she was determined not to let that change.

Chapter Twenty-one

A di stopped just inside the room and stared at the king-sized bed. *Now what? This is awkward.*

"You go get freshened up. I have a T-shirt you can use to sleep in. I'll sleep on the couch," Griffith said. "Here."

She tossed an oversized shirt to her. It was green with a Victorian styled man and woman on it and the slogan, "Absinthe, double the vision, double the fun."

"This is an awesome shirt," she said.

"Yeah, I thought so. It should work as a night shirt, huh?"

Adi kicked off her shoes. "Sure. I'll be out in a second."

When the latch clicked on the bathroom door, it was like all the wind went out of her. *I don't know how to feel. I'm hollow.* She stared at her reflection in the mirror. *Who are you? How are you supposed to move forward? Why can't you feel anything?* The longer she looked, the angrier with herself she became. *You are nothing. You have no anchor. You're just going to drift away. Those people out there, they could die because of you.* She grabbed a bottle from the counter and threw it at the mirror as hard as she could. The plastic top popped and lotion splattered across the clean surface.

"Adi? You okay in there?"

She watched the slow ooze of the cream down the mirrored glass. *That lotion feels more than you do.*

The door handle rattled and a hurried knock sounded. "Open the door. You're scaring me."

Adi looked at the door handle. She watched her hand move to unlock it, though she didn't understand how that was happening. She didn't feel connected to its movement. Then Griffith was there. She was holding her shoulders, saying something. *I can't hear you. What are you saying? Why are you here?*

Suddenly the hard, cold surface of the tub rim was under her. *Am I falling? No, not falling.* Griffith had pushed her down to sit. She was kneeling in front of her, holding her and talking.

Her words were starting to make sense. *Focus. She's talking to you.*

"Adi? Can you hear me? Are you okay? I'm going to call for help. Just hang on," she said.

"No, no. I'm okay. Don't leave me. Please," she said.

"I'm not going to leave you. I'm just worried about you."

"I'm okay. Would you hold me?"

Adi felt, really felt, Griffith's arms come around her. The empty hollowness drained away as warmth filled her. Griffith helped her up and out to the bedroom. She sat on the edge of the bed, but Griffith didn't stop. She climbed onto the surface of the bed and drew Adi down beside her.

"I will always hold you. Always." She wrapped both arms around her and did just that.

It felt so real, so good, being held this way. Adi was swept away by emotion and felt tears again on her cheeks. *These are different. These are healthy tears.* She let them flow, down her cheek, onto her neck and into her mouth. The tang of salt woke up her taste buds, letting her know she was alive. This was real.

Griffith moved her hand, light and tender, wiping away the tears, but said nothing, letting Adi feel. Her hand moved to her hair, gently running through the strands. *God. That feels so good. That feels like heaven. Like I matter.* She knew instinctively that this was what she needed. Nothing more, nothing less. Just this moment, right here with Griffith. With the soothing play of Griffith's fingers through her hair, she let herself fall asleep.

Burning, something was on fire. The heat was centered on her hand and the gun she held. "You done a good thing here. She was worthless and had to go. I'm proud of you, baby. Nobody cheats a Nerbass and lives to tell about it. Right?" Her? What? Not Ransom. Griffith! Her blood-soaked body a crumpled heap at her feet. She had to stop the bleeding. Save her. A hand gripped hers, pulling Adi away from her. Stop. I have to help her. She struggled against the grip, desperate to break away. "Adi, come on, it's okay. Wake up..."

"Wake up. You're safe."

The panic melted away as Adi realized it had been a dream. She was lying beside Griffith in the hotel room. "Griffith," she said. She frantically ran her hands up and down Griffith's body, looking for injury.

"Hey, everything is fine. You were just dreaming."

"I shot you. He made me shoot you."

"I'm fine. It's okay. No one shot me. He can't make you do anything anymore."

Adi pulled Griffith against her, the scent of jasmine replacing the smell of the gun smoke. The soft pressure of her breasts against her replacing the heavy feel of the gun. She needed her. Had to have her and the reality of Griffith removing the nightmare of her past. She kissed her then, hard. Almost too hard. Griffith pushed against her.

"Wait. Slow down."

In response, she kissed her again, but this time slower and with less urgency. It was like a slow wave of heat, like the sun warming her skin after a swim. It grew and grew, until it had a life of its own. And Griffith was kissing her back, her heat entwining with Adi's, becoming one entity.

And then the heat was overwhelming and Adi had to get out of the confining clothes that trapped it and kept it burning against her. And Griffith was stripping too. And her skin was like the softest silk against her fevered flesh. The press of her body ignited a different heat, deeper. And then Griffith's hand was against her, between her legs and moving, sliding through her wetness, inside her. Filling her. And she was crying out, breaking, gone. But Griffith was with her, catching her, cradling her, and bringing her back to earth and holding her, always holding her.

❖

The persistent buzzing of a cell phone woke her some time later. Griffith rolled away and grabbed it. Half asleep, Adi watched her scroll through an email. When Griffith rose from the bed and moved to a chair, she forced herself to awareness.

"What is it?" she asked.

Griffith smiled and walked back to her. She leaned down and kissed her, and the brush of her nipples against Adi's caused a rush of heat. "Mmmm. That's nice. Thank you."

"For what?"

"For, you know, for what we shared."

The smile turned into a grin and Griffith poked her ribs teasingly. "You mean for the sex? Huh? Is that what you mean?"

Adi knew she was bright red with embarrassment. "Yeah. That."

"No reason to thank me. You started that. I should thank you," Griffith said.

"You know what I'm trying to say."

"Yeah. I do. It was pretty amazing."

"Yeah?" Adi said. She wanted to hear it, to know it had been special for Griffith too. She wanted desperately to know she wasn't alone. In this, or anything else.

"Umm-hmm."

"Think we could do that again sometime?"

"I'm sure we can work something out."

Adi kissed her then, the wondrous softness of her lips captivated her. *I could kiss you forever. I'd never get tired of your lips. They are the softest thing I've ever felt.* When she moved away from Griffith, she had a pensive expression on her face.

"What is it? Why so serious?"

"That email? It was a friend of mine in the DEA. He wants me to meet with him in an hour," she said.

"It's the middle of the night, isn't it?"

"Not really. It's five thirty. I need to go see him. Would you come with me?"

"Why? What's this about?" Adi said.

"It's a long story, and I'm afraid it's going to upset you, but I think you need to know about it."

"Then tell me."

"I really don't want to talk about it until we're with my friend, if that's okay. He has more facts than I do. Can you trust me on this? I know it's asking a lot, but this is important."

Adi considered what Griffith was asking. *This has to be about J.B. What else could the DEA and Griffith have going on that would upset me? Am I ready for this?*

"Is T'Claude coming?"

"Not this time. Just us. Contacts don't like a bunch of people showing up," she said.

"You're asking me to trust you, and right now that's hard. I trusted you to listen when I asked you not to dig into my past. You didn't. I'm sure you had your reasons, but the danger you put me in, put us all in... You don't even know."

"You're right. I didn't listen, and I broke your trust. I'm so sorry I did that. I was thinking about the consequences to me and not about you, and that was not only wrong, but selfish. I hope you'll forgive me."

"I'm trying, but asking me to trust you without giving me any information is really hard to swallow. I want to, but how can I?"

"It's different now. I'm not chasing a story and I'm not thinking about how this can help me. All I'm thinking about now is you. Mike can help you, and that's all I care about. Later, if I can write about it without hurting you, then maybe I will. But I'll talk to you about it first. I love you, Adi. I love you so much."

Adi wanted to say it back, to tell Griffith she loved her too, but she was so mixed up right now. The best she could do was to trust her again and hope it wasn't misplaced this time. "Okay. Where are we meeting him?" She saw the slight disappointment in Griff's eyes and knew it was because she couldn't say the words yet. But she wouldn't, not until she was really sure.

"At the local DEA office. It's in Metairie, so we need to take a cab."

"We have to tell T where we're going. He'll be crazy with worry if we just disappear," she said.

"Yeah, of course. Let's shower, then we can call him. It's awfully early."

"A shower sounds great. Um. You first?"

"How about we take one together? There's plenty of room," Griffith said with a wicked grin.

"Okay." For some reason Adi was incredibly nervous. *Get it together. It's not like you're strangers or something. You just spent the night wrapped in her arms, naked. Come on, grow a pair.* She hurried into the bathroom and adjusted the water. Griffith walked up behind her and ran a hand up her back.

"It's okay, you know. I promise not to bite."

"I'm such a wuss...I'm sorry."

"No, you're not. This is all just new to you. Relax, it's all okay. Just enjoy it as it happens. Don't overthink it."

Adi turned and opened her arms. Griffith slid into them and kissed her, lightly at first, and then with more passion. She backed away and stepped into the spray of the shower, holding out her hand. Adi let herself be led under the warm water.

The press of Griffith against her back was sensual and erotic at the same time. She felt little jolts of pleasure ripple through her. And then Griffith was soaping her hair and her body. The wet slip of her breasts across Adi's back was making her crazy. And then she ran her palms over Adi's breasts, and the sensation of her nipples tightening made her moan. She felt Griffith gently pull on their tips and twist them slightly. It was too much. She turned and captured Griffith's lips, then ran her own hands down Griff's firm backside and cupped her cheeks.

Then she lifted her, sliding her wet center down the hardness of her flexed thigh. Griffith threw her head back and moaned, giving Adi perfect access to her flawless neck. She kissed the perfect skin and pulled gently at it with her lips, careful not to leave a mark. She lifted her again and repeated the motion against her hard muscle, her own body reacting as Griffith moaned again.

"God, Adi. Take me. Please. I need to feel you inside me."

She leaned Griffith against the wall of the shower and slipped a hand between Griffith's legs. She tenderly parted the folds of flesh with her hand and slipped one finger into the slick warmth.

"More."

A second finger followed, and she began to thrust into her. She pushed her thumb across Griffith's rigid clitoris as she moved into her, and Griffith cried out in pleasure. Her moans came in time with Adi's thrusts and then the crest as euphoria met rapture and she fell against Adi, completely spent. Adi's heart felt like it could burst. She felt so completely powerful in this moment, with Griff helpless in her arms. *This is trust. This is what I need to have from you, and give to you. To be this open and vulnerable with you. I love you, Griffith.*

Adi held her until she recovered, treasuring the experience, and then they finished their shower in earnest. When they were dressed, Adi called T'Claude to let him know where they were going. He wasn't happy about being left behind, but understood the necessity. They promised to phone when they were on their way back to the hotel.

The cab ride to Metairie seemed to take forever as Adi considered all the possibilities of what was about to happen. The glass tower that housed the DEA office was imposing and daunting. She didn't have much experience with high-rises. In fact, the hotel was her first. This building made her feel small and vulnerable.

"Are you sure this is the place? It's so huge," she said.

"This is it. Come on. They aren't nearly as big and scary as they look from the outside, when you're inside. The office is on the eighteenth floor."

The feeling of heaviness that hit as the elevator ascended shook Adi. She glanced at Griffith, who seemed undisturbed. *Must be normal. I wonder how it will feel going down?* Once again, she was reminded of the different worlds they inhabited. She didn't want to think about where they'd go when this was over. When they entered the office they were met by a man in a suit.

"How may I help you?" he asked.

"We're here for a meeting with Mike Hague."

"Okay, give me a second to verify." He looked at his computer for a few seconds. "Ms. McNaulty? I'll need to see your identification, please. And yours as well, ma'am."

They handed him their licenses and waited. He scanned them into his system and handed them back.

"Right this way."

They followed him into a good-sized conference room, and Adi's anxiety rose another notch.

"He should be with you in a minute. Can I get you some coffee or something else to drink?"

Griffith looked at Adi, who shook her head. "No, thank you," she said.

The chairs at the long table were comfortable, and they didn't have long to wait. The door soon opened, and a large, bearish man entered.

"Griffith, Ms. Bergeron, hello. I'm Mike Hague."

"Mike. Good to see you again."

"Likewise. Ms. Bergeron? I didn't expect you this morning, but I'm glad you decided to come. Thank you."

"It's Adi. And you're welcome."

"I don't know if Griffith spoke to you about our current case. We've been following the movements of J.B. Nerbass for the past eight and a half months. I understand you're familiar with him?"

Adi shivered. "Yes. He's my stepfather."

"That's what Griffith said. You do know the nature of his work, right?"

"You mean his drug trafficking? Yes."

"Good. We've built a scenario and I'd like to run it by you. Is that okay?"

Adi looked at Griffith, but she wouldn't meet her eye. *What's up with that? Why is she not being upfront with me? She said I could trust her.*

"Okay...I guess that's fine."

"Good. Griff wasn't sure you'd be willing to help us, but we have to ask."

"Wait. How am I going to help you? What are you talking about? I thought I was just giving you some information or something?"

"It's like this, Ms. Bergeron...Adi. We need a way to get your father to say something that incriminates him and ties this thing up nice and tidy. I think you're our solution. We want you to confront him and get us the kind of information we can use to put him away for good."

Adi felt her blood turn cold. *Confront him? I don't ever want to see him again. I spent my life hiding from him. What exactly are they expecting?*

"Don't worry. You won't be in any danger," he said.

"How can you know that? You've no idea what you're talking about. I can't do this," she said. She started to get up, feeling the need to run.

"Hold on. Let Mike tell you what he has in mind. If you can't do it, you won't, but hear him out," Griffith said. She placed her hand over Adi's and said, "Please, Adi. It might be the only way you get your life back."

Adi sat back down and turned her hand over so Griff could slide hers into it. "Go on."

"It's really fairly simple. You arrange to meet with him in a location of your choosing. We'll have all possible routes to and from watched. You'll be perfectly safe. All you have to do is engage him in a conversation about his business. He's been looking for you for a long time. I'm sure he'll be happy to see you."

"He won't. He knows how much I hate him. How much I hate what his drugs do to people. He won't believe a word of it."

"Why is he still looking for you, then?" he said.

"Trust me, it's not for a reunion. He wants me dead. Looking for me is his safeguard against my surfacing and sharing what I know."

"What do you know?"

"I…it's complicated."

"Try me. I'm pretty good at figuring things out," he said.

Adi looked from Mike to Griffith. Sweat ran down the line of her back, and she felt nauseous. Griffith gently squeezed her hand, lending her strength.

"It's okay. You can trust him," she said.

"Anything you tell me is just between us at this point. If it is something that incriminates Nerbass and we can use it, that might change, but you don't have to worry, regardless. You're completely safe here. As far as the DEA is concerned, you're an informant. I can guarantee you won't be charged with anything by us."

Adi felt Griffith slide her arm around her shoulders. She leaned into her, wishing this wasn't happening. Griff was right, Adi wanted a real life, and she knew J.B. had to be stopped, had to pay for his crimes, but she didn't want to have anything to do with him. Not confronting him meant running again, and this time she would be running from those who loved her. She'd spent the past eight years afraid. *No more.* It was time to stand up to him. She took a deep breath and willed the tension out of her body. Her voice caught as she started to speak, but she made herself keep going.

"When I was eleven, he made me shoot a man. I didn't know what he was going to do, and I couldn't stop him. I would never have pulled the trigger if I had a choice; he put his finger over mine and forced it. It was the worst thing I've ever experienced. And then—"

"What man? Did you know his name?"

"Yes. Ransom Prejean, our neighbor."

"Good. Let's stop and do this properly. We need this on the record to be able to use it against him. Come with me, please."

He led them to an interview room and asked them to wait. Adi felt her stomach cramping. *What I wouldn't give for a Coke right now. Why am I talking about this?* She looked at the door, wondering if he'd locked it behind him.

"It's okay, you know. You aren't in any trouble, I promise," Griffith said.

"How can you know that? They could arrest me. I just told him I killed a man."

"Seriously? You were forced to pull the trigger. And the other stuff? You were a child, forced to do what you did by a parent—again, not your fault. Even if they did press charges against you, there's no way you'd be convicted. What's the worst thing that could happen?" she said.

"I could end up in a jail cell."

"Okay. Let's look at that. If, which isn't going to happen, you are arrested, then what?"

"I don't know."

Griff took a deep breath and nodded. "Here it is, Adi, the big scary truth. If you are arrested, they bring you before a judge for arraignment. You make your plea and we get you bonded out. Worst-case scenario, you spend a night in lockup. The hardest part is over. You've finally opened up about J.B. and the things he made you do. Everything from here on means dealing with your past head on, instead of letting fear keep you from living. And that's better than spending your life running."

How could you possibly know that? There's nothing easy about any of this. I want to believe you, but I can't.

She dropped into the hard-backed chair and waited with building dread. When Mike returned he had a second officer with him to take notes. It wasn't an easy thing at all, but she got through her memory of the day Ransom died. They asked her about the years after, and she told them about all of it. The beatings, the bodies, the oil rig and the man there. She told them about the way J.B. arranged to ship his drugs and how he recorded the transactions. The questions they asked were reasonable, and she was surprised when she actually did feel the tension start to fall away.

"Okay, I think we're done for now. How are you holding up?" he asked.

"I'm okay. So, are you going to arrest me?" she asked.

"No. Firstly, we have no evidence that this occurred other than your story. We have to investigate the crime and see if there's any evidence that can tie up Mr. Nerbass. Giddings, here, will coordinate the search for Ransom and the others. Second, I'm going to ask you to play a bigger role, and that makes you an informant. I'll see to it that you're not implicated in this due to your cooperation with our investigation. We have to have something concrete to stop your stepfather. Your information will help, but it's not enough," he said.

"What else can I do?"

"I propose that we go through with the original idea," he said.

"But—" she said.

"Hear me out. We're much more likely to get him on this charge if you can get him to talk about it with you. He won't be able to stay away if you tell him you want to meet. We'll bait the hook just enough so he'll want to hear you out."

"But what's to keep him from just walking up to me and killing me? That's what he wants. He's used to having his way."

"That won't happen. There is a risk, but we'll minimize it. You don't have to worry. It's our job to protect you, and we're good at it."

Adi wasn't convinced, but the pinprick of light in her soul was enough to make her willing to try. They would set everything up and this thing with J.B. would be over. *One way or another.*

"Right. No time like the present."

From there, everything started happening so fast, Adi barely had time to register it all. They made detailed plans and explained everything. Other officers came and went, and the entire situation started to feel surreal. If it weren't for Griff's constant, calming presence, Adi would have bolted and disappeared into the bayou somewhere. Instead, she sat there, getting ready to face her demon.

The next challenge was to bait J.B. into a meeting they could monitor and control. This was where Griffith came in. Once they had the equipment set up, she called him and admitted to giving him false information.

"I knew you lied to me. What is your angle, McNaulty?"

"It's about your daughter, Mr. Nerbass. She wasn't ready to meet with you, but now she is."

"Oh, come on. You expect me to believe this shit? What do you take me for?"

"I'm telling you the truth. Your daughter, Merley, is here right now. Do you want to talk to her?"

"You better not be playing me this time. I'm not a forgiving man."

Griffith handed the receiver to Adi. Her hand shook as she put it to her ear.

"Papa? It's me."

There was silence on the line. For a minute, Adi thought he'd disconnected, but the agent signaled that the line was open.

"Papa? It's Merley."

"Where are you? Where have you been? I'd given up on ever finding you."

"I'm here. In New Orleans. I want to see you, Papa."

"Come to me, baby. Come to Morgan City and I'll take care of you."

"I can't do that. My life is here. If you want to see me, I'll be in Jackson Square tomorrow at ten thirty in the morning. If you don't show up, I'll know disappearing was the right thing."

"I'll be there. Don't you worry, I won't let you down."

"Okay." She disconnected the call.

"Good work. We'll have everything in place well before sunup tomorrow. You just come in and get wired, and we'll handle all the rest. Thank you for doing this," Mike said.

Adi felt like someone had thrown a blanket around her. She could see and hear what was going on, but she was detached, emotionless. *He's coming. Tomorrow.* She should be terrified, but strangely, she felt nothing.

❖

Griffith followed Adi out of the building to the waiting cab. The flash chill of the air conditioning hit and she shivered. The weighted humid air and heat of New Orleans corrected by frigid artificial temperature changes shocked her every time, just like it did in LA. She gave the cabbie their destination and sat back, watching Adi.

She'd been quiet since the meeting with Mike, even more so after the conversation with her stepfather. Griffith gave her the space she needed to digest what they had talked about, and to deal with the coming confrontation. She would wait as long as Adi needed her to. When she was ready, she would talk. Until then it was her job to be supportive. *I'm finally learning.*

The journalist in her was chomping at the bit to start writing this story. But J.B. Nerbass had caused so much damage to her soul, and Griff wouldn't make the mistake of jumping the gun and getting shut out of the healing process. She would be patient, and if supporting Adi meant losing the story, so be it.

"Why didn't you tell me what they were planning?" Adi said.

"I'm sorry, but I really didn't know what they had in mind. I knew Mike wanted to talk to you, but not that he wanted you to be involved. He never told me that."

"I'm glad you didn't know. I was worried you'd lied to me, to get me in there. But it's true. I need to finish this, to be free of J.B. and his world. I'm tired of being afraid."

"I promise I didn't lie to you, and I'm glad you're ready to move forward."

"It's weird. I should be frightened by what's ahead, but I'm not. Oh, I was at first, but now, I'm just numb. I think about what I'm going to do and expect the cramping stomach and the fear to knock me over, like it usually does, but it doesn't come. What's wrong with me, Griffith?"

"Nothing's wrong with you. You've let go of the fear, now that you see a solution ahead. You're waiting. Numb is okay, for now."

"Will you be there? Tomorrow, when I meet him? Would you be with me, please?"

Griffith wrapped her arm around Adi and gently hugged her. "Of course I will, although I don't know if they'll let me be right beside you. But I'm here and I'm not leaving. I'll be with you every step of the way."

"Thank you." Adi leaned into her, her head resting on Griffith's shoulder.

I'm here for you, Adi. I'll be here as long as you allow me to be. Griff had been a journalist long enough to know things could go wrong. And that dealing with people this dangerous had a list of potential outcomes less than optimal. But sometimes, it was necessary to get the bad guy. *Please don't let anything happen to her.* She closed her eyes and pulled Adi closer.

❖

T'Claude met them at the curb and slid into the front seat. He directed the cabbie to a place he knew in the Garden District for lunch. When they were seated, he grilled them about the morning.

"I can't tell you, T. We have to protect the integrity of the operation," Griffith said.

"Come on, you can trust me. I'm not going to do anything that puts Adi in danger."

"I know you wouldn't, but she's in danger and the way we keep her safe is to keep quiet and let the professionals handle things."

"What kind of danger?" He looked at Adi. "What are they making you do, kid?"

"What I have to do to be free of all this, T," she said.

T'Claude sighed and looked at the ceiling, his hands wrapped tightly around his glass.

"I know what you're feeling right now, T. It's hard to feel helpless to protect those you love. You're going to have to trust that these guys will keep her safe," Griff said.

"I'm not okay with that."

"You haven't got a choice, T. This will all be over with by tomorrow, and then Adi will be free."

"I don't like this one bit. You sure you want to do this?" He looked at Adi, who avoided eye contact.

"It's not a choice. It's what I need to do to be free of him forever. I want my life, T. I don't want to run anymore. Bertie…you know, what she said in her letter? It's true. I'm stuck, and I'm tired of being stuck," she said.

"I'm on your side, always. If this is how it is, then I have to accept it. You know you can count on me, right?"

"Of course I do, T. And the moment it's all over, I'll call to let you know. Thank you for coming after me."

Adi tried to relax and enjoy the beautiful meal, but the looming events made even the best food tasteless and unappealing. The waiting was the hardest thing. She willed the day to pass and the new one to dawn. She wanted resolution, needed it. J.B. had always been her personal nightmare, and she wanted him out of her life. She looked at Griffith and T'Claude. They were bantering about the food and trying to distract her.

I'm so lucky to have you both in my corner. I hope this ends the way I want it to. If not, I hope you'll lean on each other.

"What do you say, Adi?" T said.

"Huh?"

"I asked if you and Griffith want to go see some sights, get a feel for the place. Sound good?"

"Yeah, that does sound good. I need to be distracted. Thanks."

They left the restaurant and joined a walking tour across the street. They followed that with a carriage tour, and then a trip down river on the *Creole Princess*, a paddle wheeler. The day waned into night and they wound up back in the city.

Adi stopped to check out of her old place. She needed to do something about the apartment, but that could wait a while. She had also called Tujague's and let them know she wouldn't be returning for now. Maybe when this was all finished, she would stay in New Orleans for a time. It was nice to know she had options. *And then there's Griff, and whatever happens with that.*

She considered booking her own room, but Griffith urged her not to. They would all check out after tomorrow to head back to New Iberia, and it wasn't an issue for her to stay with her. When the door to their room clicked shut, Griffith made it clear that this was exactly where she wanted her to be as she led them straight to the bed.

The feel of Griffith against her, the clean fresh smell of her, intoxicated Adi. This was the place she wanted to call home. Here, in Griffith's arms. When their lips met, it was with the familiarity of a lover's kiss and the tenderness of the known. *If kissing you were the only thing left in my life, it would be full and happy. In you, I feel whole.*

"Would you hold me tonight? I want to feel you around me until I wake tomorrow."

"I will, indeed. Nothing would make me happier."

They slipped out of their clothes and lay on the big comfy bed. Griffith turned into Adi's back and held her, and Adi felt the strength of their connection as she drifted into sleep. The morning would be punctuated by fear and tension, but the night would be golden. She eased into the world of dreams.

❖

The filtered light through the partially open curtains announced a morning come too soon. It would all be over by the day's end. She would have to confront her past and overcome her fear. Today would mark the beginning of her forever. If all went as she hoped, she would walk away free and with Griffith still beside her.

So much rode on the actions of others, though. If the DEA did as they said they would, she would be safe and free. If they failed her, she would be dead. But she wasn't afraid of death anymore. Stopping J.B. was more important than worrying about her own life.

Griffith stirred behind her, and the sounds she made while waking touched Adi like nothing she'd ever imagined. She rolled toward her and kissed her sleepy face.

"Good morning," she said.

Griffith stretched like a cat, long, languid movements of her arms and legs followed by an amazingly drawn-out yawn. She opened one eye and regarded Adi.

"Morning. How are you so awake?"

"Just lucky, I guess. Well, that and I have a few things going on today."

Suddenly, Griffith was wide-awake. She sat up, dislodging the comforter.

"That's right. We have to be at the DEA by nine. We better get moving."

They showered and met T'Claude in the restaurant for breakfast. He was going to drive them to the office and stay as long as he could. They weren't sure how Mike would feel about his being there, but Adi was glad to have him along. She felt anchored with T and Griffith beside her.

Once at the office, the officers explained the body wire she would be wearing. It was concealed in the buckle of a belt. She just needed to flip a discreet switch in the buckle mechanism to turn the microphone on. The broadcast range was one hundred and fifty feet. She wouldn't have to worry about him finding any wires or attachments where they shouldn't be.

The weight of the belt felt normal, and it was actually something she would wear, so that eased her nerves a bit. T would stay at the office, but Griffith would accompany her to the square. She would serve as the go-between with J.B. When Mike explained this, Adi protested, not wanting her in danger, but he overruled her, saying there was strength in numbers, and given the amount of years elapsed, he might not recognize her. Griffith was fine with the situation. He pulled out a schematic of the square and showed her where all his people would be.

As they drove across town to the square, Adi felt like her insides were turning to water. *This is too risky. Griffith could be hurt, or worse. What have I done? He's going to kill us. We're dead. Why did I think this was possible?*

Her heart raced and her palms started to sweat. "I'm going to throw up. Stop the car."

She jumped out of the car and ran to the bushes, and Griffith was right behind her, rubbing soothing circles on her back as she lost her morning coffee.

"Stop thinking the worst, Adi," she said, "You have to do this. You can't let him control you anymore. Think of Bertie, what she wanted for you. You can do this. I know you can."

Adi collapsed against a wrought iron fence, her stomach heaving. Griffith continued to gently rub her back.

"It's going to be okay, I promise."

Swiping a hand across her mouth, Adi nodded. The driver was standing beside the car waiting for them. *Get it together. You can do this.* Adi pictured Bertie, her smile wide, sitting on the porch. Her words came back to her then. *"You all have things to do in that world. That's why you're there. Be sure and do them. Don't be stuck. Let life take a hold of you and fly free."*

But this time there was more to her message, and she heard Bertie's voice loud in her head. *"This is your time, Dink. Don't you let that man stop you. You're meant to stop him. Get yourself moving, girl."*

She stumbled forward and climbed back into the car.

"Let's go," she said.

The square had a smattering of early morning tourists admiring the cathedral. Griffith leaned casually against the iron rail surrounding Colonel Jackson, but Adi couldn't be still. She walked back and forth, dreading the coming reunion. J.B. would have his people with him; she knew that. When she had last seen him, he was small potatoes, but now, he was huge. He wouldn't come unprepared. She tried her best not to stare at the assorted agents around the square. She knew there were two agents on rooftops with sniper positions, in case things went really wrong.

"What time is it?" she asked.

"It's five minutes past the last time you asked me. Try to calm down. Worrying won't make this any easier. He should be here in the next ten minutes," Griffith said.

As she was about to respond, Griffith's phone rang.

"It's him," she said, "Hello?"

"McNaulty. I decided it would be nice to have a coffee while we meet. Why don't you and Merley walk on over here to Café du Monde?"

"That's not what we agreed to. Merley isn't comfortable being in an enclosed space with you yet."

"Let me talk to her."

"Hold on," she said. "He wants to talk to you. He wants us to walk over to the café."

"If he wants to see me, he can come to the statue as we agreed."

Griffith conveyed the message.

"I'm afraid I can't do that. Too exposed. I'm here, if she changes her mind."

She shook her head to let Adi know the situation and went back to the call. "I'll talk to her. Give me ten minutes."

"Clock's ticking."

Mike's voice came through the earpiece Adi was wearing in her sunglasses.

"Do not comply. We can abort the whole operation. Repeat, do not comply."

Adi took the shades off to halt the shouted commands.

"We can't go in there. You'd be unprotected," Griffith said.

"I want this over. He needs to pay for what he's done. Isn't that place full of tourists? Won't we be okay?"

"There's no guarantee, and Mike can't protect us in there. I say we wait him out. If he refuses to come to us, we call it off. It's a game of chicken, and we don't want to duck first."

"But I need this finished. I need to be free of him." The microphone in her sunglasses started making noise again, and she put them back on so she could hear.

"New parameters. Café street entrance covered. Agents in place inside. Suggest a meet at outer edge of patio. We lose snipers, but target covered."

"I don't like this," Griffith said.

"Just call him."

Griffith called and they headed toward the café, on the corner of Decatur and St. Anne. Adi watched to see if she noticed the movement of the various agents, but found it hard to determine who was who. As they neared the corner, the brave front she'd put on began to slip and her nerves kicked in.

Am I crazy? What am I doing? J.B. wants nothing more than to kill me. He has no intention of letting me walk away from here. Bertie? If you can hear me, watch out for me, huh?

They crossed Decatur with a horde of tourists who pushed between them, forcing her to let go of Griff's hand. Griffith walked slightly ahead and to the right of her, trying to move back but swept ahead by the crowd. Her steps slowed, and Griffith moved farther away, another woman keeping pace beside her.

As they turned and approached the outside corner of the café, she heard the racing of a car engine. There was a flash and the booming sound of gunfire. Everything moved in slow motion as she watched the red mist that haunted her dreams erupt from Griffith's chest. Her body crumpled to the sidewalk like a rag doll. Two, three others, fell, then return fire came from the café and street as agents responded. The driver of the car appeared determined to get clear, but his luck had run out. The black Kia coasted toward the restaurant across the street, crashing into one of the supporting posts.

And then time was moving again, people screaming, running. Hands held her down on the sidewalk. Sirens.

Confusion and panic filled her. She fought against the weight on her back. "I need to get up. Let me up! Griff!"

"Ms. Bergeron, stay down. We have to make sure the threat has passed."

"Griffith, she's been shot."

"Yes, ma'am. Agents are with her. They're doing all they can. Just please stay down."

"Did you get him? Is he here?"

"I'm unclear on that, ma'am. We'll sort it all out once the scene is secure and all casualties are dealt with. I'm not moving until I hear from AIC Hague. My job is to secure you."

The moaning and cries of pain entered her awareness, and she struggled to see Griffith.

"Can you tell me how bad it is? Is she going to make it? Please, please let me go to her," she cried.

"I can't tell. We should get an all clear soon. Just be patient."

Local police and emergency personal swarmed the area. Adi was finally allowed to sit up. An EMT assessed her and released her from care. She looked at the space where Griffith had fallen, but only a red stain remained on the pale sidewalk. She ran to one of the ambulances, but there was an injured man inside. She turned to race to the next ambulance when a firm hand on her wrist stopped her. It was Mike Hague.

"Ms. Bergeron. Wait. It isn't safe for you to be running around. Come over to the car."

She let him guide her to his sedan and help her sit in the back. He climbed in beside her and tapped the driver to get him moving. Adi panicked.

"Where are we going? Where are you taking me?"

"Calm down. It's over now. We're going back to headquarters. Your friend is there, Mr. Michaud?"

"What about Griffith? What about J.B.?"

"We believe this was an ambush. We don't have reason to suspect that Nerbass was even present. We thought we had eyes on him, but he had a look-alike in place, and we didn't know it until the man tried to run. You need to be extremely careful, Ms. Bergeron. Apparently, your concern that he means to kill you is valid, more so than we believed. The only positive thing from all of this is the recording we have of him and Griffith. We have something concrete to charge him with now. It's only a matter of time until we catch him."

"What good is that to me? And you didn't answer about Griffith. Where is she?"

"She took a slug to the shoulder. They transported her to University Hospital. The trauma team is fantastic there."

"I want you to take me there."

"I don't think that's—"

"Take me there now, or stop this car and let me out." She fumbled with the door handle, panic surging through her.

"Wait, wait. We can do that. Just hold on." He directed the driver to change course and they soon arrived at the hospital.

Adi tried to bolt out of the car to get to Griffith, but Hague stopped her.

"Listen, it will be much easier for me to find her. Stay with me and we'll get to her."

He led the way into the trauma center. After talking with the admitting nurse, he let her know that Griffith was in critical condition and was on her way to surgery. "There's nothing we can do but wait. I'm sorry."

"Sorry is worth about as much as bayou mud. You said you had it covered. You said..." Adi hugged herself and turned away from him. Mike had the driver return to the office to inform T'Claude and transport him to the hospital. Adi paced until he arrived, and the moment he came in she felt she could breathe, at least a little bit, again. Being in a waiting room with T was something familiar. He wrapped his arms around her and hugged her.

"She's going to beat this, kiddo. No doubt about it."

"I hope you're right. This is all my fault, T. I shouldn't have done it. I should have kept running till he couldn't find me."

"Now, don't you go finding fault. This is all on that ass, Nerbass. You didn't create this. Right now you need to focus on helping Griffith heal. Don't you dare beat yourself up. She knew the risks, and she thought it was worth it to help you. Heck, I bet that woman has been in worse situations and pulled through fine."

Hague moved away to talk to other agents who began appearing in the waiting room. Something was happening, but Adi couldn't make herself care. They'd let them know, eventually. Her only concern, the only thing she could think about, was Griffith. She watched the clock, wondering how long it would be before they had any news. She couldn't imagine for a second what life would be like without her, even though they hadn't been together all that long. It was amazing how the right person could feel like someone you'd known forever and wanted in your life for the rest of always.

"Well, we have some news about the shooter," Mike said. "It was Rafael Ortega, a thug known to have ties to the Sinaloa Cartel. He's in surgery now and likely to survive. This could be a big break for us. If we can get him to talk, we can nail Nerbass to the wall."

"That's good. What about the others who were shot?"

"There was one fatality, the woman who was walking beside Griffith. The others should survive."

"That was meant to be me. He thought that was me," Adi said.

"Hush now, you don't know that, and even if it's true, it's still not your fault," T'Claude said.

"McNaulty?" called a voice from the doorway.

"Here," Mike said.

"The bleeding has been controlled. Luckily, no major vessels were hit. Looks like Ms. McNaulty will have a full recovery. She should be in a room in about two hours."

Relief washed through Adi as his words filtered in. *She's going to be okay.* T hugged her hard and shook her shoulders a bit.

"What did I tell you? It's all going to be okay," he said.

It wouldn't be okay until she could see Griffith and know in her heart that all was well. It wouldn't be completely okay until J.B. was in a tiny concrete cell. It was all so overwhelming. She needed some space to breathe.

"I need to get some air. Can I go?"

"I'm not sure that's a good idea."

"I have to get out of here, please," she said.

"I'll go with you. We can go out to the courtyard," T'Claude said.

"Fine. Porter, go with them."

Adi paced across the open courtyard. She really needed a run more than anything, but neither T nor the agent would allow that. She did her best thinking when she ran, and she really needed to think.

Griff is going to be okay. Thank God. What am I going to do now? Will she want to be with me after this? She couldn't guess at the answer. One thing she knew was that she was done with being afraid. No more would she live in hiding. If Griffith wanted, they could stay here in New Orleans for a while. Or maybe they could go to LA. Either way, she knew she would be okay. J.B. was finished. Now he would be the one hiding, until they caught him. That couldn't happen too soon, in her opinion.

I can do anything I want. Maybe she'd open her own restaurant, a little café where she could get to know her patrons. Where Griffith could sit and write her articles and they could be together. She liked that idea.

In fact, she liked thinking about the future. She'd never had options before, and now, suddenly, there was no end to them. She couldn't wait to get back to Griff to start her life, for real.

CHAPTER TWENTY-TWO

Griffith woke, realizing after a second that she was wearing an oxygen mask. Her shoulder burned, but it was bearable. There was no one with her, but she could see people moving around just beyond the partition that marked her space. She closed her eyes and must have drifted back to sleep, because the sound of Adi's voice in her ear roused her.

"I'm here. You're going to be okay," she said.

"Hey," she said and cleared her throat. She didn't recognize her own voice, which was muffled by the oxygen mask.

"It's okay. You've been shot, but the doctor says you'll heal just fine."

"What happened? I don't remember anything."

"They ambushed us. They thought the woman beside you was me. She didn't make it. Mike says they have enough to get J.B. now for sure," she said.

A nurse entered the room to record her vitals. She removed the mask and switched Griffith to a cannula. The thought that someone had died right next to her, someone that could have been Adi but for the crowd, brought tears to her eyes. She squeezed Adi's hand tighter. "My shoulder?" she asked.

"Let me get the doctor. She should be able to answer any questions."

"Thank you."

Griff closed her eyes. An ambush. It wasn't surprising, but she was angry anyway. The DEA had nearly gotten them killed. That Adi was whole and Griffith was alive was a miracle. That Nerbass had taken the risk and attacked them on a public street spoke of his desperation. *No wonder Adi ran.* A few minutes later, Dr. Long arrived and introduced herself. Adi started to step out, but Griffith asked her to stay. Adi sat in the chair beside her bed and held her hand.

"What's my prognosis?"

"Well, the bullet entered here." She pointed to a spot high on her own shoulder, about an inch below her clavicle. "It tunneled pretty harmlessly around the bone and muscle to lodge in your third rib in the back upper left quadrant. We left it in place. Digging it out could have done more damage than leaving it, due to the nerves surrounding it. You were extremely lucky."

The bullet is still inside me? "So what should I expect?"

"You'll be moved to a regular room in the next few hours and probably stay for three days. We had to tie some blood vessels off that were damaged and we want to be certain there's no more bleeding and no infection. Long-term, some possible residual pain and limited range of motion. You should definitely plan on some physical therapy."

Griffith nodded. *Not so bad, for being shot. A few days in the hospital, therapy. Now, if I can just keep Adi by my side...*"Thank you, Doctor."

"No problem. If you have any other questions, don't hesitate to ask. I'll leave my contact information with the nurse. For now, know you'll see me again at morning rounds."

"Thanks."

When the doctor left, Adi kissed the top of her hand. "I'm so glad you're going to be okay. I was scared I was going to lose you."

"I'm glad too. Mostly, I'm glad to see you sitting there, to know that you're okay and still here."

"I wouldn't be anywhere else. T is outside. He wants you to know he's praying for you."

Griffith laughed. "Good thing. I need a few prayers. What about J.B.? Are you safe here?"

"Mike and his guys were here for a long time. The guy who shot you is out of surgery now and they're waiting to talk to him. Mike's sure they can get him to finger J.B. for this. He told me I'm not likely in danger at this point. They're thinking that J.B. arranged the hit, but made sure he was far from the location to give himself an alibi.

He doesn't think J.B. had any idea we involved the authorities, or he would have arranged a kidnapping or something. He's given me clearance to leave as long as I update him on my location. Basically, they're taking this on full force and we get to go on with our lives."

"And what is your life going to be? Now that this is done? Will you go back to New Iberia?"

"I don't know. For now, I'm staying here. I have an apartment and enough to live on while you heal."

"While I heal? You're making your decisions based on me?"

"Yes, if that's okay."

"Of course it's okay. It's more than okay. I was afraid you wouldn't want anything to do with me after all of the drama."

"I'm not sure of much right now. I don't know what's going to happen today or tomorrow, but the one thing I'm sure of? How I feel when I'm with you. I want to give us a chance. Are you good with that?"

Griffith felt like the sky had opened up and sunshine was pouring into her soul. "Yeah, I'm good with that."

CHAPTER TWENTY-THREE

The canoe slid silently through the still water of Lake Fausse Pointe. Adi dug deeper, watching Griffith in the boat ahead of her. She was paddling well now, her physical therapy was really making a difference. The cool air and sunshine were the perfect accent to the day.

"There, there it is. Do you see her?" She pointed at the weathered old cypress to the left of the boat.

"I do. It's so beautiful. Bertie would like it here, I'm sure. It's just like you told me."

Adi felt warmth wrap around her with Griffith's words. *Bertie would like it here. She'd love seeing us together too.*

"Can you see the face? In the tree bark?"

"Yes, I see her. Are we going to let her go here or right by the tree?"

"By the tree. I'll get us as close as possible." She took the craft right to the base of the grand ole lady.

"Now?"

"Yeah, here, let me help." Adi stowed the paddle and reached out to help steady the lotus shaped paper flower that held Bertie. Together they set it gently on the water's surface and watched as it slowly sank. It was done. Bertie was at rest.

"She'd have been so proud of you."

"She'd be proud of us, you mean. I'm so glad we decided to stay in New Iberia for a while."

"Me too. I'm glad you've arranged for Jose to rent the house when we go to LA so we always have a place to call home."

They'd stayed in New Orleans during Griffith's recovery, then decided to return to New Iberia and help T stabilize things at the Boiling Pot. Now that Jose was confident in the kitchen, Griffith was excited to take Adi to LA and introduce her to a whole different world.

Adi was excited too, but worried a little about how Griffith's friends and family would accept her. They'd done a lot of talking about the differences in their worlds, and there were things she couldn't imagine. Griff would have to travel for her journalism work, eventually, and they'd floated the idea of Adi opening up a little Cajun eatery in LA, but for now, it was enough they had the time to experience new things together. Deep down, she knew she'd be okay anywhere, because she had Griffith.

They would have to return to Louisiana next spring when the trial of J.B Nerbass was scheduled to begin. Griff had already written a major article that was receiving all kinds of attention, and she'd finish it after the trial. It would be rough to relive all of the things he'd done, but she was relieved he was behind bars and would likely stay there for most of his life. She'd do her damnedest to make sure of it.

"Look at that," Griffith said, bringing her back to the moment.

A stately eagle soared across the lake toward them and settled in the highest branches of Bertie's rest.

"That was perfect. And this is perfect. I love you, Griffith."

Griffith turned and smiled at her with tears in her eyes. "And I love you."

"Let's go home. T's bringing beer and Jose's bringing crawfish. We should get the water going."

"Okay, love. Let's go home."

Home. Adi liked the sound of that.

About the Author

Laydin Michaels is a native Houstonian with deep Louisiana roots. She finds joy and happiness in the loving arms of her wife, MJ. Her life is also enriched by her son, CJ, and her four fur children. Her love of the written word started very early. She has been a voracious reader all her life.

Books Available from Bold Strokes Books

A Class Act by Tammy Hayes. Buttoned-up college professor Dr. Margaret Parks doesn't know what she's getting herself into when she agrees to one date with her student, Rory Morgan, who is 15 years her junior. (978-1-62639-701-9)

Bitter Root by Laydin Michaels. Small town chef Adi Bergeron is hiding something, and Griffith McNaulty is going to find out what it is even if it gets her killed. (978-1-62639-656-2)

Capturing Forever by Erin Dutton. When family pulls Jacqueline and Casey back together, will the lessons learned in eight years apart be enough to mend the mistakes of the past? (978-1-62639-631-9)

Deception by VK Powell. DEA Agent Colby Vincent and Attorney Adena Weber are embroiled in a drug investigation involving homeless veterans and an attraction that could destroy them both. (978-1-62639-596-1)

Dyre: A Knight of Spirit and Shadows by Rachel E. Bailey. With the abduction of her queen, werewolf-bodyguard Des must follow the kidnappers' trail to Europe, where her queen—and a battle unlike any Des has ever waged—awaits her. (978-1-62639-664-7)

First Position by Melissa Brayden. Love and rivalry take center stage for Anastasia Mikhelson and Natalie Frederico in one of the most prestigious ballet companies in the nation. (978-1-62639-602-9)

Best Laid Plans by Jan Gayle. Nicky and Lauren are meant for each other, but Nicky's haunting past and Lauren's societal fears threaten to derail all possibilities of a relationship. (987-1-62639-658-6)

Exchange by CF Frizzell. When Shay Maguire rode into rural Montana, she never expected to meet the woman of her dreams—or to learn Mel Baker was held hostage by legal agreement to her right-wing father. (987-1-62639-679-1)

Just Enough Light by AJ Quinn. Will a serial killer's return to Colorado destroy Kellen Ryan and Dana Kingston's chance at love, or can the search-and-rescue team save themselves? (987-1-62639-685-2)

Rise of the Rain Queen by Fiona Zedde. Nyandoro is nobody's princess. She fights, curses, fornicates, and gets into as much trouble as her brothers. But the path to a throne is not always the one we expect. (987-1-62639-592-3)

Tales from Sea Glass Inn by Karis Walsh. Over the course of a year at Cannon Beach, tourists and locals alike find solace and passion at the Sea Glass Inn. (987-1-62639-643-2)

The Color of Love by Radclyffe. Black sheep Derian Winfield needs to convince literary agent Emily May to marry her to save the Winfield Agency and solve Emily's green card problem, but Derian didn't count on falling in love. (987-1-62639-716-3)

A Reluctant Enterprise by Gun Brooke. When two women grow up learning nothing but distrust, unworthiness, and abandonment, it's no wonder they are apprehensive and fearful when an overwhelming love just won't be denied. (978-1-62639-500-8)

Above the Law by Carsen Taite. Love is the last thing on Agent Dale Nelson's mind, but reporter Lindsey Ryan's investigation could change the way she sees everything—her career, her past, and her future. (978-1-62639-558-9)

Actual Stop by Kara A. McLeod. When Special Agent Ryan O'Connor's present collides abruptly with her past, shots are fired, and the course of her life is irrevocably altered. (978-1-62639-675-3)

Embracing the Dawn by Jeannie Levig. When ex-con Jinx Tanner and business executive E. J. Bastien awaken after a one-night stand to find their lives inextricably entangled, love has its work cut out for it. (978-1-62639-576-3)

Jane's World: The Case of the Mail Order Bride by Paige Braddock. Jane's PayBuddy account gets hacked and she inadvertently purchases a mail order bride from the Eastern Bloc. (978-1-62639-494-0)

Love's Redemption by Donna K. Ford. For ex-convict Rhea Daniels and ex-priest Morgan Scott, redemption lies in the thin line between right and wrong. (978-1-62639-673-9)

The Shewstone by Jane Fletcher. The prophetic Shewstone is in Eawynn's care, but unfortunately for her, Matt is coming to steal it. (978-1-62639-554-1)

A Touch of Temptation by Julie Blair. Recent law school graduate Kate Dawson's ordained path to the perfect life gets thrown off course when handsome butch top Chris Brent initiates her to sexual pleasure. (978-1-62639-488-9)

Beneath the Waves by Ali Vali. Kai Merlin and Vivien Palmer love the water and the secrets trapped in the depths, but if Kai gives in to her feelings, it might come at a cost to her entire realm. (978-1-62639-609-8)

Girls on Campus edited by Sandy Lowe and Stacia Seaman. College: four years when rules are made to be broken. This collection is required reading for anyone looking to earn an A in sex ed. (978-1-62639-733-0)

Heart of the Pack by Jenny Frame. Human Selena Miller falls for the domineering Caden Wolfgang, but will their love survive Selena learning the Wolfgangs are werewolves? (978-1-62639-566-4)

Miss Match by Fiona Riley. Matchmaker Samantha Monteiro makes the impossible possible for everyone but herself. Is mysterious dancer Lucinda Moss her own perfect match? (978-1-62639-574-9)

Paladins of the Storm Lord by Barbara Ann Wright. Lieutenant Cordelia Ross must choose between duty and honor when a man with godlike powers forces her soldiers to provoke an alien threat. (978-1-62639-604-3)

Taking a Gamble by P.J. Trebelhorn. Storage auction buyer Cassidy Holmes and postal worker Erica Jacobs want different things out of life, but taking a gamble on love might prove lucky for them both. (978-1-62639-542-8)

The Copper Egg by Catherine Friend. Archeologist Claire Adams wants to find the buried treasure in Peru. Her ex, Sochi Castillo, wants to steal it. The last thing either of them wants is to still be in love. (978-1-62639-613-5)

The Iron Phoenix by Rebecca Harwell. Seventeen-year-old Nadya must master her unusual powers to stop a killer, prevent civil war, and rescue the girl she loves, while storms ravage her island city. (978-1-62639-744-6)

A Reunion to Remember by TJ Thomas. Reunited after a decade, Jo Adams and Rhonda Black must navigate a significant age difference, family dynamics, and their own desires and fears to explore an opportunity for love. (978-1-62639-534-3)

Built to Last by Aurora Rey. When Professor Olivia Bennett hires contractor Joss Bauer to restore her dilapidated farmhouse, she learns her heart, as much as her house, is in need of a renovation. (978-1-62639-552-7)

Capsized by Julie Cannon. What happens when a woman turns your life completely upside down? (978-1-62639-479-7)